Sign of the Dragon

Sign of the Dragon

MacGregor Family
Adventure Series
Book Four

a novel by

Richard Trout

PELICAN PUBLISHING COMPANY
GRETNA 2007

Library of Congress Cataloging-in-Publication Data

Trout, Richard.
  Sign of the dragon / a novel by Richard Trout.
    p. cm. -- (MacGregor Family adventure series ; bk. 5)
    Summary: While in China, Chris, Heather, R.O., and
Natalie kayak on a Class IV river, discover a link between
animal exports, the illegal dinosaur bone trade, and corrupt
officials, and encounter panda poachers.
    ISBN-13: 978-1-58980-476-0 (hardcover : alk. paper) [1.
Ecology--Fiction. 2. Fossils--Fiction. 3. Poachers--Fiction. 4.
White-water canoeing--Fiction. 5. Adventure and adven-
turers--Fiction. 6. China--Fiction.] I. Title.
  PZ7.T7545Sig 2007
  [Fic]--dc22
                                        2007015300

Printed in the United States of America

Published by Pelican Publishing Company, Inc.
1000 Burmaster Street, Gretna, Louisiana 70053

For Carrol and June Pfund, wonderful

parents of Mavis, Margo, and Marcia

Contents

Acknowledgments

A special thanks to the following friends whose contributions to this series are always greatly appreciated: Dr. Neal Coates, Professor Julian Hilliard, Ann Hovda, and Yen Hwa "Tracy" Yu.

Sign of the Dragon

Prologue

Fuo River, Tibetan Highlands
222 A.D.

Minh Chu jumped from one rock to the next, slipping on the mossy surface as the cold water splashed up to his knees. He balanced himself precariously, shifting the heavy pack on his back to the left and then the right. He turned quickly to look back over his shoulder, but he couldn't see his pursuers, who were two miles behind. They too had temporarily abandoned their rafts and canoes because of the rapids and the heavy boulders that accented this part of the river. Looking ahead to plan his path, he leaped to a large boulder. His straw sandals gripped each surface as all of his body worked in rhythm to move from peak to peak, fighting against earth's gravity and the rush of the river between the rocks.

He glanced quickly toward the bank, but the steep incline would be too hard to climb and the emperor's troops could be above the river on horseback waiting in ambush. As Minh Chu jumped to the next rock, the pain in his legs began in his heels and climbed up each calf to the front of his knees. He struggled onward, never forgetting his wife, children, and why he was doing this. The last three days had become a blur, beginning with the camp of the noblemen and their plan to outwit the emperor and gain an advantage for their side. Each one of them was a man of great wealth and stature, but the price had become too much to bear. It had been acceptable at first to give up land to the emperor and then it was even tolerable to give up the peasant workers and the foreign slaves to the emperor and even to pay more taxes. But when the emperor's troops had come to take his daughter to Peking, Minh Chu had drawn the line. He and the other noblemen banded together to fight back, but the emperor's troops were too many and their weapons too advanced. So the plan had been born to strike where the emperor was most vulnerable, the solid gold statue of Lord Buddha that bore the sign of the dragon.

The emperor claimed his mother was born of a dragon. He even built a temple to pray to the dragon just as he had for Lord Buddha. But in the temple to Lord Buddha, the emperor had placed a solid gold statue and on the statue were the five claw marks of the Tienlong, the heavenly or royal dragon, which was the only dragon to have five claws. There was nothing in the universe that was more valuable to the emperor than the Buddha, and now Minh Chu carried it in the pack on his back. The pain in his right foot brought his concentration back to the rocks, and the loud rush of the river filled his ears and all of his thoughts.

He suddenly slipped and dropped between the rocks into a hole about waist deep. The cold water felt good on his legs, so for a minute he didn't struggle to get back up. Then he heard a voice yelling.

"Minh Chu."

"Minh Chu."

He looked around and saw an arm waving from the brush on the side of the rocky bank. It was his next contact. There were to be nine in total who would aid his plan to take the sacred Buddha to its final place of hiding. Once the statue was hidden, the noblemen would feel safe enough to negotiate with the emperor. He pulled himself out of the water and struggled across the rocks toward the bank. As he approached, he could see it was his friend Chi Lee.

As he reached him they embraced for a moment.

"Minh Chu, you are hours late. What happened?"

"We were ambushed at the caves. There is a traitor among us. Over half of the noblemen are dead. But I have the sacred Buddha," Minh said as he shivered.

"You have it?" Lee asked.

"Yes. We've made it this far but the emperor's men are close behind. My guess is about one or two hours," Minh said.

"Your canoe awaits you around the bend. Your next contact is in place two hours down the river. He will have horses waiting to take you north," Lee spoke.

"Thank you, my friend. Now make your escape and return to your family. Each man captured by the emperor's men took his own life rather than give up the others. It is a debt we all owe if we can stay alive," Minh said.

"Now go," Lee said as they embraced.

Lee began climbing up the bank as Minh stepped out on the rocks to travel the last hundred yards before he could reach the canoe. The leg pain seemed to disappear with his new hope of reaching the canoe and traveling the river safely again. After a few minutes he could see the boat sitting on the rocks. Soon he was pushing it off into the river and jumping inside. He kept the pack on his back in case he capsized. He reached deep into the river with the paddle, catching the current. Now the paddle became the rudder.

For two hours he bounced and rocked and swayed across the rapids, glancing at the beautiful canyon walls until he could see a rush of whitewater ahead. He leaned back into the canoe and held tight to the paddle. The canyon walls forced the river to become narrower by the second. Soon Minh felt like he was in a cave without a ceiling. Then he felt a thud on the canoe's wooden side. Then another and a third thud was accompanied by an arrow that stood straight up on the floor of the canoe.

Minh Chu quickly looked up and could see the emperor's archers on the ledges above as they rained arrows down on him. He rolled to his right and felt a sting on the back of his left leg and several thuds on his pack. The arrows kept coming and Minh felt more pain, first on his shoulder and then on the side of his face as an arrow glanced off his left cheek, making a two-inch slice. He gripped the paddle tightly and held it over his head. He felt pain on his left hand as an arrow hit between two fingers, but he still held on. Then the arrows stopped as quickly as they had begun.

Minh looked up and realized that he had traveled beyond the range of the archers and the river had picked up speed. He sat up quickly and felt the arrow lodged in his leg. He reached down and broke off the shaft of the arrow next to the skin, leaving the head sticking out the other side. Carefully he tried to inch the shaft out, but without luck.

"Aahg," he yelled over the rush of the river as blood began to pour from the wound. He hung his leg over the side of the canoe into the cold water, and the bleeding stopped. Grimacing in pain, he began to steer the canoe down through the rapids. With each dip of his paddle into the waves, massive amounts of water flooded over the bow of the canoe and into Minh's face. The cold water felt good and temporarily made him forget the pain in his leg, but the speed of the river increased as the rapids seemed to build and build. Soon there was nothing but whitewater ahead, boiling from bank to bank.

Hanging on tight to the paddle, Minh tried with all his strength to steer the canoe. It was hopeless. The river did what it willed with the tiny craft. The water level inside the canoe was about a foot deep and forced the canoe deeper into every hydraulic that rushed over a boulder. Then the inevitable happened. The bow of the canoe didn't surface and Minh held his breath as he and the canoe went under. When he realized the canoe wasn't going to surface, he let go of the paddle and swam as hard as he could upward. In two swimming strokes he felt the air on his face and gulped in all he could before a wave hit him hard and pushed him back under. On the next stroke he broke the air again and was buoyed up for nearly a hundred feet before going back under. When he surfaced the third time, he realized that the pack and the Buddha were keeping him under longer each time, but he knew he couldn't dump the precious cargo now. So many lives had been lost and this was no time to surrender. His family weighed in the balance, and if he lived and the Buddha was lost, he would have no life indeed. Minh knew that he and the Buddha shared the same fate.

Minh Chu controlled his breathing to allow for the long bouts under the water and soon he developed a rhythm. He pulled the pack with the sacred Buddha around to his chest so the balance would be better. The rapids didn't seem to slow down and he couldn't remember how long the river ran through the canyon. Then something on the left bank caught his attention.

He tried to wipe the water away from his eyes but his hands were stiff and cold. Then he saw it again. It was a person waving at him. He spirits immediately jumped and he strained high in the water to see. It was a person waving at him with both hands. He began to swim with all his strength. As he got closer he could see a long pole sticking out over the water and he knew he had to grab it. He repositioned the pack again and began to reach out as he swam. The river rushed him closer and closer. Then he saw the face of his friend Chen. He tried to smile, but his face was too cold and his cheeks wouldn't move. He tried to wave but his shoulders wouldn't flex to allow his arms above his head.

He began to panic, worrying that he would be unable to grab the pole. He was only seconds away and he had to reach it. Then suddenly a current pushed him against the wall of the canyon and he went under. Struggling, he pushed himself away and tried to break the surface. He began to cough violently as he sucked in water. He pushed again off a rock and was suddenly vaulted through the air over the rapid. Minh felt a sting on his neck as the pole flew through the air in a sweeping motion and hit him. Reflexively he grabbed at the long object, wrapped his frozen fingers around it, and shoved it under his right arm.

He suddenly went underwater as his body stopped moving and the river rushed onward. He hit the wall of the canyon and felt the sting of his lungs, begging for air. As he broke the surface, he gulped in breaths of air and was pulled into an opening in the wall of the canyon. He opened his eyes and could see Chen smiling at him just a few feet away. Then, as he was dragged across wet rock, the world suddenly stopped moving. All he could hear was the echo of the river's rush and his own breathing.

"Minh Chu, you're safe. You made it," Chen comforted.

"I'm still alive, so my family is still alive," Minh said and forced a smile on his still frozen facial muscles.

Chen laid a blanket over him and rubbed him briskly to return the heat to his body. After an hour, Minh began to look around and noticed a small fire in the cave. Chen leaned over and tried to pour some tea down his friend's throat. It felt good, so Minh drank it all and looked up at him.

"Thank you, my friend," Minh said.

"No, Minh, it is I who should thank you. It is all of the noblemen who should thank you for your risk and sacrifice. We are now close to being able to bargain with the emperor. Without your courage, we would still be giving our daughters to be his wives," Chen said.

"I must keep moving. Where am I?" Minh asked as he stood up, lost his balance, and sat back down. The pain in his leg returned and he felt the small shaft of the arrow protruding from his leg.

"You're wounded," Chen realized.

"An archer's arrow found its target," Minh replied.

Within a few minutes, Minh was lying on the blanket and Chen had heated a small knife and was cutting the arrow out of Minh's leg.

"It is a small tip," Chen said and pulled out the remainder of the arrow. Minh lay quietly thinking about his family and listening to the roar of the river. He felt the sting of the hot knife as Chen cauterized the wound and closed it carefully. Tears escaped his eyes, but his voice was still silent.

"You're as good as new," Chen said.

"Where is the land entrance to the cave?" Minh asked as he sat up and sipped more tea.

"It's quite a ways up the cave system. It opens into a forest that surrounds the river canyon for many miles. You . . ." Chen stopped in mid-sentence, coughed, and grabbed his chest.

Minh looked up and saw the tip of an arrow sticking out the front of Chen's chest as his friend fell dead to the rock floor of the cave. Minh looked quickly toward the river and saw two canoes with four of the emperor's men stopped at the entrance of the cave. The men struggled against the current to hang onto the rocky entrance and climb out of the canoes. One archer, still sitting in the canoe, fired a second arrow into the cave toward the small campfire, just missing Minh Chu by inches. Minh grabbed his pack with the sacred Buddha and stiffly ran into the darkness of the cave, pausing only to grab a glowing stick from the fire. Another arrow whizzed by, glancing off the rock wall with a crash and an echo.

Minh didn't look back as he moved across the cave. He heard another arrow streaking through the darkness with the small glowing stick as its only target. It crashed against the rock wall of the cave just a foot away. He had no time to admire the aim of the archer but only to find another path through the black cave, hoping he could discover the path to the surface.

He noticed a dark hole across the main room and ran for it. The pain in his leg had long been forgotten, the pack firmly on his back to block the archer's arrows. As he reached the blackness he looked over his shoulder and could see shadows around the fire. More than one man had made it from the rushing river into the cave. He quickly stepped into the hole, which was a rock corridor, and started walking quickly, holding the small burning stick in front of him. He knew he would be out of light soon and darkness would seal his fate. He picked up speed and began to trot, the pain in his leg returning, but he ignored it and never lost a step. His dried sandals began to clap on the rocky floor, but he knew he was far enough ahead that they couldn't be heard. He came to another room in the cave system and held the small stick out in front of him. It was a magnificent underground river. Minh couldn't see the other side, but to his left was a wall that reached up into the darkness with scratch marks all over it. Minh reached out and felt them. He recognized them immediately.

"Bear cave. This is good. There will be a useable entrance somewhere. But where?" he wondered and put the stick in his mouth with the glowing ember end near the right side of his cheek.

He reached into the deep scratch marks and began to climb the wall. With each step, his fingers and his toes found the ancient pathway of the bears, leading, he hoped, to their lair. Knowing that winter was not upon him, he also hoped that he would be alone. As he ascended, the roar of the river seemed farther and farther below him. He knew he had been climbing for ten minutes, carefully maneuvering the wall and its hidden pathway. Finally he reached up and there was nothing more to grab. He had reached the top. Slowly and carefully he edged his aching body over the top of the wall and lay still on his stomach for a full two minutes.

He took the stick from his mouth and blew gently on the ember at the end and it came to a flame. Light jumped across the room at the top of the wall to reveal piles of bones from bears and ancient stacks of bear spore. He was happy there were no live bears present. Minh sat up and looked around and felt safe for the first time. He rubbed the wound on the back of his leg and felt warm blood. Then he heard voices echoing through the cave. Quickly he took the small ember and set it inside the skull of an ancient bear and piled more bones around it. He feared he would lose his only light, but he couldn't afford to take a chance.

Soon the voices were closer and then a light broke into the darkness below as three men charged through and stopped at the river's edge. Minh sat back from edge and breathed very slowly. The men looked around and said something, then left the way they came. Their voices and footsteps faded in the distance and Minh began to breath deep again. Then he remembered his small torch and turned around. He felt for the bear skull and swallowed hard as he realized the ember had gone out. He had lost his source of light.

Minh knew that if there were no way to tell all of China that the nobles had the sacred Buddha then the emperor could claim anything he wanted and there would be no bargaining. Sadness came across Minh when he thought that his life ended when the ember died. He lay on his side, filled with fatigue and sadness, and soon fell asleep.

Minh Chu had no concept of time when he awoke in the darkness of the cave. He touched his eyes to be sure they were open. He blinked repeatedly. Feeling around him he found the pack and the Buddha. He opened the pack and was startled to see a little light. He could actually see the outline of the top of the pack, so he opened it fully and more light poured out. Minh reached inside and pulled the Buddha out, and the top of the bear landing lit up. He blinked again and again as he looked at the Buddha and could see a precious stone mounted in the belly that glowed much brighter than his small torch had. He had heard of such minerals and smiled for the first time in hours. He turned the Buddha around and watched the path of the light as it showed him the interior of the cave.

He slowly got to his feet and held the small Buddha in front of him as he walked around the landing. When he was confident there were no other exits, he slowly put the Buddha back into his pack and slipped over the side of the wall. In a few minutes he was standing next to the underground river. Minh Chu took the Buddha from the pack and began to walk the ancient bear trail alongside the river, going away from where the emperor's men had headed.

As Minh moved farther along he was awed at the beauty of the cave, the mineral deposits hanging from the ceiling and protruding from the floor of the cave. Then he discovered a small pool of water that sheltered many other beautiful formations, nothing like he had ever seen before. But the trail was still there, where bears had walked in total darkness for centuries, using their noses to find their way to the lair at the top of the wall. Holding the Buddha carefully, Minh finally came to an incline that looked like a natural stairway to the outside world where water had eroded into the rock formation.

Within minutes he was at the top of the incline and standing next to a rock hallway that smelled like moss and tree bark. A small draft washed across his face and he sensed he would soon be out of the cave. Holding the Buddha in front of him but tight to his chest, he limped his way through the small hallway and began to see light. Putting the Buddha back into the pack he began to walk faster until he came to an opening that was covered by vines and roots. Crawling and forcing his way through it he stepped out into the forest that Chen had talked about. In the sunlight, he could see where his friend, probably with the help of some local villagers, who sympathized with the noblemen and knew the cave well, had cut through some of the roots.

Walking quickly, Minh finally reached a clearing in the forest and looked up at the afternoon sun. The heat felt good on his face. Looking around he found some flowers and weeds and picked them. He wadded them up in a ball and stuffed them into his mouth and began to chew. He knew he had a long walk before his next contact would greet him with tea and food. Minh needed energy and he knew he had lost blood.

After about an hour he found the edge of the forest and could see the village at the bottom of the hill. From there he would go north by horse to find a safe home for the Buddha. Then it would be time to negotiate with the emperor.

1

Boulder Fields

The metal arm of the winch, called a boom, extended ten feet over the rim of the canyon and was anchored in the back of the olive green Dongfeng, a Chinese-built truck. Four men in military green khakis worked feverishly to control the stress on the winch and balance the bright red K-2 tandem kayak, full of gear and supplies, to prevent the sharp, jagged rocks of the canyon wall from damaging the new boat.

"Let her down," Chris MacGregor shouted from forty feet below the canyon rim. Another man interpreted quickly in Chinese and the men who worked the winch responded immediately. The problem was not the weight of the boat but the age of the winch. This was the third boat to be lowered two hundred feet in the last hour. The landing had to be perfect because this was the only available sandbar for miles on this small tributary feeding into the Fuo River, just northwest of P'ingwu, in far western Sichuan Province. To make matters worse, the larger two passenger K-2 kayaks had to dodge not only the two single passenger K-1 kayaks occupying most of the sandbar but also Heather and R.O. MacGregor and Natalie Crosswhite.

The red kayak reached Chris and he touched it lightly out of an impulse to steady its sway, when suddenly he heard a grinding noise and looked up in a panic. He could see blue smoke filtering over the rim of the canyon, and had it not been for the roar of the river, the voices of several very worried Chinese would have echoed back to him. The red kayak came to a halt for just a second before beginning to plunge toward the river. Chris pushed off the canyon wall, hanging tightly to the repelling rope, and yelled to warn of the danger below.

"Wow, this river is so cool," R.O. said as he watched the flow of the water downstream.

"I can't believe Chris talked Mom into this," Heather replied. "But I have to admit, I love rafting. We rode the Grand Canyon rapids on the Colorado River once and it was awesome."

"I do too. My family used to vacation in Crested Butte and we would go rafting every summer," Natalie said.

Chris was screaming with all his might, but no one below could hear him over the roar of the river. Chills erupted all over his body as he saw the red kayak fall and begin spiraling toward R.O., Heather, and Natalie, dropping at the end of the cable like a spider in a mad dash toward its prey.

"Natalie!" Chris yelled, when suddenly he heard a screeching noise from above the rim. The K-2 began to slow down and then quickly came to a halt. His heart was still pounding out of his chest as sweat ran down his face from under his helmet.

"I wonder when Chris is coming down," Heather said and looked up. "Oh my gosh," she said and jumped backwards against the canyon wall. She instinctively put her hands up and touched the shiny red side of the kayak, which was two feet above her head. It took Chris five seconds to repel down the canyon wall onto the sandbar.

"You guys nearly got flattened by this kayak," Chris

gasped, out of breath from the fast descent.

Natalie had followed Heather's lead and was pressed up against the canyon wall."What happened?" she asked excitedly.

"Either the winch is old or this boat is too heavy," Chris replied, his heart still pounding.

Natalie stepped over and put her right arm around Heather.

"That was close," she sighed.

"No kidding," Heather agreed.

R.O. looked up from the water's edge.

"Wow, that was a close call," R.O. said as he sat next to the river on a large boulder.

"Too close," Chris replied, deciding to change the topic of conversation and focus on something less traumatic. "How's the water temperature?" he asked.

"Not too bad. It's about forty-eight degrees. It will probably warm up once we're out of this canyon and farther south toward the Yangtze," R.O. said.

"It's the Jinyang, Ryan. Mom's going to quiz us on the major rivers when we get back to Beijing in two days," Heather said. "And besides it's late November and there's no such thing as heat this late in the year."

Chris, still shook up about the near accident, took a deep breath. He knew that complaining to the Chinese army crew that lowered the boat would do no good, so he focused on calming down Heather, Natalie, and R.O. and getting on with the kayak trip.

"That's why we're wearing dry suits and rafting shoes. Ten minutes floating in this water would suck out all your body heat. The dry suits will give you enough time to swim downriver and get out," Chris explained. The four of them untied the K-2 tandem kayak and lowered it to the sand. It was the heaviest of the three boats because it had room for extra breakdown paddles, ropes for climbing in an emergency, a first-aid box, blankets in dry bags, food, and water.

Everything was ready to go except the guide, who had fallen sick the night before.

Chris had studied a map of the river and felt confident enough to lead them on this small adventure before being immersed in political dinners in Beijing. After about twenty minutes of repacking gear, they were ready to go.

"Let's look at the map together," Chris said as the others gathered around. He laid the vinyl map across the top of the yellow kayak. "This tributary is rated as a Class III river. That means it's going to be a challenge but it won't kill us. We will travel about ten miles and with the flow as it is now, that means about forty-five minutes before we reach the fork in the river. Hey, R.O., pay attention," Chris said as R.O. watched a large bird overhead.

"These marks here," he said and pointed to some dots on the river at the fork, "represent a heavy boulder field. The army guys up top said to stay left. If you go right, then you'll be pulled into the right fork, which is a Class IV. Remember the ratings? Class III is a challenge, Class IV is scary, and Class V is downright terror. We don't want Class IV or V. So as we approach the boulder field, everyone line up single file to the left. Heather and R.O. will go first, then Natalie, and then me."

"Do I have to ride with Heather again?" R.O. whined. "I mean, I always have to ride with Heather. She got to drive the dogsled in Alaska. . . ."

"O.K. Stop the whining. You take the blue K-1 single, I'll take the yellow K-1, and Heather and Natalie can take the red K-2 tandem. Everyone be sure to tighten the straps on your life jackets and pull the buckles tight on your helmets.

Knives should be at easy arm's length on your vest in their scabbards in case you have to cut yourself free of the boat. Once in your boats, tighten the cord on your spray skirt and be sure the gasket is in place. We don't want anyone sinking the first mile. I have a GPS locator and tracking device attached to my vest," Chris said as he patted the small, wallet-sized, yellow plastic case. "Our friends on the rim can track us and have orders to come get us if we don't show up at Meinyang in two days. We can also use the device and a map to find our way out. Is everyone ready?"

"Yes, let's go. I'm getting hot in this dry suit," Heather said.

"O.K. Let's shove off," Chris said as Natalie stepped into the back seat of the K-2. Heather hopped in the front just as Chris gave it a big shove. The girls hit with a splash and were fifty feet downriver in a couple of seconds, digging into the water to straighten their course. R.O. was fast behind them as Chris gave him a big heave to.

With the tension of the canyon descent behind him, Chris smiled as adrenaline rushed in his veins. After a shove and a hop he was in the river and in his kayak all at once. A quick tug pulled the spray skirt tight. He began to pull deep with the paddle to catch Heather, Natalie, and R.O., in the fast-running river. As he looked ahead at Natalie a warm feeling passed over him.

The cold water splashing across the boats and into their faces felt good as the large waves bounced off the canyon walls and large boulders. Everyone had already begun to overheat from the thermal gear and paddling. The first five miles were the challenge that had been foretold by the map. R.O. caught up with the girls and proceeded to splash them as he zipped by.

Natalie just laughed, and for awhile they were all stroking well in the water until a large but rather calm hydraulic separated them and propelled them through a quarter mile of easy rapids. Chris waved his paddle at Heather and Natalie, pointed downstream, and then patted his helmet. He had lost sight of R.O. and immediately began looking for him. Then suddenly Chris realized what was about to happen. There had to be a large hydraulic or a small waterfall ahead, so he began paddling as hard as he could. Natalie and Heather saw him and did the same.

Within seconds they could hear the roar of the water

crashing over twenty-foot-high boulders and at the last second Chris caught a glimpse of R.O. down the river. The river reached out and grabbed his kayak and hurled it between two large boulders the size of small houses and sent him airborne for two seconds. Leaning back and pushing on his footrests, Chris held on tight to his paddle as the kayak nosed into the river and went four feet under. Struggling to paddle, he soon broke the surface only to see Heather and Natalie follow him through the hydraulic and over the falls. The power of the river was immense. Sucking in air Chris looked ahead and could see R.O. with his paddle raised over his head laughing and floating backwards. The girls bobbed to the surface and blew a mouthful of water into the air and took deep breaths. Their boat drifted over to Chris; he reached out for the loop on the front end and pulled them close.

"Still warm, Heather?" Chris asked, shouting over the roar.

"No, I think I've cooled down a bit," Heather replied and forced a smile.

"Are you all right?" Chris shouted to Natalie.

"Yup," she choked out as she coughed up water. "Better than a mouthful of Oklahoma dirt in the spring," she replied.

At that moment, R.O. bumped Chris from the side and let out a big "yee-haa, ride 'em cowboy," and then paddled away in a frenzy.

Chris remembered the boulder field was straight ahead. R.O. was already fifty yards in front of him, and he knew he had to catch him to keep him bearing toward the left. The boulders were the size of trucks and created super-fast lanes for even the best kayakers. Chris pulled hard with his paddle while Heather and Natalie stayed on his tail. They were all thinking the same thing. Catch R.O! But the boulders weren't cooperating. Just as they would gain speed, a large boulder would create a new hydraulic and the water would spin the kayak first to the left, then to the right. Only once or twice did Chris catch sight of R.O.'s red helmet.

Then another boulder spun Chris all the way around and he could see Natalie's green helmet and Heather's yellow helmet as they bobbed up and down on the whitewater.

Making a quick reversal, Chris motioned for them to go left as they were coming out of the boulder field. The canyon split right in front of him, and his heart sank as he saw R.O. take the right tributary. He had no choice but to follow. He motioned the girls off to the left, but they ignored his signal and bore into the right tributary behind him. Now it was going to be a more difficult battle than ever. Chris pulled hard with his paddle. His mind worked quickly and he estimated that he could catch R.O. and beach him and the girls would follow. They would then use their ropes and climb out of the canyon to safety.

Suddenly they hit the first rapids and Chris knew they were all in trouble. He was going under water after every hydraulic. A professional wouldn't last two miles in this, he thought to himself, and he hadn't even gone a half-mile. Finally, he spotted R.O. as his blue kayak was launched over a ten-foot boulder. Chris had no time for emotion, just resolve, as he dug his paddle deeper into the water and pointed toward the same hydraulic. The girls had witnessed it all and steered to the left and a shorter drop.

Chris became airborne behind R.O. and was shocked to see his brother still upright and paddling as he shot across the rapids. Holding his breath, he plunged underwater for three seconds and then back to the surface. He spun his straight-blade paddle around and righted himself. He came up next to R.O., caught his eye, and yelled at him.

"Follow me!"

R.O. couldn't hear him but knew the meaning of his expression. He quickly slowed his kayak, pulling in behind Chris, and the three kayaks now raced down the river at breakneck speed, all four teenagers white-eyed and living on adrenaline by the second. A little skill and lots of luck led them for nearly two miles as the roar got louder and louder. Chris could tell it wasn't a waterfall but steep canyons and a narrow river. He knew he had to find a safe place to ground the boats, but time was running out.

The sharp turn to the right threw them all up against the smooth canyon rim, where millions of cubic feet of water rushed by. The scraping of the fiberglass kayaks couldn't be heard over the roar of the river, but Chris could see that all three boats were losing their paint. He felt a slight chill and knew the girls would be suffering soon. As they came out of the turn, a knot formed instantly in his stomach as he saw the boulder field dead ahead. There was only one opening big enough for a kayak. He used his paddle as a rudder and glanced back to see that Heather and Natalie were following his lead.

Once Chris lined himself up with the opening he began to paddle quickly, fighting the many forces of the river that tried to drag him toward the smaller openings and bigger rocks. He fought hard as the paddle slipped in his cold, · gloved hands and he gripped tighter, afraid to look back. In seconds he was at the opening and the force of the water lifted him two feet higher as he went through. The hydraulic shoved his boat to the right, where he bounced off two smaller rocks and was forced back into the main stream of the river. He looked back as R.O. zipped through the opening and was sent airborne right toward him. As the blue and yellow kayaks hit, Chris could sense that his yellow boat had received some damage but he couldn't tell how bad it was since he was riding low in the water. R.O. was lighter and his blue boat rushed by and ahead.

Chris looked back again just in time to see the red K-2 pop up from being submerged. Both girls again spat out a mouthful of water and shook their heads, trying to free the water from their helmets. He knew they couldn't survive too many of these. The river opened up a little and seemed to slow; however, it was still a Class IV and paddling had become exhausting. Chris knew that if he was cold and getting tired, the others had to be exhausted. The view ahead wasn't offering much hope, either. The boulder field went on and on and the canyon walls were getting taller and taller. Climbing out now looked impossible.

"Think!" he yelled aloud.

At that second he spotted a pile of rocks ahead on the right and started waving his paddle toward the other two kayaks. R.O. saw him first and nodded his head. Finally Natalie spotted his waving paddle and nodded and pointed her paddle toward the rocks. They were about a hundred yards away and closing fast. The boulder field was still a massive maze of rock with two large hydraulics dead ahead. A cluster of gargantuan boulders posed like a giant gate guarded each one. Chris paddled with all his might and the others followed his lead.

"What's he going to do?" Heather shouted to Natalie.

"I'm not sure, but I think he's going to try to wedge his boat into the rocks," Natalie shouted back.

"He's crazy," Heather replied.

Natalie nodded her head in agreement and stroked hard with her paddle.

Chris was only fifty feet away when he suddenly jammed his paddle into the water deep as a rudder and turned his yellow kayak sideways. In two more seconds he quickly leaned to the right as the boat slammed into the two boulders that guarded the entrance to the hydraulic and flipped upside down. He heard a crack as R.O. collided with his kayak and careened onto the pile of rocks with one end out of the water.

"Paddle hard and push toward R.O.," Natalie yelled to Heather and pushed her paddle deep.

Heather pulled with all her might and felt the scraping sound of the rocks on the right and R.O.'s blue kayak on the left.

"Get out and pull on the loop quick," Natalie yelled to Heather.

R.O. was already pulling his kayak another foot out of the river when he turned to help Heather. The second he let go, the blue kayak was yanked back into the main course of the river and catapulted over Chris's yellow kayak and disappeared downstream. Heather slipped on the wet rocks but immediately got back up and pulled harder with R.O.

"Pull," Natalie yelled, not yet able to get out.

The weight of the boat finally shifted and it began to slide onto the pile of soccer-ball-sized rocks. Natalie yanked at the spray shield rope and climbed out as quickly as she could. The three pulled the heavy red boat farther away from the river until they were standing at the wall of the canyon.

"Oh my gosh. Chris," Natalie gasped and put her wet, gloved hands to her mouth.

"Chris!" R.O. screamed.

"Chris!" Heather joined in as fear filled her thoughts and her eyes filled with tears.

Natalie tried to yell but the lump forming in her throat wouldn't let her.

"Chris," she whispered.

All three teens crawled across the rocks with R.O. reaching the top of a big boulder. Chris's kayak had gone through the hydraulic and was floating in pieces down the river.

"Wow," R.O. said softly as he spotted a piece of it moving in circles in a whirlpool fifty yards downriver. The sides of his mouth turned down and tears began to escape his eyes. He shivered from head to toe and turned to look at the girls, several feet below him. As he shook his head, they both burst into tears and began sobbing. Natalie then put her arms around Heather and pulled her close. R.O. sat down on the big boulder and put his face in his hands and let out a small whimper.

Twenty minutes passed while the kids didn't move as they mourned over the loss of Chris, their big brother and protector. R.O. finally slid down the boulder and walked over to the girls and fell into a group hug with them.

"What will we do?" Heather managed between sobs.

"I don't know. We'll think of something. Maybe he's still alive downstream or somewhere," Natalie said.

"Nobody could survive that river, not even Chris," R.O. said as he wiped the tears from his eyes.

"Don't say that," Heather said. "Chris can do anything."

"Wait, did you hear that?" Natalie asked and stood up.

"All I hear is the river," R.O. replied.

"No listen, there it is again," Natalie said.

"I heard it. It's faint. It's a whistle," R.O. said.

Natalie tugged at her dry suit and unzipped the first few inches. She pulled out a plastic whistle on a long black string lanyard. With one blow she let out an extended whistle and then stopped. Taking in another breath she blew again.

From a distance, a shrill return whistle could be heard bouncing off the canyon walls. Then there were two more blasts.

"He's alive," Heather shouted.

The three kids started jumping up and down. R.O. slipped on the rocks and nearly fell into the river.

"O.K., what do we do?" Natalie said to herself. "He may be hurt, a broken arm or leg, or maybe he's laying on a rock barely alive."

"Stop that," Heather said. "I don't want to think that way."

Then they heard another whistle blast and R.O. climbed back up on the boulder. Within seconds he spotted Chris's blue helmet.

"There he is. I see him," R.O. shouted down to the girls.

Natalie and Heather climbed to the top with R.O., where they spotted Chris on the other side of the river.

All three began waving as Chris waved back from the entrance of a cave.

"Is he waving for us to come over there?" Heather asked.

"I think he is," Natalie answered.

The three waited as they saw Chris work his way along a narrow ledge, carefully stepping from the top of one large boulder to the next, until he was twenty feet away and perched just across from them.

"We thought you were dead," R.O. shouted.

"Me too," Chris shouted back and smiled.

"Get the rope. Tie one end down and throw it to me," Chris shouted back.

"Roger," R.O. said as they all climbed down and started unloading the supplies from the battered red kayak.

Thirty minutes passed as they took out the supplies and tied the rope to a large boulder. They looped it so that the rope could slide over the top. R.O. climbed back up and with a big swing heaved the rope across to Chris. Chris barely moved to catch the perfect throw; he smiled and winked at R.O., who grinned with pride. R.O. then noticed the blood on Chris's face and his ripped dry suit. Chris scurried across the boulders and found a tight place to tie the rope so that it was suspended above the river between the two giant rocks.

"He's not thinking what I think he's thinking, is he?" Heather asked, looking at Natalie.

"Yes, we better regain our courage because I think we're all going across to the other side," Natalie replied.

"Go get any supplies you can bag. Cut off the excess rope and make loops. Then make a pull rope for me," Chris shouted to R.O. over the noise of the river.

Thirty more minutes passed as R.O., Natalie, and Heather fashioned all of their supplies into three bags and fixed the ropes as directed.

R.O. climbed back up and lifted the supplies to the top. He tied a loop on each pack and then to the main rope and tossed the pull rope to Chris. This time he missed and it dangled down into the river. He pulled it up and threw it again. This throw was perfect and Chris started hauling the supplies over. It worked like a rope chain and soon all three bags were on the other side and secured on a group of rocks away from the river.

"Now, I want you to take your life jacket, unfasten it and then refasten it with the rope on the inside. Got it?" Chris said.

"Yes," R.O. shouted back.

"Then just drop off the side and pull yourself across hand over hand, and use your feet," Chris shouted.

R.O., with his trusting spirit, never hesitated as he followed instructions to the letter. Soon he was dangling over the hydraulic just four feet above the water and pulling himself to the other side. Chris reached out and grabbed his right wrist and pulled him up the rock. After he released the rope from his vest, he hugged Chris without saying a word.

Natalie and Heather were now crouching on the boulder across the stream.

"I can't believe I'm doing this," Heather said.

"We've done worse?" replied Natalie.

Heather refastened her life jacket and squeezed the water out of her gloves. With a small step she knelt down, rolled upside down, and was at once suspended over the rushing river. Heather pulled herself quickly to the other side. Soon she was crawling up on the giant boulder and embracing Chris and R.O., before stepping gingerly to the other side of the canyon. Finally Natalie tightened her helmet and slid slowly across the boulder before dangling over the hydraulic.

Natalie was barely halfway across when Chris felt a slight vibration in the rope. Suddenly it broke free from the boulder on the other side dumping Natalie into the middle of the raging river.

"Get off the rock!" he shouted to R.O., who danced like a deer from one rock to the next to reach Heather.

Chris swiftly wrapped the pull rope around his waist, tied a knot and leapt into the hydraulic following Natalie's rope into the whitewater rushing up and across his face. The rush of the water pulled him vertically downriver and filled his jacket with icy water as he slid along the rope. He suddenly felt Natalie as his legs brushed against hers, and he grabbed for her life jacket. They were now at the bottom of the hydraulic with the pressure wave passing over them.

Chris yanked his knife free from the scabbard on his vest, and with one slash he cut the rope. They were jerked into the full course of the river and surfaced about forty feet down river from the boulders. As they bobbed to the surface, Natalie gulped in air and began choking.

"Breathe then blow, I got you," Chris said as he let go of the knife and it sank to the bottom of the river.

Natalie tried to breathe, but the waves submerged them every ten feet.

"Hang on. We're going into the canyon wall in about thirty seconds, twenty . . ." Chris shouted.

Natalie nodded as she continued her struggle to breathe.

"Ten, here it comes," Chris said as they slammed into the curved wall of the canyon. They slid along the rock surface of the wall, worn away by thousands of years of rushing water. The jagged edges of the rock ripped and tore at Natalie's suit and what was left of Chris's.

"Roll over and look at me," Chris shouted.

Natalie caught her breath and obeyed immediately.

"When I say now, reach up as far as you can. There's an opening about a hundred yards away," Chris shouted.

The raging river delivered them to the cave entrance in a matter of seconds. At the last second the main stream departed toward the center, and they rushed toward the opening.

"Now," Chris shouted.

They stretched and found the rugged rock floor of the entrance and gripped it tightly.

"Hang on as I pull up," Chris said.

In seconds he was crawling out of the river on his belly, reaching down for Natalie. He pulled her by both arms into the dark entrance and away from the water. There was an eerie silence as both teens lay on their backs shivering and breathing deeply. Several minutes passed before either moved. Chris sat up and looked at Natalie.

"Are you all right?" Chris asked.

She leaned sideways and pushed herself up into a sitting position.

"I better go back and get Ryan and Heather. They'll think we've both drowned," Chris said.

"Yes," Natalie responded. "They'll be worrying for sure."

"I'll move as quickly as my cold feet will let me," Chris replied. "Take off the vest and as much of the wet clothing as you can."

Natalie removed her battered helmet just as Chris stepped out of the cave. He began creeping along the narrow ledge toward Heather and R.O. After a few minutes he stopped and blew three sharp blasts on his whistle and got three back from his two relieved siblings. An hour passed before Chris, R.O., Heather, and three bundles of supplies were all in the cave with Natalie.

Heather dropped her bundle on the rock floor of the cave as R.O. stepped in behind her.

"This must be the coolest cave I've ever been in," R.O. proclaimed. "Do you guys remember Carlsbad Caverns? You know with all those stalacmites and stalagbites?"

"Stalactites," Chris corrected as he unloaded the packs and passed out the only three bottles of water to survive the canyon.

"Yea, those too," R.O. replied as he took off his helmet and watched Chris retrieve three bottles of water.

All four took big drinks and drained the bottles. Chris and Natalie leaned against each other on the floor of the cave and soon put their helmets and vests back on for warmth. R.O. lay down with his head resting on one of the bundles as Heather sidled over to Natalie.

In minutes they were all asleep. Outside, the river rushed by as it had for thousands of years. The day passed and the sun went down while the teens slept inside the remote lair of the ancient river gorge.

2

Four Point Five

Chris was the first to wake up and found Natalie curled up against him. R.O. and Heather were sleeping peacefully, both hugging a supply sack and with their backs touching. He wished he had brought a camera when he suddenly remembered he had one in the watertight first aid kit. He hesitated to dig in after it because of his exhaustion. He felt like he had been clearing an East Texas forest with an axe from the ache in his arms and shoulders. His need for aspirin quickly overcame his hesitation, and he began digging through the pack to find the first aid kit.

As he explored the bag, his mind drifted to his mom and dad back in Beijing. He thought how this was supposed to be an uneventful two weeks in China, seeing the sights while his dad, zoologist Dr. Jack MacGregor, attended an environmental conference about China's new Three Gorges Dam.

He blinked and realized that the cave was eerily lit although the entrance was as black as midnight. He gently slid a bag away from Heather; she barely moved. Untying the rope he opened the netted bag and saw that two light sticks had been activated and were the source of the yellow-green light. Taking them from the bag he found they illuminated most of the cavern. In the bag, he found six more light sticks that hadn't been activated and breathed a sigh of relief.

"Wow, that's cool," R.O. said as he sat up and rubbed his eyes.

"We've been sleeping for about six hours. It was nearly noon when we hit the water and it gets dark about five this time of year. So we're one hour into the night," Chris informed as he glanced at his watch.

"Is anyone going to rescue us?" R.O. asked.

"Sure. The homing chip inside the GPS device on my vest will tell them exactly where we are or help guide us out of here," Chris said. He felt down the front of his vest and frowned.

"That's going to do a lot of good," Natalie said as she sat up, having listened to the conversation.

The GPS device was gone. Only the fastener and a piece of yellow plastic remained on Chris's vest.

"Well, who knows? It might have saved my life. You know, a sharp rock or something . . ." Chris said.

"No something else about it, Chris," R.O. interjected quickly. "Nothing out there but rocks and river. I never even saw one fish!"

"What now?" Heather asked as she sat up against the cave wall. "I'm cold."

Chris began to rummage through the small bags and found the first aid kit. He also found his small digital camera and two more light sticks.

"That's eight," he said.

"Eight what?" Heather asked.

"Eight light sticks left. Enough to get us through the night in the cave until we can get back outside tomorrow and wait for a helicopter to come looking for us," Chris replied with optimism.

"Let's explore the cave," R.O. said excitedly, grabbing a light stick as he stood.

"Wait, no one leaves the group," Chris said.

"Roger. I was just going to walk around. I do need to go find a place to, you know," R.O. said and raised his eyebrows.

"Me too," Heather said and stood up.

"That's three," Natalie joined in.

"O.K., R.O. and I will go to the left side of the cavern and the girls go to the right side of the cavern. That way," Chris replied and pointed. "Use your compass. That would be due north. The girls go due south. The river is due west."

The boys walked toward the left. The girls headed to the right with a light stick, which revealed a narrow, worn path.

"Chris," Natalie shouted, hearing her voice echo in the cavern. "There's a pathway over here."

"We'll be there in a minute," Chris replied, following R.O.

After a few minutes everyone had taken care of business, and R.O. and Chris had joined the girls on the narrow pathway. They began to walk across the cavern toward a dark tunnel, about fifty yards away.

"Can I go first?" R.O. asked.

"No one is going in there tonight," Chris said and stared back at him. "In fact, give me the light stick. I control the light so that means I control the cave."

"We may be the first humans in centuries to be here." R.O. replied.

"Another day, little brother. We all need to go back and huddle together for the night. I noticed a plastic box of cookies in the bag and some kind of candy. I'm a little rusty on my Chinese, so I couldn't tell you what the flavor of either is," Chris said and started leading them down the path toward the entrance. They could hear the river's roar as they drew closer to their makeshift camp. Within minutes, all the bags were emptied and everyone was munching on cookies and dark chocolate candy.

The cold was starting to set in again. Chris had bare legs up to his hip on one side and to the knee on the other. Natalie wasn't much better as she had lost a sleeve on her right arm. To make matters worse, they were still wearing their rafting shoes over wet socks. In an effort to stay warm, they zipped up their damp vests and fastened down their helmets. Their gloves were helpful in retaining heat since most of the water had drained from them.

The river had drained their energy and once they had a little food in their stomachs they all fell asleep again. They lay stacked together like wood with R.O. and Chris on the outside and Natalie and Heather on the inside. As trained young explorers they knew when to stop their sibling rivalry and pay attention to the dangers of nature and protect their lives.

Four hours had passed when Chris abruptly sat up straight. The two light sticks had burned out and it was pitch black except for the face of his diving watch. Likewise, he could see the faces of the other three glowing watches. Then he felt something, the same thing that had awakened him.

"Natalie, Heather, R.O. Wake up!" He said loudly enough to cause an echo.

The three teens awakened just as Chris ignited a light stick.

"What is it?" Heather asked first.

"I don't know. It's a strange vibration of some kind. I can't put my finger on it," Chris replied just as a large rock fell from the ceiling and landed about ten feet away, causing a concussion like a shotgun blast.

"O.K. That explains it," Chris shouted, jumping to his feet. "Earthquake. Grab everything quick, now. We've got to get moving toward the tunnel."

"Won't the tunnel cave in?" Heather asked over the noise.

"Do you want to go back to the river?" Chris shouted as he picked up a pack.

Heather knew the answer and quickly grabbed the supplies that were strewn on the cave floor. Everyone was on their feet, picking up supplies as quickly as they could, when two more boulders dropped thirty feet away, and the cave began to rumble. Just as Heather picked up the last light sticks and the box of cookies, the floor began to rise under her feet.

"Chris, Chris," she screamed as it lifted her one foot higher than everyone else.

"Let's go," Chris said as he grabbed her arm and pulled her toward him.

He tossed a light stick to R.O., who dashed toward the path leading to the tunnel making a splendid catch without breaking his stride. They found the path quickly, with R.O. in the lead followed by Natalie, Heather, and Chris. The cave was moving all around them as if it were a living animal waking from a century's long slumber; Chris heard a splashing noise and knew that the river had invaded the cave. He didn't look back, knowing he couldn't see it anyway.

"Faster, the river's coming into the cave," he shouted.

Heather suddenly stopped.

"What are you doing?" Chris shouted.

"I dropped the cookies," she yelled back.

"Forget them. We can't stop," he said as he suddenly felt water on the back of his bare legs.

"Run, run, run," Chris shouted and held on to Heather's arm, pulling her behind him.

In seconds they were all running in eighteen inches of water and losing the trail. Rocks and boulders were splashing all around them, some bouncing as high as two feet in the air.

"I see it. Straight ahead," R.O. said as he sprinted through the water, soaking Natalie with each stride.

Chris was the last inside the tunnel. He thought about them drowning like rats in a hole as he ran inside.

"It's an ancient stairway," Natalie said.

"Then up we go. Can't take a chance on the river rising or the cliff wall sinking,"

Chris replied.

"Is it safe?" Heather asked quickly.

"Safer than drowning and if it all falls in, it won't matter anyway," Chris said solemnly. "So keep moving."

Chris could barely see Heather and Natalie so he kept his eyes on the glow from R.O.'s light stick as he climbed above them. The stairs began to turn inside the narrow opening, creating a spiraling effect. Every few steps one of the adventurers would slip and fall. Soon they all had banged up knees and elbows. Their wet shoes didn't give them much traction or comfort. Then the earth moved again and the rumble echoed through the tunnel.

"Heather, give everyone a light stick and pass the rest down to me," Chris commanded as he instinctively looked up at the ceiling of the passageway.

"Did you feel that one?" Natalie said.

"How big of a quake, Chris?" Heather asked.

"I can only guess. Maybe a four or a four point five," Chris replied as he climbed behind them. "The science camp I went to," he said as he breathed in deep, "let us stand in an earthquake simulator. I'm guessing that it's maybe a four point five. A five would have knocked us down. But I'm also guessing that if it were really big, we wouldn't be standing here talking," Chris replied.

"No, we'd be in the first stages of worm bait," R.O. called back down the tunnel.

R.O. stepped out of the stairway tunnel into a small cavern. Natalie was next and in minutes they all stood with their arms lifted high and light shining on the walls of the big room.

"Where are we?" Heather asked expecting Chris to be able to answer.

"I don't know. I'm guessing we're about a hundred feet above the river but two hundred feet from the surface. The canyon was over two hundred feet deep when we entered the river and dropped another seventy-five feet during the run before we bailed out," Chris replied, walking around shining his light on the walls. "I just can't tell. We moved so fast and climbed in the dark. There's no way to really know how high we are in the cliffs of the canyon. Walking in the dark can play tricks on you. Look at this," he said and pointed his light stick toward a pile of rocks. "Some of the rocks were shaken loose here but I don't see . . . wait. Yes, I do. Look over there."

"That's quite a rock slide," Natalie said and walked over next to him and took his hand in hers and squeezed. Chris looked at her.

"There's something unusual about that pile of rocks. There aren't any sharp cuts. Looks like a pile of rocks that used to be a pile of rocks," Chris said.

"Are you saying that the rocks didn't come from the earthquake? I mean the earthquake caused them to be the way they are but someone had originally stacked them there first. They just didn't fall off the cave wall." R.O. said.

"Yes, that's pretty much it," Chris said.

Chris started to climb the pile of rocks carefully, holding the light stick in his mouth. In a few minutes he reached the top and sat on a small boulder.

"Stand away from the rock pile in case we get an aftershock," he yelled down.

He then took his light stick and heaved it through the hole at the top of the pile. It sailed through the air and bounced to a stop, lighting up a room on the other side.

"O.K., listen up you guys. I'm going over the top and into the next room. Someone put these rocks here for a reason and maybe it's to hide the way out," Chris finished and began to gingerly climb toward the opening at the top of the rock pile. A minute passed before he reached the top and then waved another light stick as he disappeared into the next room.

He was gone for ten minutes and the teenagers' light sticks had begun to die one by one. Natalie took one out of her vest pocket and broke it to give them light just as Heather's light stick went to black. Several more minutes passed before Chris appeared out of the hole.

"It's a sight you won't believe. Come up one at a time.

Place your foot on each rock firmly. Don't rush it. Heather goes first, then R.O. Natalie, sorry, but you're last," Chris said.

"That's O.K. I know why," Natalie said, taking her helmet off. She shook her long, auburn hair to work out the tangles.

Before long, all four kids were at the top and perched to go through the opening.

To their surprise, they saw a small door-like gap about four feet high and three feet wide. The light stick that Chris had ignited glowed in the room below them but the room wasn't the normal yellow-green color. They were shocked to see hues of pink, blue, orange, and red. Even more surprising were the walls of the room. They were covered with beautiful murals that wrapped all around the cave leading up to a rock stage where five Buddha stood in different poses, as if they were holding court.

"It's magnificent," Natalie gasped as she stepped through the doorway and down into the room on rock stairs. "My friend Louise would die to see this. She loves Asian art, especially ancient Asian art."

"I thought Louise was in medical school," Chris said as he led the way.

"She is, but art is her passion," Natalie replied.

Without another word, R.O. and Heather followed Natalie through the rock entrance to the floor of the room. Chris walked over to the rock stage and climbed up on it. The others held their light up to the painting and gazed at all the detail.

Soon Chris was back down on the floor, holding a small ceramic container in his right hand. With his left hand, he retrieved his camping lighter from a vest pocket and ignited it. He held the lighter up to the small cup-like pot and it immediately flared a red and orange flame.

"Wow. You found a torch," R.O. said.

"A torch nearly as old as the one I burned in Egypt," Chris replied.

"This was probably one of the world's first lanterns

fueled by gun powder, a low-grade mix that would burn slow and emit enough light without exploding. There are several more up there," Chris added.

"And not too soon," Natalie said as she dropped her light stick on the floor of the room as it began to die out.

"You'll also find another stairway at the back of the stage. My guess is that it leads to the surface," Chris said.

The other three teens cheered and their voices reverberated around the room. Soon they were all dancing in a circle until R.O. broke the chain and spun away, twirling and colliding with the wall under one of the murals. He sat there and looked where he had hit and squinted hard in the dim light.

"Hey, look at this," he said to the others who ignored him for his antics. "Hey, listen to me. You should look at this," R.O. demanded and got up.

Chris let go of Natalie's hand and walked over to him.

"What is it?" Chris asked.

R.O. reached over to the wall and peeled off what appeared to be a form of plaster. As the piece of ancient plaster fell to the floor something shiny appeared in the hole. Chris dusted off the wall. He then pealed off another piece of plaster and by that time the girls were standing behind him. With both hands he reached into the hole in the wall and pulled out a solid gold statue of Lord Buddha.

"A gold Buddha," Natalie whispered.

"Oh my, gosh," Heather responded.

"What can I say? The treasure finder Ryan O'Keefe MacGregor strikes again. Give me five, no ten," R.O. said and turned to Heather who ignored him.

"What's this above the hole," Heather asked and put her hand on the wall.

Chris leaned down and held the ceramic lantern next to the wall while holding the gold statue in his other hand.

"It's a dragon," Chris said.

"A dragon?" Natalie asked and leaned closer.

"How cool." Heather said. "Why would a dragon be in a cave with paintings about Buddha?

"I learned in my eastern religions course at the university that the Chinese mixed the mythology of dragon worship with Taoism and Buddhism. It has something to do with dragons and ancient emperors being related," Natalie said. "I can't remember it all but some emperor claimed to be related to a dragon. So they had several different kinds of dragons for royalty, the air, water, and something else I can't remember. But only the royal dragon had five claws. The other dragons had three or four claws."

"No kidding. I'm impressed you remembered all that," Heather said as she reached out and touched the dragon painted on the wall over the hole. "This dragon has five claws and is holding something round in the right foot."

Chris looked close and touched it.

"Sure is. Must be important," he replied.

He then took the statue over to the stage and dusted it off with his still damp gloves revealing a stone in its belly. It was only about six inches tall but probably weighed about three pounds. The gold glistened from the glow of the four newly lit lanterns and sent rays of light bouncing off the cave wall. It was a supernatural illumination as it mixed with the beautiful pink and green of the murals.

"What's that?" R.O. asked, pointing to the stone.

"I don't know. It's doesn't look like a precious stone, a diamond, emerald, or ruby. It looks more like a mineral. I've heard of these kinds of minerals before. It's a compound of some sort. See how it glows," Chris said and held it up high.

"I have it. I know what these paintings are," Natalie said as she walked around with the small ceramic lantern. "It's the life of Lord Buddha."

"How do you know that?" Heather inquired.

"Louise and I were in London for spring break and one of the museums had a replica of a cave very similar to this. The guide said that the Chinese loved painting the life of

Buddha in hope of garnering as many blessings as possible as they studied his teachings. Look at the stage. Those are five different faces of Buddha probably representing Chinese government or society or whatever. A mural with four different scenes and a gold Buddha buried in the wall. It's got to be that," Natalie stated convincingly. "There could be other treasures in the wall. Dragons watched over the earth, brought rain, protected treasure, and had magical properties. Unlike European dragons that were mean, Chinese dragons were kind and helpful. They could even fly magically without wings."

"You must have made an A on that exam," Heather said admiringly.

"I did," Natalie smiled.

"I'll give you guys a one-half cut of the Buddha. I get the other half. Just be lucky I share it at all," R.O. said and patted the statue on the head.

"The statue stays here," Chris said. We still have to find our way out and we don't know who we can trust. This is, after all, the People's Republic of China. We just can't walk into a local police station and say, 'look what we found.' There are all kinds of international implications. They could say we stole it and put us in prison."

"Good thinking, Chris. The statue stays here. I'm ready to go," Heather said and climbed up on the stage.

Chris walked over and put the statue back into its two thousand-year-old hiding place and piled the plaster up around it, covering it the best he could. Without saying a word he climbed the stage, walked between the life-size Buddha toward the rear entrance and entered the stairway followed by Heather, Natalie, and R.O. The kids began climbing again.

The journey to the surface was tiring and by now they were beyond fatigued. Stopping every twenty steps or so, they took in deep breaths of the stale air of the tunnel.

"Check your packs and dump anything unnecessary.

You don't need extra ballast," Chris said as he stood straight up.

"I can't go anymore," Heather pleaded to Chris. "Can't we stop longer than two minutes?"

"O.K. Everyone down and try to get comfortable," Chris replied.

It was only a matter of minutes before all were asleep. They were curled up tight on the steps and Natalie was leaning against Chris's legs.

Heather was the first to awake when the earth shook again.

"Earthquake," she shouted as they all woke up.

"It's probably just an aftershock," Chris coolly stated. The vibrations started to slow down. "Time to get going."

"That felt good. We needed the rest," Natalie replied as she tightened her helmet strap.

Slightly refreshed they all fell in behind Chris as he continued the climb toward the surface. No one spoke as they walked for what seemed like an hour in the narrow tunnel, their ancient lanterns still glowing after thousands of years of rest.

"Finally," Chris said, stepping into a small room that was damp and musty. "Watch out," he shouted as a bat flew by. "That's a great sign you guys."

"Where there's a bat, there's an opening," R.O. piped in.

"My lantern just burned out," Natalie said and set the ceramic cup on the floor.

She moved in closer behind Chris.

"We're going to follow the cave wall until we find another tunnel or the opening," Chris said and picked up the pace.

"What if all the lanterns go out?" Heather offered nervously.

"Then we'll use our lighters and just keep going. We have no choice," Chris retorted.

The group became quiet as they walked along the cave wall, stepping through piles and piles of bat guano.

"This is disgusting," Heather said.

"I once read that you can get rabies from bat urine that floats in the air of caves," R.O. said.

"Ryan you are so enlightening some times," Natalie said and blew at a lock of hair that had fallen in her face.

"I think I see a shadow of something ahead. It's not a cave wall," Chris said as they all huddled together behind him. "It's late so there won't be any light outside. We'll have to stop here and take our chances later after the lanterns burn out or we move forward in the dark."

"What is it?" Natalie asked.

"It's a massive root bank from trees on the surface. My guess is we are between ten and one hundred feet from the surface, but we can't see the light to follow the openings in the root." Chris answered.

"I vote we go forward and take our chances," Heather said.

"Me too. I'm tired of the cave," R.O. agreed.

"There's a large space here next to what I think is the last stairway to the top. I think we should try it. The lanterns will be gone in a few minutes then we'll just be hoping that there's enough light from our lighters to lead the way," Chris said. "O.K., that's the plan. We start climbing. Secure the packs. Knock out the ashes and put the lanterns in one of the packs. Heather, leave your lantern on the floor next to the opening so we can look down and have a reference spot. Up we go," he said confidently. He stepped up to a large tree root, grabbed, and began to climb. He knocked the guano off his shoes and took another step.

"Hey, watch out. I don't want that bat dung in my face," Heather exclaimed.

"Sorry," Chris said and kept on climbing.

In a matter of minutes all four teens were squirming up through the massive root complex as if they were climbing a large oak tree back home in Texas. The spaces were large enough for a human and the lack of dirt and debris allowed them to have a firm hold with each step.

"This is too awesome," R.O. said as he stepped on a large root.

"It's really dark, Chris," Heather complained as she stepped up behind Natalie.

"Chris, I can't see any light from the lantern," Natalie said.

"It must have burned out. We've climbed about ten feet. Keep going. I want a sound check from everyone every minute," Chris said.

"R.O."

"Check."

"Heather."

"Check."

"Natalie."

"Check."

"O.K., now let's keep talking and I want everyone to say something no matter how dumb it is. I want to hear your voices," Chris called down the root hole they were following.

"I'm hungry. I'm tired. I want a fluffy pillow and bed. I want a warm coat. I'm still cold from Alaska. Never warmed up for a minute," Heather stated.

"I want a big turkey dinner for Thanksgiving," R.O. answered.

"With cranberry sauce, dressing, hot rolls, and butter," Natalie joined in.

"And a big pecan pie, my favorite," Chris replied.

"Don't forget the whipped cream," R.O. interjected.

For the next thirty minutes they discussed the food they wanted for Thanksgiving, their favorite dinner of all time, the worst food they had ever eaten, and how they all wanted dry socks.

"I feel a breeze," Chris shouted.

"Me too," Natalie said.

"Here it is. It's a big opening to a rock surface. Everyone stop. R.O., you there, buddy?" Chris asked.

"I'm here dude. Just keep moving," R.O. shouted from below Heather.

"I'm climbing through a hole between the roots. I'm going up and out," Chris yelled with each step and reach.

Natalie followed as quickly as she could, continuing to scratch her knees on the roots through the torn dry suit that was now shredded beyond recognition. She felt Chris's strong hands as she reached for the surface and he pulled her through the opening. Heather was next, followed by R.O. The kids sat quietly in the cold breeze and looked up at the bright stars in the sky. The radiance of the full moon allowed them to see each other's faces and the shadows of the trees around them. Heather began to cry and everyone huddled around her.

"We made it," Chris whispered. "It's alright now."

"I know. I am just so exhausted," Heather replied.

"We all are. So let's go find help," Natalie said as they stood up and stretched their arms and legs.

Chris and R.O. grabbed a pack and started off through the dimly lit forest.

"Stop for a second," Chris said. He pulled out his compass and ignited his lighter. "We need to go that way," he said and pointed toward the east. "That's away from the canyon and the river and toward the village I saw on the map."

R.O. ran to the front next to Chris as they weaved through the forest. Over an hour passed before they broke free from the tree line and were standing in a plowed field.

With little left of their dry suits, they were all shivering from the cold. The small fire they had started nearly thirty minutes before had long lost its power on their bodies.

"There's the village," Chris said as he pointed toward a few speckles of light coming from fires near a cluster of houses.

With resolve encouraged by the fact that they had finally re-entered civilization, the kids walked faster and climbed over a dozen stone walls that divided the fields before they entered the village of dirt streets, no automobiles, and nearly two hundred houses. Corralled animals awoke as the visitors walked by, baaing, mooing, or snorting. Within minutes people stepped from the dwellings with oil lamps in their hands. They were staring at the strangers in red, blue, green, and yellow tattered dry suits that were dangling from their bodies. Their equally colorful helmets and the dried blood on their faces gave them the strange appearance of aliens who had just landed and battled to capture the planet Earth.

The kids stood watching as the crowd began to grow and a roar of voices speaking in Chinese surrounded them.

"Anyone speak English?" Chris asked.

The crowd became quiet, almost shocked that these aliens could communicate.

A small, almost frail old man stepped from the crowd.

"I speak English," he said very clearly. "You must be the Americans that the army has been looking for. They have been very worried about you since the earthquake."

"Yes, we are Americans," Chris replied.

"Texans too," R.O. popped off.

The crowd erupted in more talk with the word American being heard clearly.

"You must be very tired and hungry. We were told you were riding the river when the earthquake came. I am amazed that you were able to climb out of the canyon and walk to our village. You must be very strong," the old man said.

He then turned to the crowd and barked some orders. It soon dispersed. Only four people stayed and walked closer to the teenagers and stood next to the old man.

"We'll share our warm homes with you tonight and give you something to eat. The army will be notified by radio. They will be happy to see you are still alive. It would have been embarrassing if you had died in the river," the old man said.

"Embarrassing? Maybe really terrible would be a better way of putting it," Heather stated.

Soon the kids were being led through the streets and into

a modest home of three rooms. Tea and soup were fed to the Americans, who drank it down quickly.

Shedding their destroyed clothes, and taking off their wet socks for the first time in many hours, they wrapped up in blankets next to a warm hearth. Soon all were asleep on soft pillows and grateful for having survived yet another ordeal in their voyage around the world. But little did they know that China had more dangerous adventures to share.

3

Thanksgiving in Beijing

Shortly after dawn, Chris, Natalie, Heather, and R.O., were awakened by a young woman. She was dressed in a plain, brown tunic suit that was well worn but neatly pressed. She spoke broken English and passed out a set of clothes that resembled hers.

"Warm socks," Heather said as she thanked her and bowed her head in respect.

The old man, who had greeted them several hours before, walked into the room.

"Good morning MacGregors and you as well, Miss Crosswhite. An army helicopter will be here soon to take you to Mienyang and from there you will be flown to Beijing to meet your parents. I have been informed that the success of your kayak adventure has been shared with our government and they are pleased that you established what is called 'a first' for that tributary of the Fuo River," he said and smiled.

"Success. Did he say success?" Heather asked.

"Yes. We're alive so that means it was successful," Natalie said as she stood up with the blanket wrapped around her and waddled into the next room to change. Heather followed.

The old man and the young woman left the room and all the kids dressed quickly, putting their dirty and damaged rafting shoes back on over the clean socks. Chris and R.O. picked up the two remaining packs and went out the door. The streets were full again but this time with a company of soldiers in uniforms, arms, and packs. Chris and R.O. stood perfectly still as Natalie and Heather walked out and stood behind them. The old man walked over to them.

"I apologize that I didn't introduce myself. I am Hao Lu. I am what you would call the mayor of this village. I sent a radio message when you arrived last night to the People's Liberation Army to inform them of your safe arrival at our humble village. The soldiers have been here for an hour waiting for the sun to rise. They will escort you to the landing site of the helicopter," he said as the young woman who had brought them the clothes reappeared with a wooden box in her arms. The old man took the box and turned toward Chris.

"It has been an honor to have you stay in our village. No Westerner has ever done so, and we would like for you to have this gift to remember this day," he said and handed the box to Chris.

"Thank you for your help and your hospitality," Chris said and took the box. They bowed in unison.

The commander of the troops gave an order in a low voice and the soldiers came to attention.

"They are ready for you to go. Have a safe journey, Mr. MacGregor," Hao Lu said and bowed again.

"Thank you," Chris replied and bowed back.

The four teens then walked over toward the soldiers and fell in behind them. R.O. waved at the villagers who were watching and they all waved back. As he tried to bow and walk, he stumbled and nearly fell down not having realized that the modern custom is to only bow one's head. They traveled behind the Chinese troops for nearly a mile before they began to hear the thumping of the rotary blades of a helicopter. As it neared, the troops stopped and the officer in charge walked over to Chris.

"Please wait here," he said in perfect English.

"Do they all speak English?" R.O. asked.

"I would imagine just the people in authority do," Natalie answered.

"Sikorsky S-70A Black Hawk. I would have never guessed," Chris said.

"A Black Hawk?" R.O. inquired.

"Sure is. I think China has only a few hundred helicopters in the entire country. At least that's what the Western nations believe. But the demand is estimated to reach ten to twenty thousand this century," Chris replied.

"I wish I could remember facts like that," Heather said and smiled.

They stood still and watched the camouflage painted aircraft drop in smoothly for a landing and begin to decelerate the blades. The army officer hurried over to them and put his radio back in his belt holder.

"We are ready for you to board. Have a safe journey," he said and bowed.

An aviator jumped out of the side door and ran toward the teens.

"Follow me please," he said and took off in a run toward the helicopter.

"O.K., let's run," Natalie said and took off behind him.

Within minutes they were all aboard and strapped inside the big Sikorsky that was outfitted as a war bird. It was equipped with external canons and shell boxes strapped to the insides. Sitting on a hard plastic bench, the kids watched as the Chinese pilot increased the rpm, and the massive rotary wings lifted the aircraft into the air. No one spoke a word.

Chris took out his compass and checked their bearings. The helicopter was flying forty degrees northeast.

"Natalie," he shouted over the noise and the ear protectors

they had put on. "We're going the wrong way. Mienyang is 150° south. We're headed northeast," he said and pointed to the compass.

He then leaned across the space toward the front of the helicopter and got the attention of the aviator who had accompanied them into the aircraft. He was neither the pilot nor the co-pilot. Chris held out the compass for him to see and then said Mienyang. The Chinese aviator smiled and replied.

"No Mienyang. Xi'an."

"Oh. Thanks," Chris stated.

"What's Xi'an?" Heather shouted.

"Another city. My guess from looking at a map of China is that it is about three or four hundred miles away. We'll be there in a couple of hours if we don't have a head wind. This baby will fly about 162 mph or 140 knots," Chris said.

"Ever since you got your pilot's license in Italy, you've turned into an aviation geek," Heather shouted back to him.

Chris just smiled and Natalie gripped his arm tighter.

"I'm hungry," R.O. yelled over the noise.

Within seconds the aviator had opened a box on the side of the seat and produced a package of something that was round, hard, and looked like a big cookie. He took one out and took a bite and handed the package to the kids.

"It's a sweet bread of some kind," Natalie said as she swallowed a big bite.

They all ate one and R.O. grabbed a second. Time passed quickly as the explorers quietly gazed out at the country-side called the breadbasket of China, the most fertile land in the nation.

Before they knew it the city of Xi'an could be seen. The Black Hawk circled a military landing strip and set down next to a large hangar where two army trucks were parked. A twin engine Aero Commander was parked next to the trucks. Like the helicopter, it too had a Chinese flag paint-ed on it. As soon as the helicopter landed, the kids were ushered off the Black Hawk and then on the airplane. A female aviator greeted them once aboard.

"Please fasten your seat belt. We will be in Beijing in one hour. Your parents have been notified that you will be arriving at the airport and someone will be there to welcome you. Your mother sends word for you to remember the dinner tonight at the American embassy. They are busy with activities all afternoon and will gladly meet you there at 5:00 p.m. You'll have a few hours to rest and prepare for the dinner once you get to your hotel. There are facilities in the back of the airplane if you need them," the uniformed officer said and walked back to her seat behind the pilot's section.

"What was that?" R. O. asked.

"A very efficient person," Natalie answered.

"We have to go to a dinner?" Heather asked incredulously.

"I forgot about that. We were supposed to finish the river early last night and then catch a flight from Mienyang to Beijing. We would have been there by midnight and had a whole day free before the dinner," Chris said.

"What dinner?" Heather asked again.

"It's a dinner for people associated with Three Gorges Dam, the giant dam project over the Jinyang River that will be finished in about five more years. This is the first time the Chinese government has agreed to listen to some of the environmental concerns that other nations have and Dad is part of the American delegation," Chris said.

"Well, I'm taking a long, hot bath and an equally long nap before I even think of getting ready," Heather said.

"Ditto that," Natalie replied and smiled at Heather.

"Hey, I just remembered. Tomorrow is Thanksgiving," R.O. shouted.

"That's right. Mom said that yesterday, no, day before yesterday before Chris talked her into letting us go rafting." Heather jabbed.

"Who knew it was a Class IV river?" Chris answered.

"We know, who knew," Natalie said and squinted her

eyes at him. "And now Chris MacGregor is in the record books for a 'first' on a Class IV river in China."

"Well, I didn't know it was going to get that bad and if it hadn't been for you, little brother, we'd be in Beijing right now seeing the sights," Chris retorted.

"I can't figure out why Mom won't be at the airport. After all, we survived a Class IV river, an earthquake, a dangerous climb from the center of the earth . . ." Heather started.

"Center of the earth, was it? That's a stretch," Chris cut in.

"Well I learned it from the king of stretches, prince fibber himself, Chris MacGregor," Heather said and laughed.

"That's a good one, Heather," Natalie said. "Maybe your parents don't know about all of this. You know how secretive the Chinese are about everything. Maybe they want to save face."

"Suits me just fine. The less explaining I have to do about anything, the better off I am," R.O. declared.

The cabin warmed up and the kids drifted off to sleep. Before they knew it, the aircraft was landing at the international airport in Beijing among all the giant airliners delivering tourists, Western contractors, and diplomats from all over the world. A taxi ride to the hotel through the bustling capital of the People's Republic of China was an adventure in itself. Streets were being resurfaced after decades of neglect, and high-rise office buildings and apartments were springing up everywhere. It was typical of the growing pains of a third world country making the jump into the twenty-first century. There were fewer bicycles and more cars than ever before, but the cyclist was still the dominant person on the street. In Beijing the automobile is merely the dream of a dawning middle class, as an attainable personal wealth staggers far behind the rest of the world.

As the kids stepped out of the taxi, Chris paid the driver. They walked up the magnificent marble steps of the new hotel. After checking in at the front desk and finding out which suite their parents were in, they took the elevator to the twenty-second floor and found the suite, twenty-two, twenty-two.

"That's pretty cool," R.O. said as they pushed the door open.

"This is really beautiful," Heather agreed as they walked in and browsed around.

"Kitchen, sitting room, four bedrooms. Guess we'll be bunking together, Heather," Natalie said as she turned to R.O. "Don't say it. I'm not a poet."

"Together, Heather. Sure sounds like a rhyme to me," R.O. grinned.

Chris ordered room service for everyone and the food arrived thirty minutes later. Chris headed for the shower while the others began to eat hot soup, hamburgers, fries, and down a few soft drinks. By the time Chris emerged clean, with hair still wet, the food was scattered over the kitchen with his portion set to one side on the table. Heather and R.O. were still eating and not saying a word. Chris joined them and devoured a hamburger. One by one the other teens left and headed for the showers. R.O. was first, followed by Heather, then Natalie.

They were all sound asleep when the front desk rang their room with a complimentary wake-up call.

"Mr. MacGregor?" the front desk manager asked.

"Yes, this is Chris."

"It's four o'clock and your driver will be here in forty-five minutes," he said.

"Thank you," Chris replied and got up. He had barely walked a step when he felt the jabbing pain in his shoulders and hips.

Walking stiffly through the suite, he began waking everyone. The girls rushed off to do their hair, but he had to wrestle with R.O. three times before he moved. The rooms were full of activity as the four teens got ready. They dressed in the clothes that they had been instructed to wear from the note left by Mavis MacGregor.

It was late November in Beijing and the high temperature for the day was 42°. There wasn't any snow on the
ground, but the Siberian Express had brought its cold tem-
peratures straight across Mongolia into China. At five minutes until five, the front desk called and told them that the
car had arrived and was waiting. Chris wore a blue blazer,
red tie, and gray pants, with R.O. looking nearly alike.
Heather had on burgundy, wool pants and jacket. Natalie
stepped from the bedroom in a lavender dress and matching wool jacket.

"You look great," Chris said.

"Thanks," she replied.

"Let's go," Chris declared and herded them out the door.

"Wait," Heather said and rushed back inside. She snatched
up her pink parka and put it on over her wool blazer.

"Cold?" R.O. asked, raising his eyebrows.

"I'm glad mom sent these bags on to China from Alaska.
Clean clothes and warm coats are the best," Heather said,
ignoring her younger brother.

The speedy elevator covered the twenty-two floors in
seconds. The elevator doors opened and they walked into
the lobby. A young Chinese woman with a PRC Navy dress
coat greeted them and led them to a waiting car. Her shoulder epaulet revealed that she was a lieutenant. Her English
was perfect and the kids were surprised to learn she had an
engineering degree from Purdue.

The sun had vanished from the sky and it was again
dark in China. The trip to the American embassy took only
ten minutes. Upon arriving the young Chinese lieutenant
escorted the teens to the front portico. Two U.S. marines
opened the doors, and they entered into the large foyer.

"This is where I leave," the Chinese lieutenant said. "I'm
to join our delegation for the dinner. I'm sure we'll meet
later. Goodbye."

Chris, Natalie, Heather, and R.O. stood and looked at the

huge crowd gathered in the main ballroom of the embassy. They had seen this many times before. Slowly they walked toward the multitude of people but decided instead to nestle themselves against the drapes in front of three floor-to-ceiling windows. Then they spotted their mother talking to two Chinese men. R.O. took off in a dash through the crowd. As he reached her he slowed to a measured walk and stood right behind her, smiling at the two men. They smiled and bowed, and Mavis looked over her shoulder.

"Ryan, sweetie, when did you get here?" Mavis asked and gave him a big hug followed by a kiss on his cheek. "Now, don't wipe it off," she said softly, winking at him.

At that moment, Heather walked up and hugged her while Chris and Natalie stood by.

"We'll see you at dinner, Dr. MacGregor," the two men said and walked away.

"Natalie, did you keep them in line for me?" Mavis asked and smiled.

"I tried," Natalie replied.

She then turned to Chris and gave him a hug and a kiss on the cheek. Leaning back she reached up and wiped the lipstick off his cheek. When R.O. saw this he started to vigorously rub his cheeks, just to be sure.

"Well how was the rafting trip? Was the water cold? Bet you had fun, didn't you?" Mavis asked and looked at each one individually who stood there quietly.

"Great fun, Dr. MacGregor," Natalie answered.

"Natalie. What did I tell you in Cairo? You're to call me Mavis," Mavis said.

"Mavis, sorry," Natalie replied.

"And how about you big guy? Enjoy the rafting?" she asked as she turned to Chris.

"Sure mom. It was a lot of fun. Ran a few rapids, got a little wet. The usual stuff, you know," Chris responded, never losing eye contact with his mother. "The Chinese army guys really took good care of us."

Heather looked around like she was trying to locate someone in the crowd, using her best skills to avoid eye contact with her mother.

"Yes, I'm sure. Dr. Sherri Biggs, our liaison here at the embassy, said they are the best unit in China. You know, for rivers and all that sort of adventure stuff. She said they send visitors out with them all the time. Well, let's look for your father. He was with a group of Chinese environmental scientists a few minutes ago. Glad you guys had a fun two days. You'll have to share it with your father and me later," she said and turned to look through the crowd.

"You bet," R.O. retorted and caught a glare from Natalie and Chris. "I know, I know," he said and put up his right hand in front of him in a defensive posture.

Mavis walked into the crowd as the kids looked around the room.

"Well, another city another banquet. Don't we ever get tired of this?" Heather asked.

"Nope, good food is always on the horizon," R.O. answered and walked away.

"O.K., I know I'll regret this but I'm following him," Heather said and walked off.

"How about you? Hungry yet?" Natalie asked.

"It's Thanksgiving. Who wouldn't be?" Chris responded and led Natalie by the hand.

4

Major Yufan Chen

The embassy ballroom was crowded with people representing major foreign interests in China. Ambassadors from the United States, Europe, and Russia were on hand for the big party and to be sure that their presence was recognized. There were engineers from Japan, who were specialists in turbines for the many new dams that China was building across the country in their attempt to harness the dozens of rivers that ran wild and killed thousands each year. There were environmental groups from America and Europe who opposed the dam because of loss of habitat for the varied wildlife in the way. They all knew, however, that China listened to no one but its own leaders in Beijing and possibly to the new entrepreneurs scattered along the coast from Shanghai to Hong Kong. But if there was an outside chance that industrialists could earn a new contract or foreign nations a new treaty, it was worth the effort.

"Chris, I'm so hungry," Heather commented and looked up at her big brother as they came to a stop in the crowd, having lost track of the food line.

"Me too," said R. O. as he looked toward the tables being set. "I don't see a buffet table anywhere."

"I don't think there is one," Natalie stated as she looked across the room.

"I see it," Chris announced. "It's in the next room."

"See ya," R.O. said and headed that way.

Heather, Chris, and Natalie followed him through the crowd until they noticed Alaska Senator Lynn McMillon talking to their Dad. They detoured to that direction.

"Jack, I'd forgotten that your kids came to China with you," Senator McMillon said and shook Chris's hand.

"Hey Dad," Heather said and gave him a hug.

"Hi honey, how was the float trip?" Jack asked. "Hey bud," he said and grabbed Chris by the arm.

"Hey Senator McMillon, I've got a question," R.O. said and looked up at him. "Heather said that you were so scared of the mule ride down into Grand Canyon that you had to hire a helicopter to fly you out. I said no way a senator from Alaska would be afraid of that. I mean, I've traveled all over the world and been in lots of jams, just like our kayak trip down the canyon yesterday and the earthquake. I said that there would be no way you would be that scared. Right?"

Chris, Heather, and Natalie grew tense. Jack just looked on in awe and bewilderment.

"Well Ryan, I can't lie. The story is true. I lost all sense of balance on the mules and was definitely feeling uncertain about the trip back up the canyon," the Senator said. "It could have been an inner ear problem or something."

"So basically you're saying you lost it," R.O. said.

"O.K. That's it. No more interrogation." Jack said, knowing how to get rid of them. "I apologize, Senator. Kids, go find food and get busy eating."

They didn't need coaxing and quickly made their way into the buffet room in seconds, R.O. again in the lead.

"I don't know what any of this is," R.O. said as he looked at the vast array of Chinese dishes.

"Amazing," Natalie said and walked up behind him.

"Noodles, cabbage something, more noodles, chicken with mushrooms, noodles, something fried, red stuff, brown stuff, green noodles, egg looking pancakes, gravy, yes, beef with broccoli," Heather said and started filling her plate.

"Chicken soup's good. I just can't believe people would put that slimy egg stuff in their soup like we see back home," Natalie said. "Whatever happened to chicken and rice or tomato soup?"

"You guys are a bunch of wimps," Chris said and starting serving a little bit of everything on his plate. "After the cookies by the river, I'll eat anything."

The kids, except for Chris, were all back at a table picking at their dinner and sipping hot tea when Mavis walked up.

"Oh, I see you found the Chinese food buffet. The Roast Peking Duck looked delicious and the stuffed mushrooms are heavenly," Mavis teased. "But the American buffet is in the other room."

R.O. stood up and looked at Mavis' plate full of turkey, dressing, cranberry sauce, corn-on-the-cob, lime Jell-O with walnuts, and a big, hot roll.

"Man, I'm tradin' this plate in for a new one," he said as he headed for the American buffet room.

"Don't stop. I'm right behind you," Heather said.

Natalie just smiled and followed Heather.

"O.K. big boy, what's the plan?" Mavis said to Chris who by now had cleaned his plate.

"I liked my food, mom. But one can't pass up turkey on Thanksgiving. I mean it would be un-American," he said and smiled. He leaned over as he stood up and kissed his mother on her cheek. "Be back in a minute."

"You guys are too funny," Mavis said and sat down.

Meanwhile at the buffet, the kids were piling up the food on two plates each.

"I saw pecan pie on the dessert table," Heather said.

"I'm so hungry. I had forgotten just how much and the

smell of the Chinese food didn't stimulate anything," Natalie joined in as R.O plucked two black olives from a large salad bowl and downed them.

Ten minutes later everyone was back at the table and wolfing down the food as fast as they could. They appeared to have not eaten for days and if it weren't for the hamburgers that Chris had ordered, the observation would have been true.

"Dr. MacGregor?" a well dressed Chinese man said.

"Yes, I am," Mavis replied, as she patted her mouth with the red cloth napkin.

"Pardon my interruption of your meal, but my name is Yufan Chen. After the ordeal your children experienced with the Fuo River Canyon, I have been asked to accompany them during your stay in China," he stated. "Your special envoy, Dr. Sherri Biggs, invited me to the dinner tonight so I could meet the children in a less formal setting," he said and bowed.

"What ordeal? Why do they need protection?" Mavis asked and stood up.

"It's not a problem, Doctor," Chen replied. "It's an honor for me to be with your family."

"Who are you with?" Mavis asked as Mr. Chen sat down next to her.

"I'm not sure I know what you mean," Chen responded.

"Who are you attached to, what agency hired you?" Mavis asked politely.

"I am Major Yufan Chen with the Peoples Armed Police. Dr. Biggs has a copy of my credentials for you to examine," he replied.

"Why is the Central Military Commission interested in my children?" Mavis asked more sternly.

"It is because of their experience in the River Fuo and their miraculous return this morning. We want to ensure their safety while you are guests in the People's Republic of China. As an officer in the People's Armed Police, I will have all the means I need at my disposal to protect them."

"What?" Mavis gasped with her mouth wide open. She turned to Chris, who had just returned from the buffet line. "I'm really getting tired of these surprises. The Kodiak experience was enough to give me gray hair and an ulcer in my stomach. What did you guys get yourselves into this time?"

"Mom, it's a long story and best told tomorrow when we're all rested," Chris tried to bargain.

"I want to hear it now," she insisted.

"We went kayaking, but we made a wrong turn and ended up on a Class IV river," Chris began.

"Class IV? O.K., I need coffee. Ryan, find me a cup now. Black," she ordered as he hopped up from the chair and took off in a run. Her English accent was getting thicker the more nervous she became.

"We made it down the river for a few miles but had to abandon the boats when the going got rough. We found our way into a cave and crawled to the surface," Chris continued as R.O. walked up with a waiter at his side.

"Black coffee?" the waiter asked as R.O. sat down.

"Thank you," Mavis answered and turned to Major Chen. "I apologize for the confusion, but my husband and I had yet to learn of the incident."

"Yea mom, it was really cool when Chris flipped upside down in the river and had to bail. We all thought he had drowned and Natalie and Heather started freaking out. But Chris would never do that. He's the man! He swam to a cave downriver and we all had to cross a boulder field on a rope about three feet above the rapids. I mean it was cool. Even Heather went across without falling in. But the knot came out when Natalie was over the rapids and she fell in. Chris cut the rope and went in after her," R.O. stated quickly and then filled his mouth with mashed potatoes.

"That's enough, R.O.," Chris said from across the table.

"No, please continue. But swallow your food first," Mavis demanded and stared at Chris with squinted eyes.

"Well, we got to the cave and started exploring when the earthquake hit and water started filling the cave. We found some old stairs to the surface and eventually made our way out. I mean there was this old . . . ouch," R.O. said as Chris kicked him under the table.

"Major Chen, I will be more than happy for you to babysit these four children. I'm sure Natalie's parents in Oklahoma would approve as well," Mavis said and eyed all four teenagers who were now eating and not looking up.

"As I said, Dr. MacGregor, it will be my pleasure. Although they may not be able to see me personally, I will be present at all times. It's been wonderful meeting you and I look forward to seeing you in the morning for your trip to the Great Wall," Major Chen said and got up, bowed his head, and walked away.

"I will need another cup of coffee soon," Mavis said. "Now, I'm going to enjoy some turkey and cranberries, and if I hear anyone breathe deep, cough, or even blink an eye, I promise I will lose my cool like you've never seen. I understand it was an accident that you found yourselves in a death-defying moment, but it was also my understanding that this was going to be a two day river rafting trip, a quick trip back to Beijing, and then some sight-seeing for a few days. How in the world you three, four, excuse me Natalie, manage to make something so small into something so big is beyond my imagination." Mavis remarked as she sipped her hot coffee. "We won't bother your father with the details right now. We'll save them until after the dinner tonight. Got it?"

All four teens agreed by nodding their heads.

"I could use another hot roll," R.O. said and hopped up.

Across the grand ballroom two Chinese generals huddled with two Chinese men dressed in black silk business suits. The shortest and thinnest civilian in the group seemed to be getting all the attention. He wore a four-inch jade dragon. The dragon hung from a gold chain across his blue tie.

"We've been able to divert the Fuji Heavy Industries' dirt

moving equipment to the Tibetan Highlands from the Three Gorges Dam project which is entering its final stages," the younger of the two generals said and sipped his drink. "We have only a few weeks to use it before it's missed and we have to return it. Then new equipment arrives and we continue the cycle."

"Excellent. How are the mining efforts?" Ku Jong Wu, one of the two civilians, asked.

"Progress is being made, sir. Our engineers tell us that the uranium ore is high quality," another general responded. "But isn't it dangerous to speak of it here?"

"Not at all, general. Only rats hide behind doors and in caves. Our society will rule China someday from the public square. It's safer here in the embassy of the naïve Americans than in our own houses of government. Maybe I should rent a room from them to conduct our business," Ku Jong Wu said and they all laughed.

"Good. Our customers around the world have orders to fill, gentlemen," Sen Li, the other civilian said. "Mr. Wu and I will be returning to Hong Kong in the morning to continue our bidding process for the ore. We also have many other investments brewing for the four of us."

"But Mr. Li, isn't four an unlucky number? I mean, the Gang of Four have all met their doom for their efforts to control China," a general commented.

"Have no fear of the past mistakes of a few. It will be the four of us and the people of China. We will deliver the people of China into the twenty-first century at the expense of the Western powers," Sen Li said and they all nodded their heads in agreement.

"And for the newest member of our society, have you made your final commitment?" Ku Jong Wu asked.

The young general carefully held out his left arm so only the four men could see it. Mr. Wu grabbed it and pushed up the general's sleeve and military watch, revealing a fresh tattoo the size of a large coin. It was a black ring with five triangles spaced equally around the inside rim of the circle.

"Very good, general. Now all of us wear the *sign of the dragon*. Soon thousands more will join us, and the dragon society will again rule all of China as it did once before," Wu said and smiled. "It will again proudly appear on our flag, a symbol of our power."

"We will control the People's Liberation Army, the markets in Hong Kong, the Pearl River Delta, and industries from Shanghai to Macao. Those factories that now make jeans, shoes, and shirts for the world will gladly welcome a much stronger climate," Sen Li said. "Soon our electronics industries will outpace India and South America combined. Shipping will increase and we'll control wood imports from Canada and Scandinavia. And then we will reveal even more surprises about the natural resources we have exploited for our movement.

"By the time these industries surrender part ownership to us it will be too late," Ku Jong Wu followed. "Our uranium business will sprout a new China with nuclear partners around the globe. While the British and the Americans are watching the plutonium enrichment process, we'll ship the raw ore through Burma and India."

"So it's important to keep all of the foreign attention focused on the Three Gorges Dam, the so-called environmental problems, the drainage, the displacement of our people, and China's ability to make its own fuel. By the time the dam is finished, we'll have enough control of the army to move on Beijing and the six other military regions of our country. Until then, we'll use American capitalism to collect cash and buy new friends," Sen Li said. "The more uranium ore we mine and ship, the more natural resources we use, and the more oil we buy from the Middle East, the more we destabilize the Americans. Beijing now wants to build a military that can out-shoot the Western nations and take Taiwan by force. Doing it our way we will simply bankrupt the West from the high cost of energy and make them paranoid about a nuclear war that will never happen."

The two generals then took a drink and mingled into the crowd with only the two civilians left together.

"I'm going to Manchuria to take care of one of our investments before we meet in Hong Kong," Ku Jong Wu said. "You'll like the immediate cash flow from this one."

"Then I will gladly meet you in Hong Kong later this week," Sen Li replied.

As Jack and Mavis MacGregor mingled in the crowd, they didn't know they had delivered their family into a cauldron of deceit and revolution in the heart of the People's Republic of China.

5

Great Wall of China

---⬭---

Dr. Sherri Biggs walked into the lobby of the hotel and met the MacGregors when they stepped off the elevator. As she passed out their itinerary, she also handed them tickets for a box lunch they could buy at a public canteen located near their destination for the day, the Great Wall of China.

All morning long the family had been buzzing with excitement to see the country's most famous landmark.

"There will be all sorts of people there, trying to sell their wares. The government is very open about this now and wants the average person on the street to make extra money. It's a way to keep the people happy and to bring American dollars into the economy," Dr. Biggs explained as they made their way out on the street.

The kids were dressed in clean parkas and jeans. A trunk full of clothes and coats had been sent from Alaska, while their soiled ones were being sent to a laundry in Beijing. It was Mavis's efficient way of staying on top of having clean clothes for five people hopping from continent to continent. She was already packing and saving clothes for their next stop on the yearlong journey around the world.

"Good morning, Dr. MacGregor. Dr. Biggs," said Major Chen as he walked up with two men at his side. He was dressed in the uniform of the People's Armed Police and a matching wool overcoat.

"Good morning, Major," Mavis replied.

"Well, I'm off," Dr. Biggs said. "Always good to see you, Major." She walked out and stepped into an American embassy car and was driven away.

"I regret that you have chosen to take the tourist bus, Dr. MacGregor. I have a car waiting to take you to China's greatest monument to our history and freedom," Major Chen said.

"A bus," Heather said and frowned. "Mom, a car would be better."

"A bus is just fine, Major," Mavis replied and smiled at Heather.

"I'll have one of my people on the bus with you," the Major stated.

"That's so unnecessary. We're experienced travelers and can get along just fine," Mavis responded.

"Then our presence will be all around you. It's your choice. Please have a good day," he said and bowed his head. All the MacGregors tried to bow in return with R.O. practically touching his head on his knees.

The MacGregors moved outside toward a group of tourists preparing to board the bus and immediately started grumbling at Mavis.

"Won't do a bit of good. We need to act like a normal family once in a while," she said.

"Well, where's dad if we're supposed to be normal?" Heather asked sarcastically.

"Heather, you know he's working," Mavis replied.

Soon the kids were on board the bus and headed across Beijing to the Great Wall of China. R.O. had already struck up a conversation with one of the teachers on the bus, who was part of a large delegation visiting China.

"Texas. So you're from Texas?" the teacher asked.

"Yes, and my mom, my brother Chris, and his girlfriend, Natalie, but she's from Stillwater, Oklahoma, and my mom's from England originally. So that just leaves me, Chris, and my sister, Heather. She's the blonde over there in the striped beanie. But then that was last summer we were from Texas," R.O. said and took a breath. "We're from other places now."

"That could be complicated. My name is Joyce. What's yours?" she asked.

"Ryan O'Keef MacGregor, but everyone calls me R.O.," he replied.

"O'Keef, that's Irish isn't it?" Joyce said.

"Yes ma'am, but my mom said her English and American relatives dropped the 'e' on the end. It used to be O'Keefe ending in the 'e' in Ireland. Now it's O'Keef without the 'e'. Just like my last name MacGregor. Some families don't have the 'a' either. So it could be 'mc' McGregor or 'mac' MacGregor but my mom's Irish relatives still have the 'e' and my dad's Scottish relatives still have the 'a'. So you pronounce them the same but spell them different. Either way is fine with me. Did I confuse you?" R.O. asked.

"No, I'm good Ryan O'Keefe MacGregor, with the 'a' and the 'e' this time," she said.

"I kind of like the 'e'. I mean I have the 'a' so I might as well have the 'e' too. You know, I think that from now on it's going to be Ryan O'Keefe MacGregor with the 'e' and the 'a'. How's that? R.O. asked.

"Works for me," replied Joyce.

As the bus unloaded, R.O. sidled up to Mavis.

"I'm thirsty mom," R.O. commented and headed for the counter that sold the refreshments.

"I could use a cup of coffee," Mavis said. "Let's all get something and hit the bathrooms before we go up on the Wall. Looks like a long walk back. It'll be time for lunch by then and we'll use the tickets Dr. Biggs gave us."

Thirty minutes passed before the MacGregor group was on the massive structure that traveled 4,163 miles across China. For centuries, known as the greatest human feat of its time, the Great Wall served as a symbol of the power of human ingenuity and determination. Ravaged by the Mongols, the Chinese created this barrier both to intimidate the enemy and to create a sense of security for her people.

Nearly four hundred miles to the northeast a private jet landed at a small airstrip on the north side of the city of Shenyang. As the turbines whined to a stop, a black BMW drove up. Two men stepped out and opened the back doors of the car. Ku Jong Wu and a young female assistant stepped off the aircraft, pulling their winter coats tight around their necks. In five minutes they were in the automobile and driving through a warehouse district, where row upon row of abandoned factories all looked the same. Only the rust marks gave them individual identities.

The BMW approached one of the warehouses, stopped at the door, and honked twice. Two men came out through a small door and approached the car. They were carrying Avtomat Kalashnikov rifles, also known as AK-47s, and wore plain brown coveralls. Ku Jong Wu spoke to them and the men ran back inside the warehouse where they began to open the larger overhead door. The car entered the building and the door closed behind it. Ku Jong Wu and his female assistant, Jing She, stepped from the car and were greeted by a man wearing a navy, pin-striped business suit, red, silk tie, and a black, wool overcoat. He could have been a stockbroker in London from his appearance. All three bowed to each other.

"Mr. Wu, Miss She. I am honored by this visit," the man said.

"Mr. Leung, how can I stay away; the message I received is so full of great news," Wu said. "So I brought along Jing She, an expert in these matters, to verify that what is being reported to me is true and accurate."

"But Mr. Wu, my honor is above suspicion. If my assessment of the goods is not as you've been told, you will have my resignation immediately," Leung said.

"No, Mr. Leung. I will have your life immediately," Ku Jong Wu stated without blinking his eyes.

"I understand," Leung said and bowed again.

"Now show us what the British scientists discovered," Ku Jong Wu ordered.

The three of them walked through a warehouse that was full of crates and large plaster eggs the size of small automobiles.

"Miss She, how does it feel to walk through a maze of money?" Wu asked.

"It always feels good when someone values what we value," she replied. "I'm excited to view the discovery."

"How much farther, Mr. Leung?" Wu wondered.

"Through this door. We try to control the temperature and humidity in this room because the discovery was found in sediments of an ancient clay lakebed. While it is fossilized, the matter and overburden around it may be volatile to expansion and contraction. We wouldn't want it to crack," Leung said and unlocked the door.

The three walked through the doorway and Ku Jong Wu reached inside his coat and pulled out a Chinese-made Makarov 9 mm pistol and loaded the chamber. Leung stopped quickly.

"Don't be alarmed Mr. Leung. This is just to insure that you will do all the right things while we are with you," Ku Jong Wu said. "Miss She, would you please take Mr. Leung's weapon."

"Yes, sir," she replied and reached inside Leung's coat where she found a holstered Smith and Wesson .40 caliber pistol. She handed it to Ku Jong Wu.

"A very fine weapon, Mr. Leung. Explain to me why one of my employees carries a well-made American handgun and I still carry this relic of the Cold War? Never mind, let's proceed," Ku Jong Wu said.

The trio walked over to a concrete platform that had a plastic cover draped across the top of it, suspended from the ceiling by a series of springs and levers. Leung grabbed a red vinyl lever and pushed up carefully. The spring-loaded device gently lifted the protective covering from the platform while a set of lights came on at the same time. The covering was now standing perpendicular to the table with the object in full light.

"Magnificent," Jing She said and unfastened the buttons on the front of her white wool coat revealing a black, silk dress underneath and a strand of white pearls around her neck. She looked more like a glamorous woman of Hong Kong high society than an advisor to a powerful industrialist. She put on a pair of glasses and leaned closer to the object. "You say there are only two others like this in existence and this is by far the best of the three? It's definitely a *Caudipteryx zoui*, a feathered dinosaur with forearms and claws. It couldn't fly, so it ran on two powerful legs. Mr. Leung, it's just what your documents say it is."

"What do the British scientists say about the specimen, Mr. Leung?" Ku Jong Wu asked.

"The Scot says for certain it's a *Caudipteryx zoui*, but the English says he would like to test it more and examine it longer," he replied. "It's embedded in one ton of rock."

"I see. And where are the British paleontologists today?" Ku Jong Wu asked as he walked around the room and looked at the hundreds of fossils sorted here and there.

"They are taking a day off from their work, sir. They weren't keen on coming back to China in winter, but I instructed them that the final work needed to be completed on this specimen or they wouldn't receive the academic credit they desired," stated Leung.

"You, of course, were able to keep them away from the brilliant forgeries we have hidden in our warehouses, weren't you, Mr. Leung?" Wu asked as he continued to walk around the room making Leung nervous.

"Yes, sir. No one went near them. Many are crated and ready to ship to Hong Kong, sir," Leung replied.

"Very good, Mr. Leung," Ku Jong Wu said. "And when are the British coming back to the warehouse?"

"Tonight, sir. They want to take one last look before they fly back to London," Leung answered. "They indicated that a day of study is all they needed. They wanted to focus on the impressions of the feathers in the rock and make more impressions to take back to England."

"Do your people here know the procedure?" Wu questioned.

"Yes. I even called and told Jing She about it," Leung said.

Ku Jong Wu turned immediately to Jing She in a rage.

"And you failed to inform me? And you, Mr. Leung, risked a twenty million dollar fossil with a telephone call? The bankers in Singapore would be very unhappy if the fossil slipped through their hands and was confiscated by our government. I can't afford to have my one billion dollar alliance with the bank become public. They wanted the fossil for their corporate offices and, of course, the small investment that it brings."

In an instant, Ku Jong Wu pointed the Makarov at Jing She.

"And who else has called you to ask about the fossil?" Wu demanded.

Jing She took her glasses off and tears welled in her eyes.

"No one. I meant to tell you, but I knew we would be coming today. I wanted you to have the joy of knowing everything at the same time," she said as the glasses slipped from her right hand and crashed to the floor. She bowed her head, expecting the gunshot from the Makarov to be the last sound she would hear.

"Mr. Leung, no calls should have been made. You should not have risked being listened to by the police," Wu said and pulled the trigger. Leung fell dead on the cold floor of the warehouse. The echo resounded off the metal walls. Running footsteps could be heard as two men burst through the door with their automatic rifles leveled at Jing She.

"I am fine. Thank you for your rapid attention. Dispose of this incompetent and be quick about it," Ku Jong Wu ordered.

Wu walked over to Jing She and wiped a falling tear from her cheek with the back of his left hand, the gun still held firmly in his right.

"What have we learned today, Jing She?" Ku Jong Wu asked softly.

"To trust no one, sir," Jing She answered, keeping her head bowed.

"Very good. We wouldn't want to lose our valuable animal in stone, would we?" Wu asked.

"No sir," Jing She replied and looked up.

"Now let's go find additional customers for our other fossils," Wu commanded and put the Makarov pistol in his pocket. "You have much to learn. Mr. Chang and Dr. Cheng will be here in two hours, to begin moving the operation to Hong Kong."

Half an hour later, Ku Jong Wu and Jing She were back in the private jet, flying southward.

The aircraft landed in Beijing, while Ku Jong Wu talked to Sen Li on a secure line.

"Yes. All is well. The fossil is worth at least twenty million. The other items will reach a total of one hundred million dollars on the black market. Are your agents ready?" Wu asked.

"Yes. They're ready. This should provide us with some cash flow as we seek out trade partners and transition our government," responded Mr. Li.

"Indeed, it should," Wu said and turned off the small telephone.

Jing She stood nervously nearby with her hand inside her coat pocket, gripping a small Walther PPK pistol. From now on she would trust no one.

6

Caudipteryx zoui

———————————◼————————————

Major Yufan Chen stepped from the police car and walked up the steps of the brown, brick building located adjacent to Tienanmen Square. Cold, blustery winds kept most tourists at bay, but the bold ones forged ahead across the square taking what photographs they could with their cameras. Beijing had once again become an international city of great importance. While the government still carried a heavy hand with its people, it had moved forward as a manufacturer of goods that the Western world could not live without. With more and more foreign contracts at work in the large factories of the Pearl River Delta and smaller factories across the nation, the standard of living had been growing by about ten percent annually for the last ten years. With the increase of the living standards came the desire for more energy. Oil had to be purchased from foreign sources, but water was a resource that China could afford. It was China's rivers that gave them hope to supply what the Middle East and the United States could not.

There were no markings on the building or signs in the hallway as the Major walked steadily toward an elevator. A uniformed army private held the door as the Major stepped in. Two female clerks stood back and didn't enter the elevator as the doors closed. Soon the compartment stopped on the tenth floor and the stainless steel doors opened. A soldier carrying a small automatic rifle was standing there as Major Chen stepped out and into the room. He walked forward toward a freestanding metal detector and stopped. He opened his coat, took out a semi-automatic pistol, and laid it on the small table next to the detector.

"Is that all, Major?" the female attendant asked, looking him in the eye.

"Yes. I only carry my smaller weapon when I'm in the capital city," replied the Major with a smile.

"Please walk forward," she instructed.

Yufan Chen stepped through the detector and the young woman handed him back the German-made Walther PPK 7.65 semi-automatic pistol.

"Now place your hands on the black pad on the table, Major. You know the procedure," she stated and turned on an instrument that sucked air from around the Major's fingers and palms.

"Small weapons first, explosives, and then radiation. The three greatest threats to our government," he said and raised his eyebrows.

"No, Major Chen," said a voice behind him. "Those are only the means to cause a threat. The major threats to our country are the lies that the West tells about us. If they would speak the truth about our government, we would all live in harmony."

"Lin Wong, my old friend," Major Chen said. "What brings you to Beijing?"

"The same as you," the tall man replied and embraced the Major. "The world is visiting us to tell us how to build our great dam and save all the little fishes at the same time. Don't they know we are in a race to save our people and our country? The sea is full of fishes to save and then to eat."

"Spoken like the party spokesman that you are," Major Chen said.

A large door at the end of the room opened and the noise of people talking could be heard. "I think they're ready for the last two arrivals," Lin Wong said and walked toward the doors.

As Wong and Chen entered into the room, several people turned to look at them while others ignored their presence and continued talking. In the center of the room was a large, mahogany table with ten chairs around it. Stationed behind the table and around it in a semi-circle were five smaller tables with four chairs each. Chen and Wong separated and moved toward their assigned table, where they bowed and greeted others and sat down. As three men and two women entered the room, it became quiet. Two of the men were dressed in plain, dark, business suits, while the third was in a Chinese air force uniform. The women wore dark pantsuits with no jewelry or refinement of any kind. One of the women remained standing while everyone else sat down.

"We have called this meeting of our council to discuss issues that have come before the Central Committee and the Politburo. I was asked to represent them today as was Ming Lee," the woman said and nodded toward one of the men in a business suit. He neither acknowledged her recognition of him nor of anyone else. "The Three Gorges Dam is moving along at a rate of development that shows the courage and ingenuity of our people. The world would like to see us fail so that the West can continue to reign in superiority over us. Our former allies, the Russians, continue to subvert our ties to our Asian allies. However, we can prevail as long as we continue to move forward with the dam. Our new contracts with Saudi Arabia, Venezuela, Kuwait, and Iran will meet our growing energy needs for years to come. As all our new dams come on line, the electrical power will light our cities and our factories. The farm belt of the Sichuan Basin is no longer big enough to feed our people. If we want them to continue to work, then we must continue to feed them just as we fuel tractors, factories, and ships," she stated and sat down quickly.

Ming Lee stood up and looked across the room with a straight expression on his face.

"As members of the Central Committee you know how important each of you are to the future of the People's Republic of China. You are a select group from the People's Liberation Army, Ministry of National Defense, Central Military Commission, People's Liberation Army Air Force, and the People's Armed Police. Our chairman sends this message: 'As foreign guests travel across our vast nation, please be advised to maintain the integrity of our government and the privacy of our communications. Everyone on the Central Committee was not invited today. Those members should not be informed of this meeting. Five senior officers of the People's Armed Police were invited today as a reminder that all laws pertain to all people, including guests,'" Ming Lee proclaimed and pointed toward the table where Major Chen was seated with four high-ranking officers. He sat there quietly, motionless, as was expected when a superior was speaking.

"General Feiran is here to assure us all that the Central Military Commission and the People's Liberation Army are at our disposal. Their job is to protect our people and our government from foreign aggression and acts of treason," Lee said and nodded toward the general. "If you are approached by Western news media, you will be kind and gentle and redirect their inquiry to the Ministry of Information. This protocol should be shared with the members of the National Party Congress and all administrators within our thirty governing units. The administrators for Guangxi, Inner Mongolia, Ningxia, Tibet, and Xinjiang will be notified by the Central Committee through private communiqués," Lee continued.

Major Chen fought back sleep as the member of the

powerful Central Committee droned on for nearly an hour. The room grew warm from being overheated by the forty or so bodies that sat in the chairs and, of course, his wool uniform. He knew his presence was merely ceremonial to remind the various officials that they weren't above the law; even though, they had more freedom, more money, and more prestige than the common Chinese citizen did. Although he hated this part of his job, he knew that if he wanted to continue to get promotions that fed his family and provided for a nice place to live and the opportunity for his two sons to go to college abroad, he had to be there, at least for now.

To pass the time, his thoughts lingered on the new opportunity that was about to happen. Yufan Chen loved being a policeman and tracking down the violent criminals that preyed on innocent Chinese and tourists, a threat that intensified as people began to earn more money from better paying jobs and the increase in free enterprise businesses. He had intentionally stayed away from the political side of the enforcement process, but now he yearned for this new opportunity and awaited it anxiously.

Suddenly he heard the chairs around him move and realized the meeting had come to an end and everyone was getting up. Pretending to follow suit he stood up and quickly began to worry that maybe he had fallen asleep, but he didn't see anyone look at him. His career would have been over in an instant.

Lin Wong walked over to him and shook his hand.

"If you're ever in Hong Kong, you must stay with my family," he offered to Chen.

"I will certainly do so. I go there a few times a year to bring back fugitives. It would be tempting to transfer there and work among the glitter of China's gem on the sea," Chen responded and smiled.

"Your family would love it. It's more like London and

Tokyo than China, but don't tell anyone I said that," Lin Wong said and started to move away.

"Be careful," Chen warned. "Hong Kong could corrupt you."

"Not me," Lin Wong smiled and walked away.

The three superior officers to Major Chen walked up and stood around him.

"Yes," Yufan said and bowed his head.

"How is your surveillance of the renowned American, Dr. MacGregor?" one of them asked.

"My people are with him every hour of every day. I have people with all of his family as well. Dr. and Mrs. MacGregor will attend the environmental conference in Shanghai later in the week. The four children will fly to Chengdu and spend three days in the Wolong Panda Reserve," replied Major Chen, looking each of his superiors directly in the face. He was never one to shy from authority.

"Good. We want maximum protection. The American F.B.I. informed us of the plot to kill Dr. MacGregor last week in Alaska. We don't want that to happen on Chinese soil," a colonel said and put on his large broad-brimmed officer's hat.

"I will guarantee their protection," Major Chen said and bowed his head slightly.

The three senior officers walked away as the room emptied and left the major standing alone. Within minutes he was on the street and stepping into the back seat of the unmarked police car.

"Marriott," he said and the driver sped away from the curb.

The tour bus stopped at the Marriott; the group of teachers and the MacGregor clan unloaded.

Once inside, Mavis made her way to the front desk to collect their messages.

"Thank you," she said to the clerk in Chinese as she opened an envelope.

"Who's that from, Mom?" R.O. asked as he stood nearby. Chris, Natalie, and Heather were already stepping into an elevator.

Mavis looked up. "What's happening, honey?"

"Just thought I would ride up with you," he replied.

"How about you? Who's the mail from?" R.O. asked again.

"It's a note from a paleontologist friend back home in England," Mavis answered with a smile.

"He sent it from England?" R.O. asked.

"No, honey. He's in China, but he's from England. It's a telephone message he left for me," Mavis explained, reading the note that had been written by the front desk clerk.

"How'd he find you?" R.O. asked.

"He says he called your father's office back home and they told him where we would be today."

Mavis pulled a small cell phone from her purse and dialed the number on the note.

On the third ring a man's voice answered.

"Hello," the voice said.

"Nigel, is that you?" Mavis asked and smiled.

"Who else might be trying to find you in China, my dear Mavis," Nigel sarcastically responded.

"What on earth are you doing here in the winter? Mongolia must be freezing," Mavis inquired and sat down in a big chair in the lobby.

"You won't believe what these, well, I can't say what they are lest you blush, Mavis. But they called Julian in Edinburgh and told him that if we didn't come to China this week, they would turn the specimen over to another team, and they would get the credit for the find and the research. I mean they are dreadful to deal with, don't you see?" Nigel said in exasperation.

"What specimen are you hiding from me Nigel? I haven't heard about a new one. Obviously, you and Julian have found something and kept it quite the secret for some time," Mavis answered back.

"Well, dear, it's been a secret. The Chinese are very protective of their finds. If we had secured it in Mongolia, there would be no discussion or politics. But this specimen was found north of Shenyang," Nigel began as Mavis cut him off.

"Shenyang, that's *Caudipteryx zoui* territory. Aren't those formations late Jurassic to early Cretaceous?" Mavis said as goose bumps spread across her arms from the excitement of the news.

"My dear Mavis, you are still sharp as a tack. *Caudipteryx zoui* it is, and she is a beautiful specimen, lying neatly on one ton of rock. The feathers are immaculate," Nigel informed.

"Nigel, I'm just beside myself. I can be there in four hours or sooner. When can I see her?" Mavis asked.

"Julian and I are staying in a house provided by the company the Central Government contracted to oversee the dig and the transportation of the fossil. Mavis, we have nearly two truck loads of other specimens that have emerged from the area in the last two years," Nigel said.

"Nigel, I must admit, I've been a mom in Texas far too long and have missed out on all the excitement. But I've got to see her. I'll arrange a flight and will be there in four hours or sooner, maybe by eight o'clock. Can I reach you at this number?" Mavis asked.

"Yes, it's a loaner phone that the company gave me. Julian and I plan on leaving tomorrow morning so don't be late. We can spend the night browsing through the new fossils and looking at the *Caudipteryx zoui*," answered Nigel.

"Have you named her?" Mavis asked smiling.

"No, we decided that if we could find you we would wait to do that," Nigel said.

"Nigel, you have always been my champion. If it hadn't been for Jack, well, those are fond memories," Mavis said.

"Likewise, dear. See you soon," Nigel said and disconnected.

Mavis got up from the chair excited from head to toe

about the new discovery and a chance to get back into the paleontology game for just one day. She dialed the U.S. embassy on the way to the room. Once there, she and R.O. found everyone lying around. Jack walked through the door a few minutes later.

"Hi, babe. Did y'all have a good trip?" Jack asked as he kissed Mavis.

"Yes. It was wonderful. What a monument to strength and ingenuity the Wall is," she replied.

"It was so cold, Dad," Heather said as she sipped on the cup of hot cocoa she had just made in the tiny kitchen.

Chris and Natalie were bundled together in a big chair, asleep. R.O. began fiddling with the television trying to find an English language station.

"I think these people are speaking French or something," R.O. said ignoring everyone.

"I have great news," Mavis exclaimed. "Nigel and Julian are in Shenyang with a new dinosaur find and I'm going to see them."

"When?" Jack asked and took off his coat.

"Right now. I called the embassy and they arranged for a private plane to fly me to Shenyang. I leave in an hour. It's a one-hour flight. Julian and Nigel have a private home, and they'll take me to the warehouse where the fossil is located. Jack," she said excitedly. "It's a *Caudipteryx zoui.*"

"A feathered dinosaur!" R.O. exclaimed. "Can I go?"

"No," Mavis replied. "Sorry, you kids are all going with Major Chen in the morning to Chengdu. There's a military aircraft flying that direction and he has seats on it for everyone. Your father is off to see the Three Gorges Dam. Chasing pandas will be an enjoyable three-day adventure for you. When I get back from Shenyang, I'll head west to join you," Mavis stated with an authority that was rarely questioned.

"Pandas. Yeehaa," R.O. exclaimed excitedly.

"Ryan, do you mind?" Natalie said as she woke up.

"Well, you better get going. I'll see you off," Jack said

and sat down.

After packing a small bag for the overnight trip and putting on her heavy parka, Mavis and Jack left the room. No one noticed they were leaving except for a "have fun, mom" from Chris. They all knew how much she enjoyed seeing new fossil specimens, especially since she rarely had the chance to back home in Texas. An embassy car drove up just as Mavis and Jack were walking out of the hotel.

"Be safe, babe," Jack said and embraced her.

"You know I will," Mavis replied and kissed him.

"Give my regards to Nigel and Julian," Jack said as she stepped into the car.

"I will. See you soon, love," Mavis said and closed the door.

The Beech Baron flew steadily into a headwind but made good time because of its two powerful 325 hp Continental engines. With a range of over a thousand miles, the Baron could easily reach Shenyang and return to Beijing without stopping for fuel. Darkness had fallen across the continent and Mavis was amazed at the totality of the blackness on the terrain below. An occasional factory was lit up for a twenty-four hour production schedule, but the lights from farms, highways, and small towns that were normal in England and America were non-existent. She knew that people lived below; however, there were no signs of a modern civilization.

She remembered her flights over Africa; there were plenty of fires from villages to light the way. Not so in the cold and barren plains of the province of Inner Mongolia. Only when the high winds forced a detour across a brief stretch of the Po Hai Gulf of the Yellow Sea, did she spot a fleet of well-lit fishing boats standing out like small floating Christmas trees. Finally, the lights of Shenyang appeared on the horizon.

The Baron, even with the modern runway, descended with ease with only a light buffeting from the wind. It was a smooth landing and the airplane taxied up to a row of hangars that was being used by foreign businesses and embassies.

"Thanks, Charlie," Mavis said to the pilot. "I don't know when I'll be ready to go back. We'll probably be up all night."

"No problem, Dr. MacGregor. Dr. Biggs instructed that I shouldn't return home without you. There's a small hotel here just for Western pilots. I'll catch a few winks and you can call me when you're on your way back to the airport," Charlie said as he helped her out of the plane.

"I'll ring you. There's my ride," Mavis said as she waved at Nigel and Julian, who were driving up in a Russian-made VAZ Lada automobile.

Mavis smiled really big as the faded red, four-door sedan came to a screeching halt.

"Nigel, is this how you pick up all the girls?" she asked, unable to contain her laughter. Julian hopped out first.

The tall Scotsman with red hair walked around the front of the Lada and gave Mavis a big hug.

"Long time no see, lassie," he said in his strong Scottish brogue. "Pretty sad we have to fly all the way to China to see our long lost, Texas-Englishman."

"Yes, it is," Nigel answered as he walked up and hugged Mavis. "You're as beautiful as ever, Mavis. Being a mum does you quite well."

"Gentleman, are we here to flatter each other or to name your new girl?" Mavis asked as the wind blew her auburn curls across the shoulders of her white hood.

"Right on," Nigel said. "Never one to get off task, were you Mavis?"

"She's the same as twenty years ago," Julian remarked.

"Well, professors, I saw you both only two years ago when I was visiting my mum on Harrington Street in London. Have you forgotten? What's this twenty-year business? Makes a girl feel aged around the likes of you," she said as she climbed into the Lada and closed the door tight.

She searched for a seat belt but there was not one to be found.

Everyone was happy to be together again. In their younger days, they had been a famous team of paleontologists, searching the world for the rarest of fossils lost in the various rock layers of the planet. But it was Mavis who chose to leave the team and move to Texas to raise a family, for her love, Jack MacGregor.

"Now, who is this corporation that the Chinese pay to control the site and the fossils?" Mavis asked as she adjusted her coat in the car. The rusty floor was allowing more than enough air inside the Lada to keep her from becoming warm and comfortable.

"We don't know," Nigel replied as he drove.

"It's run by a Mr. Ku Jong Wu who flies into Shenyang in a Lear jet. We've heard he runs a conglomerate in Shanghai," Julian said from the back seat. We have to deal with a Mr. Chang or a Dr. Fong Cheng. I get their names confused most of the time."

"We've learned the past two years that if universities are on a dig sometimes they have to find a Chinese corporate sponsor. The government sends in their paleontologists, but the semi-private companies pay for the equipment and supplies. Then they get to claim some of the fossils," Nigel said.

"We think that the companies are skimming the fossils just like the mafia skims cash. They take the fossils that fall by the wayside and move them through the black market to paying customers," Julian added. "The university's academics either don't have a clue or are too afraid to say anything."

"Who are the customers?" Mavis asked.

"We can't say for sure, but I have a suspicion they're private collectors or companies who want to make an investment in the fossils for economic gain," Nigel responded.

"Amazing. Corporate investors in dinosaur fossils instead of the stock market," Mavis quipped. "Twenty years ago who would have thought? Go figure!"

"Don't you remember about ten years ago when a

Japanese bank bought a full grown Triceratops from a group in the States? Dug her up in Wyoming, assembled her in Ardmore, Oklahoma, and shipped her to Japan. Now she sits in the lobby of a bank," Julian stated matter of factly.

"Disgusting," Mavis said. "Such specimens belong in museums so scientists can study them and the public can learn to adore them as much as we do."

"Preaching to the choir, lassie," Julian said.

"Here it is," Nigel said as he drove through an alley between two large rusting warehouses on the south side of Shenyang.

"What is this, an airport?" Mavis asked.

"It's a private one. We couldn't let your embassy pilot land here. It's too risky. It doesn't have all the runway lights and controls. We tried it once and nearly ended up in the warehouse. Don't know how that chap lands that Lear jet here," Nigel replied as he turned off the motor.

As they stepped from the Lada, two men with automatic rifles came out of the warehouse.

"They're the guards. No worry," Julian said as he led the trio toward the building.

After recognizing the scientists, the guards let them enter and made a call on a cell phone.

"Let me get the lights," Nigel said as he walked toward a fuse box and pushed up the control lever. The lights came on with a loud bang.

"Wow," Mavis commented as she saw the tables and walls lined with fossils. There were also several standing free in the middle of the room. "It's Christmas already. How do you contain yourselves?"

"We have to. This is what we've found the past two years. The Mongolian pieces are back in Britain. We have to negotiate every bone, tooth, or claw with the Chinese. They claim to have museum space even before we make a find," Julian said as he took off his hat.

"I am so impressed," Mavis said as she handled as many fossilized bones as fast as she could.

"Don't get overly impressed, love. You haven't seen our girl yet," Nigel said and opened another door and stepped through.

Mavis and Julian followed as he turned on more lights. All three were quiet, nearly reverent as they walked up to the *Caudipteryx zoui*. The specimen was clean and well lit. One hundred and twenty million years since its last breath, it still looked as though it were running after prey. Mavis reached out and ran her fingers across an impression of several feathers.

"Oh my. This is my first time. All of my life, I've always been too late to be allowed to research or handle a feathered specimen. They're always behind the glass, on the wall, or in the vault and never within my reach," she said as she stroked more feathers.

"My dear Mavis, she's all yours for the moment," Nigel responded. "That's why we called. At first we didn't want to get you involved because we don't quite know what's going to happen to her."

"This Wu fellow has kept our discovery very quiet. When we left here in August, this girl was still incased in a lot of overburden, mostly ancient clay. We could see about two-thirds of her. When we arrived two days ago, she was, as you see. Pristine. Perfect. Clean," Julian said.

"The Chinese technicians must have been working on her night and day for months. There's not as much as a tool scar on the feathers. She's perfect," Nigel said and caressed part of a leg. "This would have taken a year or more in a lab in England."

"Is she a forgery?" Mavis asked suddenly.

"No. She's genuine," replied Julian. "If she were a forgery we could tell. I would guess she would bring fifteen to twenty million at auction. Don't know if a university could afford her but a national museum could."

"What about the British Museum?" Mavis asked.

"When we first heard from the Wu fellow, I called a friend there to find out if they had heard any news through the grapevine. You know, word gets around. Graduate students talk, always looking for a better deal," Julian answered.

"What did they say?" Mavis asked and unzipped her parka.

"Nothing. They hadn't heard anything. The only buzz right now is about a complete T-Rex skeleton somewhere in Montana or Wyoming, but no one's talking, so we don't know where it is exactly. No word out of China when here sits before you one of only three specimens of its kind in the world, and the best of three feathered animals that runs and doesn't fly," Julian said.

"My friends at Cambridge are working on what we brought home last summer from Mongolia. This is the only major fossil left but only Julian and I know about it," Nigel said.

"Nigel, didn't the ancient Chinese believe that dinosaur bones were really dragon bones and would grind them up and eat them?" Mavis inquired.

"Certainly did," he replied. "In fact most of the workers on the dig are very superstitious. It dates back to when an early emperor claimed his mother was born from a dragon, "Julian added. "That started all the lore about different types of dragons with different powers and different types of claws and such. It mixed with their religion and became sacred stuff after that."

"Chinese had four and five claws, Korean dragons had three, or maybe that was the Japanese dragons," Nigel said. "Can't remember which."

"Seems mysterious to me," Mavis said.

"And that's the way I want it," boomed a voice from behind them.

Mavis, Nigel, and Julian turned around to see Mr. Chang

and the female paleontologist, Dr. Fong Cheng, standing just inside the door.

"Mr. Chang, so good to see you," Nigel said and started to walk toward him.

Dr. Cheng pulled a Walther 9mm pistol from under her coat and pointed it at him. He stopped and froze in his tracks.

"What's this about?" Mavis asked loudly and started to move.

"Stay there, Mavis," Nigel said without looking back.

"Professor Wells, you have been warned about bringing people here or even telling someone about our arrangement," Mr. Chang said and walked up to Nigel. "So I am going have to kill you to prove my point."

"No, wait," Mavis said, thinking quickly. "I'm Mavis MacGregor. My husband is Dr. Jack MacGregor and we're guests of the government. I demand to know what this is all about."

Mr. Chang walked by Nigel to within three feet of Mavis. He carefully took off his leather gloves and smiled at Mavis. Before she knew it was coming, he slapped her across the face with the gloves causing her to lose her balance. A drop of blood escaped the corner of her mouth and tears formed in her eyes.

"How dare you," she said as Julian stepped forward and grabbed her by the arm.

"He'll kill you, Mavis," Julian said calmly. "I've seen his kind before."

"Professor Hilliard offers good advice, Mrs. MacGregor," Mr. Chang said and put his gloves back on.

Dr. Fong Cheng walked over to Mr. Chang and whispered in his ear.

"My assistant informs me that she has heard of your husband and of you, Dr. MacGregor. How unfortunate that you chose to visit your friends tonight. Now I will have to kill you as well," Mr. Chang said and pulled his pistol from inside his coat.

"But you will lose the scientific notoriety that you

wanted for your *Caudipteryx zoui*," Nigel said quickly.

"But you see Professor Wells, I'm no longer in need of your endorsement. My customer is convinced and is willing to pay in gold. Since you and Professor Hilliard know too much about my feathered dinosaur and this warehouse full of fossils you have suddenly become a liability. I promise to be painless and to place your bodies in the same ancient lakebed in which you found this great specimen so that someday your bones will be of great value," Mr. Chang stated and laughed loudly, his voice booming off the metal walls. "It's just your bad luck to have come here tonight, Dr. MacGregor."

"So you would kill an American citizen whose children are in the protective custody of the People's Armed Police?" Mavis tried to reason.

"Dr. MacGregor, my family owns the People's Armed Police and nearly every other branch of government in China. Fear previously reigned over my people. Today it is money and fear," Mr. Chang said and pointed the gun at Mavis. "Those whom I can't buy, I kill. Isn't that the American and British way?"

"There's an American embassy plane waiting at the airport for my return. The embassy knows I came to Shenyang to see a dinosaur fossil. It is common knowledge that you and your corporation in Shanghai oversee the dinosaur digs for the Chinese government. And soon everyone will know that this *Caudipteryx zoui* is a fraud," Mavis said.

"A fraud!" Mr. Chang yelled and turned the gun toward Julian. "You said it was authentic," he said as he pointed to Nigel. "And you, Dr. Cheng, said it was authentic. And how does the MacGregor woman know so much about me? Who do I kill first to get the truth?"

"She's bluffing," Fong Cheng said and pointed her gun toward Mavis.

"Then why are the barbules asymmetrical on this row of feathers?" Mavis asked and ran her hand across an outcropping of feathers on the left front grasping arm.

"That's a lie," Dr. Cheng shouted and walked quickly

toward the stone fossil. Before she had taken three steps a gunshot rang out and she crumpled dead to the floor. A pool of blood began to form around her shoulders.

Mr. Chang walked over and looked down at her.

"Obviously, Dr. Cheng was protecting something or she wouldn't have gotten so nervous about it," Mr. Chang said and moved closer to the big fossil. "I think I will kill you one at a time . . . but not tonight. You may prove more useful alive until my customer can collect this beautiful specimen. I must say, Dr. MacGregor, you had me going for a minute. Do you play Texas poker? You obviously fooled the late Dr. Cheng. She was weak and would have been in the way. I owe you much gratitude for exposing her. I had been thinking about firing her for some time."

The two guards had just arrived with their rifles pointed at the three scientists.

"Take these people to the holding room. I will call for a removal squad to take them in one hour," Mr. Chang ordered as they nodded to him.

"You can't get away with this," Mavis screamed, as she was pushed with the barrel of a rifle from the room.

"Dr. MacGregor, this behavior is so unbecoming for such a beautiful woman," Mr. Chang said. "You should be pleased that I chose to shoot Dr. Cheng through the heart rather than in the head. Her family will be less traumatized when they see her body. Just remember that. And how many children do you have in China?"

Mavis instantly became weak but didn't show it. As the scientists were pushed into a small closet-sized room, they breathed a sigh of relief as they heard the dead-bolt slide into place.

"Mavis, I'm so sorry. I had no idea," Nigel said.

"You couldn't have known," Mavis replied. "I'll be missed around nine in the morning when the pilot wakes up."

"We may be long gone by then," Julian said as he looked around the small room.

"But where?" Mavis asked.

7

Chengdu to Shenyang

The phone rang; it was the complimentary wake-up call. Chris reached over and hit the off button on the telephone base to silence it. He then looked around and felt for his Rolex Submariner and checked the time. It read 7:30 a.m.; getting out of bed, he noticed that R.O. was snoring, because the polluted air of Beijing was irritating his allergies. He put on a pair of pants and walked into the main living area of the suite. At the same time, Natalie emerged from the ladies' side. They lightly embraced without saying a word and headed for the percolating coffee pot that Jack had left them an hour before. Next to it was a note.

Left for the Three Gorges Dam at 6:30. Mom will be back later today or tomorrow. Who knows? She loves the fossil business! Don't forget, you're to meet Major Chen at 9:30 for the flight to Chengdu. See you all in three days. Have fun and keep a short leash on Ryan. Love Dad.

"Well, it looks like we're on our own in the middle of China," Natalie said.

"Yes, I guess so," Chris replied and smiled at her 'happy

hair' pointing in all directions. She caught the look and returned it.

"What's to eat?" R.O. asked as he walked into the small kitchen that adjoined the sitting room.

There was a knock at the door. Natalie answered and was greeted by a smiling busboy with a white box in his hands.

"Room service ordered by Dr. Jack MacGregor," he said.

"Chris quickly arrived and tipped him as R.O. grabbed the box and headed into the kitchen in a hurry.

"Donuts!" R.O. shouted.

"Dad must have ordered these before he left," Chris said.

"You think?" Natalie laughed.

"Yea, I think," Chris smiled. "It's still early though. Mom usually thinks for all of us until about ten in the morning. She would have ordered cereal and fruit."

"Or gruel that tastes like dirt," R.O. said loudly as he munched into a chocolate donut.

"What's all the noise about?" Heather asked as she walked into the room.

"Survival food for the panda trip," R.O. replied loudly.

"Do you mind?" Heather asked covering her ears.

"No, I don't mind," R.O. shouted back.

"Hey, cut it out, Ryan," Chris said. "I have specific orders to keep you on a short leash and here's the note to prove it." Chris tossed the note over to R.O.

"Yum," Heather said as she bit into a cream filled donut. "Where's Dad? Did Mom get back from Shenyang yet?"

"Dad left early for the dam. There's a conference there today and tomorrow. Mom won't be back for a couple of days. That's my bet. You know how she gets when there's a dinosaur lurking in a mountain nearby," Chris answered and chewed on a pineapple Danish.

"O.K., then I'm first in the shower on our side," Natalie said. She carried a cup of coffee in one hand and a cherry donut in the other as she left the group.

"Everybody shower first. I'm going to guard the

donuts," R.O. said. "Besides I need to study this blender." He unplugged the white blender on the counter and pulled it toward him.

"What are you building now?" Chris asked as he sipped his coffee.

"Top secret, for my eyes only," R.O. replied. "What would they do if I took the motor out of the blender?"

"They would put it on the hotel bill. They'll charge us sixty dollars for a twenty-dollar blender that they made here in China for two dollars," Chris informed.

"Good. No one would notice," R.O. said.

Chris left for the other shower while R.O. went to his suitcase and found his mini tool kit.

By nine o'clock, all four teens were dressed in outdoor gear and putting the final touches on their backpacks.

"O.K., listen up everyone. Mom would go through a checklist so here it is. Extra socks, winter hiking boots, thermal underclothes, knit caps, gloves, down parkas, snow goggles, pocket lighters, survival knives, utility belts, flashlights, two MREs each," Chris announced.

"Those are awful," Heather interrupted.

"They're just dried fruit and meat," Natalie said.

"Two meals ready-to-eat," Chris continued. "One pocket first aid kit complete with sutures, superglue, changes of underwear, sunglasses, sun block, lip balm, eye drops, allergy pills, cold medication, and anything personal you want to take that doesn't weigh over five pounds."

"Everybody ready?" Natalie asked as she stood next to Chris.

"If we have to, let's go," Heather said and pulled her cap over her blonde hair.

Soon they were on the street where Major Chen was standing next to a van, doors already open.

"Good morning," he said and bowed. He wore an olive green casual uniform that resembled the SWAT uniforms back in the States.

"Good morning," everyone replied in near unison.

"That sounded weird," Heather said.

"We must hurry so the aircraft is not kept waiting. It's a scheduled flight of the People's Liberation Army," Chen said as he got everyone inside.

The drive across bustling Beijing to the military airport took only forty-five minutes. The van was cleared through two security checks and drove out on the tarmac directly up to the aircraft.

"Antonov AN-12," Chris whispered not meaning for anyone to hear.

"Very good, Mr. MacGregor," Major Chen said. "But the aircraft is a duplicate of the Russian version. Ours is called the Yun-8. It has been a very good aircraft for many decades and continues to be fitted with new parts as our needs change. I need not remind you that photography is not allowed while you are near or on the aircraft."

"Very cool," R.O. said peering out the window as they drove up to the giant transport plane.

The back end of the Yun-8 was open and lying at an incline toward the tarmac, with a hold large enough for trucks, helicopters, or just about anything that a battle theater would need. The kids tossed their backpacks over their shoulders and followed the Major up to the ramp.

"This is where I will leave you. Two of my people are already on board waiting for you. They will accompany you to the Wolong Reserve where the officials of the reserve will greet you. You will be taken to the remote boundaries of the reserve where tourists never travel. You will be in safe hands for the next three days. Enjoy your flight and give my greetings to any of the giant pandas you may see," Major Chen said and bowed. He turned around quickly and walked away.

A female officer walked down the ramp.

"I am Captain Wan Yi. I will be your escort to Chengdu," she smiled.

"Hello," Natalie said. Everyone else then began to greet her, with R.O. bowing four or five times.

Within minutes a whining noise from the cables pulling up the large ramp could be heard as the four teens were strapping into their seats. Only Chris could see out a small window next to a side door. The seating area was much like a hollow tube with wires and cables lining the inside walls. Two large containers, each the size of an automobile, were locked into place about twenty feet away. The Yun-8 made a lumbering scuttle down the runway then suddenly lifted off the ground. The craft climbed quickly to a cruising altitude of twenty thousand feet.

Captain Yi had explained to the kids how to use the oxygen mask attached to each seat if they felt light-headed. The pilot would keep the aircraft below twenty thousand feet since there were passengers on board; however, the Yun-8 could easily fly to thirty thousand feet if needed. With a cruising speed of over four hundred miles per hour, the nine hundred mile flight to Chengdu would take two and a half hours. They would be there before noon.

Mavis, Julian, and Nigel awoke when the dead-bolt turned in the closet door. On the floor and leaning against each other to stay warm, the night had passed slowly for the three scientists. Only a thin ray of light had shown through the opening in the door. One of the armed guards poked the barrel of his automatic rifle through the opening just to be sure everyone was still being compliant.

"Get up," the guard ordered in English and swung the door wide open.

"An agreeable chap early in the morning," Nigel quipped as he struggled to get up with a right leg that had fallen to sleep.

Mavis was the first out the door, where four armed men greeted her. Julian and Nigel followed.

A man in a business suit walked up from behind them.

"Mr. Chang sends his greetings this morning," he said.

"Please tell Mr. Chang we'll cooperate on one condition," Mavis said in a heavy British accent, which always happened when she was around her native tongue.

"Dr. MacGregor, you do not name the conditions, but since you offered one, I will humor you. What is your request?"

"Tell Mr. Chang that I feel that he should take that pistol of his and blow his brains out," Mavis declared with a cold face.

"Mavis, old girl where did that come from?" Nigel asked.

Julian let out a small laugh then caught himself.

"Your condition is both crude and unacceptable," the man said. He reached inside his coat and pulled out a CZ 75 9mm pistol. He walked over to Mavis and put the barrel up against her forehead. "But Dr. MacGregor, I could blow your brains out, if you prefer."

"Not necessary," Mavis answered softly.

"Then we are in agreement about cooperation?" the man asked.

All three scientists nodded.

"Most excellent. We're going to get along very well. Now if you will follow me, please," the man said. "If you are cooperative, then I won't feel compelled to bind your arms. If you aren't, I may kill you."

The scientists were led out of the warehouse where they could see dozens of people beginning to load and pack the fossils in huge crates. A giant forklift was lifting a crate that was most likely holding the *Caudipteryx zoui*. Mavis was nudged gently by the barrel of one of the guards for lingering in the line and watching the workers.

It was a dreary, cold morning when they left the warehouse. The red Lada was gone and they were led to a paneled truck and told to get into the back. The man in the business suit walked over and stepped into a black Mercedes. It resembled a diplomatic limousine but with an extended body. Two guards climbed into the truck with the three scientists and sat next to the door as it closed. Mavis pulled her parka up around her neck and zipped it to her chin. She tried to fluff out her hair releasing some of the tangles from the night in the closet.

"I don't suppose they'll beat us if we talk," Mavis said to Nigel and Julian.

"No talk," one of the guards said and pointed the rifle at Mavis. She nodded her head and raised her eyebrows. The truck began to move.

After thirty minutes they stopped and the back door of the truck was opened. It was obvious they were at the large state-run airport on the outskirts of Shenyang. The man in the suit appeared at the door.

"Put these over your heads and then put your arms out in front of you," he said and tossed black, cloth bags toward each of them. After they had positioned the bags they each extended their arms.

"Ouch," Mavis yelped as plastic wrist clamps were secured tightly around her wrists. The two men said nothing.

"You will be led out of the truck. Do not stand up straight or you will hurt yourself. When you are on the tarmac, you will be led to an awaiting aircraft. You will be boarded and flown out of this city. If you cooperate, you might have a slim chance of telling your story to your families someday. If not, you will be dead. Have a safe flight," the man said and walked back toward the Mercedes.

The captives were lead to an aircraft and helped on board. Buckled in and still hooded, they didn't talk. Ten minutes into the flight their hoods were yanked off. A young woman in a business suit stood before them while the four engines of the aircraft droned noisily outside the cabin. The plane was empty. They were the only passengers and Mavis could see that they were each separated by several rows.

"Dr. MacGregor, I will be your host. You may call me Ashley. I will serve you and your colleagues something to eat and drink during your flight," the woman said.

"This is too bizarre. The last gentlemen puts a gun to my

head and you want to serve me wine and cheese," Mavis responded.

"I'm sorry. We don't have wine and cheese. But I can offer you tea, coffee, soda, bottled water, sandwiches, crackers, and, of course, peanuts," Ashley said.

"How sweet of you, Ashley. Would you happen to have a pair of scissors so I can cut these restraints off my wrists? They're beginning to hurt," Mavis replied and held them up to her.

"Let me see if I can find something else," Ashley replied in perfect English but with a Chinese accent.

In a few minutes she returned with a pair of police handcuffs. She carefully cut the plastic and then replaced it with the chrome handcuffs making sure not to close them too tightly.

"There, Dr. MacGregor. That should be better. But if you should misbehave, I will squeeze them as tight as the plastic ones. Is that clear?" Ashley asked.

"I understand. Thank you," Mavis answered as she rubbed the red areas of her wrists. "I think I'm ready for a cup of coffee, please. Nigel," she shouted. "Tea or coffee, dear."

"Tea of course," Nigel replied.

"Coffee for me," Julian shouted.

Ashley stood up quickly and looked at all three of them. One of the armed guards rushed down the aisle toward them.

"We're not going anywhere, Ashley. So you might as well let us talk. What are we going to do? Escape?" Mavis said with a silly smile on her face.

Ashley spoke in Chinese to the men and soon Nigel and Julian were on rows adjacent to Mavis. A few minutes later they had their drinks and sandwiches.

"Our captors seem to have changed their tunes about us being dispensable," Julian said and sipped his coffee.

"I don't know if that's changed," Mavis said. "Could be they are lulling us into a false sense of safety."

"The box cars before the gas chambers," Nigel responded.

"Exactly. We must keep our wits about us. Even though we are definitely outgunned, a chance to break away may come," Julian continued.

"Outgunned is an understatement, old boy," Nigel said.

"There's no way the *Caudipteryx zoui* could be on board. It would take a large cargo aircraft. The other fossils weren't ready to go when we left. So we're either ahead of them or going somewhere entirely different," Mavis commented and sipped her coffee.

"From the size of this aircraft, where we're going won't be just a short hop and jump away," Nigel said.

Ashley came back down the aisle.

"I hope you are comfortable. My superior said that you may sit together but can only talk when I say so. You have had enough talking for now. It's time to sit quietly," Ashley said.

"And what if we're not through talking?" Julian asked and looked her in the eye.

Ashley quickly raised her hand, which brought one of the armed guards running up the aisle. When he had reached the three scientists, Ashley pointed to Julian. With a fluid swing the guard brought the butt of the rifle into contact with the left side of Julian's head knocking him from his seat onto the floor.

"You are through talking," Ashley said and walked away.

Mavis and Nigel pulled the half-conscious Julian back into his seat and buckled him in. Blood was pouring down the side of his face; they tried to blot it with the napkins from the food trays. Mavis pulled off her silk scarf and tied it around his head to cut the circulation to the scalp. Her white down coat was quickly becoming covered with blood. The engines droned on as the aircraft cruised the skies over China.

A thousand miles away to the southwest, the engines of the Yun-8 effortlessly pulled the hefty aircraft through the winter skies of China. The four teens had exhausted themselves of talk having made this same trip only two days before.

"I'm sick of flying," Heather said and unscrewed the cap off a bottle of water.

"I'm not. Beats buses and cabs," R.O. replied.

"I like to fly. I never got out of Oklahoma much until I met you guys. I mean, my summer job in Grand Cayman was only my second time to fly on an airplane. Then I went to Egypt, springbreak in London, and now China. Chris," Natalie said and gently touched his hand. "Is there any way I can stay for the whole trip this time? I can take six months off from college and I promise to pay my own way."

Chris took her hand in his and looked at her.

"You'll have to discuss that with mom and dad and your parents," Chris answered.

"That was cold. I mean, you didn't even say maybe if, or yes if, or anything nice," Natalie said.

"Chris are you in for it now," R.O. laughed.

Chris just glared at him as Heather pulled out a small paperback book she had brought along to read and turned to the other direction, trying to stay out of the discussion.

"Ryan, mind your own business," Natalie said and looked back to Chris.

"That's what I meant. I mean if they said yes, that would be terrific," Chris replied.

Natalie leaned over and kissed him on the mouth and saw his eyebrows rise.

"O.K., I know I show too much affection. I'll be better," she said sheepishly.

"Thanks," Chris stated.

"And thank you," she said as she pulled away.

"I'm about to hurl the donuts," R.O. said as he grimaced.

Heather kept reading her book, knowing what was going on.

The loud drone of the motors inside the military aircraft was conducive to sleep and the kids were soon out. They began to wake when the big landing gear dropped, and the aircraft began its descent.

"Well, we're here," Chris announced, and everyone starting stretching and squirming in their seats.

"Where's the bathroom?" Heather asked.

"I think we should wait until we're on the ground," Natalie said. "I think the head is up those stairs, but I bet they won't let you up until we land."

"I can wait," Heather whined as the airplane made its final approach.

Ten minutes later the ramp was being lowered and the kids felt a cold breeze blow inside the aircraft. Captain Wan Yi appeared and escorted them down the ramp where a van was waiting. On the side of the van in Chinese characters was written, "Wolong," with a panda painted next to it.

"Hey, Chris. Remember the cheetah spots painted on the safari vans at Tsavo Station?" R.O. asked.

"Sure do little brother. These look pretty cool, too," Chris replied.

Captain Yi led them to the van. They crawled inside the cabin while their gear was being stored in the back.

"Captain, I have to go to the bathroom," Heather called out before she closed the door.

"We will take you to facilities right now," the Captain said and closed the door.

"Sir, this is Charlie. Let me speak to Dr. Biggs right away," the embassy pilot said into his telephone.

"This is Dr. Biggs."

"Dr. Biggs, this is Charlie. I flew Mavis MacGregor to Shenyang last night and I was scheduled to meet her this morning at the airplane but she hasn't shown up yet," Charlie said on his cell phone as he walked toward the Beech Baron.

"Has she called in?" Biggs asked.

"No. I tried the number and no one answers. I have the

numbers of her two colleagues and they aren't answering, either," Charlie answered.

"I'll notify Major Chen. I'm sure it's all a misunderstanding," Biggs said.

"I don't think so, doctor. Dr. MacGregor was certain she would be back no later than ten and it's past twelve now," Charlie said.

"Stay near the aircraft and I'll call the Major now," Biggs assured and hung up.

"Major Chen, please," she said after waiting only a few seconds.

"This is Chen."

"Major, we may have a problem. Dr. Mavis MacGregor never returned from her meeting with her two colleagues from England," Biggs said.

"I wasn't aware that she had such a meeting," Chen said quickly.

"I apologize, Major. It was my oversight. The meeting was last night in Shenyang. An embassy plane flew her there but she didn't return this morning," Biggs said.

"I didn't see such a request for a flight to Shenyang," Chen said.

"We didn't make one," Biggs replied.

"Dr. Biggs, I am responsible for every movement that the MacGregors make while in our country. I will need all the information you have about her colleagues and where in Shenyang they were to meet," Major Chen said showing his displeasure in the tone of his voice.

"Yes, Major," Dr. Biggs said and hung up.

Major Chen dialed the number to the People's Liberation Army headquarters.

"I need a fast plane to take me to Shenyang as soon as possible. Yes, a MiG will do. I will be at the base in fifteen minutes," he said and walked out his office door followed by two junior officers. "Call Major Lee in Shenyang and tell him the People's Liberation Army Air Force is flying me in one of their fighters to the base. I will be there in thirty minutes. Have him meet me and tell him to find the warehouse where the dinosaur bones are stored. That's where we'll begin our search for Dr. MacGregor," Chen said and stepped into a waiting car.

He suddenly stopped and stepped back out of the car and came to within two feet of the junior officers.

"And be sure to emphasize to Major Lee, that if Dr. MacGregor is not at the warehouse we must locate her by the end of the day or we'll be relocated to a place that is definitely undesirable. Is that understood?" Chen asked. The two officers quickly saluted as he got back into the car.

8

Rivers, Bears, and Skyscrapers

Jack's flight from Beijing to Sandouping took approximately ninety minutes on the embassy's passenger jet. It was just enough time for him to review some of the geological documents he had, concerning possible tectonic plate shifts due to gigantic dams. What concerned him about the massive Three Gorges Dam was the actual weight of the water behind the dam and whether it would affect the many fault zones that traced across the earth nearby. He also wondered if the water was going to impact the wildlife upstream in central China.

He was looking forward to hearing his old friend, Dr. Gary Houlette, renowned geologist, address that subject. In August he had listened to Dr. Houlette lecture about the silt build-up behind the Aswan Dam and its impact on the Eastern Mediterranean. He was proud of the fact that he and Houlette belonged to an elite club of scientists who moved about the globe frequently, trying to get a handle on the growing global crises of the environment.

The landing was smooth and the drive to the conference building next to the two-mile-wide dam was made in about an hour. As Jack stepped from the car, an officer with the People's Armed Police greeted him.

"Dr. MacGregor, I am Lieutenant Mei Ling. Major Chen has instructed me to be with you all the time during your stay," the female officer said and bowed slightly.

"Thank you, but I'm sure I will be fine. You see, I made it all the way here without a problem," Jack pointed out and smiled. "However, the drive was nearly as long as the flight."

"China is a vast land of varying terrain," the Lieutenant replied.

As Jack turned and threw his light bag over his shoulder, the Lieutenant stepped in front of him. Jack came to an abrupt halt.

"There is one more thing, Dr. MacGregor," she said.

"And what's that?" he asked, becoming annoyed.

"Have you heard from Mrs. MacGregor today?" she said without blinking an eye.

"No, I haven't. Is there something wrong?" Jack asked and lowered his bag to the ground.

"The American embassy contacted Major Chen and informed him that she had not returned from her meeting with the British paleontologists in Shenyang this morning," the Lieutenant said dryly.

"I see. Well, she gets lost in time when she's around her dinosaur bone buddies. I'm sure she's fine," Jack replied.

"The pilot who flew her to Shenyang is the person who called in her absence," the female officer said.

Jack didn't say anything but it was obvious from the expression on his face that the wheels in his brain were turning quickly.

"When did he call in?" Jack asked.

"Thirty minutes ago. Major Chen will be in Shenyang in another fifteen minutes to talk to the pilot," she replied.

"Thirty minutes? How will he get there so fast?" Jack asked.

"He is a passenger on a MiG-23 fighter jet supplied by the

People's Liberation Army Air Force," the Lieutenant replied.

"I see. If he's going there so quickly then he must be concerned," Jack said.

"We are always concerned about every guest in our country," she replied.

"I should go there too. Take me back to the airport," Jack said quickly.

"That's not necessary. Major Chen is in control of the situation and as far as we know, Mrs. MacGregor is still in some dusty warehouse examining dinosaur bones, as you have said. It's best if you stay with your itinerary and attend Dr. Houlette's discussion of the geological strata under our new dam project. Your opinion as a scientist will be greatly welcomed by the government of China and the scientific world. If there's a need for you to be concerned, we'll be happy to inform you of that and when," the officer said stiffly.

"I understand you clearly. But I will contact the American embassy to verify your story, if you don't mind," Jack said and lowered his bag to retrieve his telephone.

He punched in the number to the embassy and heard the ring. When the receptionist answered he asked for Dr. Biggs.

"Sherri Biggs," she answered.

"Dr. Biggs, this is Jack MacGregor. I'm at the Three Gorges Dam and just heard a rumor about Mavis being missing. What's the scoop?" he asked.

"Well, Dr. MacGregor, at the moment, we don't know anything. Our pilot called in this morning saying she didn't come back to the airplane. I reported it to Major Chen since he has been adamant about staying in control of your family's movements ever since the kids got lost kayaking," she said.

"Lost kayaking? I didn't hear about this and I saw them all last night. And what about Mavis' two British friends? Has anyone talked to them?" he asked.

"We're not that far along yet. I have a consulate in Shenyang and have asked the liaison there to meet up with the pilot and find the warehouse and the scientists.

I'm sure everything is just fine. It takes a lot of work for a high profile person like your wife to go missing in China. Just a matter of miscommunication, I'm sure," she said.

"I tend to agree. Mavis likes to get lost when she's wrapped up in a *Triceratops* skeleton or something similar. Just keep me updated. I don't like to get information through the People's Armed Police. That can be alarming sometimes," Jack said.

"There's no doubt about that, Dr. MacGregor. You call me since I don't know your hourly schedule." Dr. Biggs said. "She's not answering the telephone I gave her yesterday, so I need to hear from you."

"I will do that. Thanks," Jack replied and pushed the disconnect button on the cellular phone.

He looked up at the Lieutenant and spoke.

"I'm ready to find Dr. Houlette. Let's go," Jack said.

The Lieutenant smiled and began walking toward the conference center. The center had been specially built for events like this. The world has come to China to praise or criticize the largest dam project in human history. The Chinese were always willing to entertain suggestions; whether or not they followed them was another story entirely.

"Whew, I feel better," Heather said. "I was about to pop."

"O.K., listen up you guys," Chris said and gathered them all around. "We've got three full days of hiking planned in the panda reserve. From what I've read, this place is very primitive. The bamboo grows all year round; therefore, the Panda's don't hibernate. They're active and always looking for the bamboo that's not covered with snow. There are over fifty Pandas in captivity near the main compound and visitor center but that's on the other side of the mountain range. It looks like we're going to the wild side of the reserve, away from all the tourists. We'll get more information as we go along. So if you even think you're getting a blister, stop and tell me. I don't want to cut this trek short because we weren't paying attention to our feet. We'll camp out for two nights and then we're on the plane back to Beijing. Now is all of this clear?" Chris informed.

"Got it," Heather said first.

"I'm with you, Chris," Natalie replied and winked at him making him smile.

"R.O.? Do you understand?" Chris asked.

"Sure do, big brother," R.O. answered and looked away.

Chris reached down and spun him around so they were now face to face.

"Mom's not here to threaten you with homework or a trip to Georgia. But you know the Police Captain out there by the plane. If you mess up, you'll be tied to her for three days, literally. When you eat, sleep, or go to the bathroom, she'll be your shadow.

Got it?" Chris voiced.

"Roger, I got it," R.O. said with wide eyes as he glanced out to the Yun-8 sitting on the tarmac.

"O.K., let's go have some fun and find us a bear," Chris said and they all gave him high fives and headed back out to the painted van.

Sen Li walked over to the floor-to-ceiling window on the nineteenth floor of the skyscraper overlooking Hong Kong harbor. He puffed hard on a green cigar, creating a cloud of smoke that filled the room. His view of the harbor and Kowloon was magnificent. Five people entered the room carrying briefcases and laptop computers.

They sat down around a mahogany table and waited for Sen Li to turn to them.

He stood and stared out the window for a couple of minutes, ignoring his guests. No one uttered a word. Then he casually turned around, walked to the table, and sat down in a red, leather chair.

"Let's begin. Miss Chen, please summarize the activities of the last week," Sen Li politely stated.

"Shipping accounted for sixty million tons of containerized goods to California. You had twenty-two active ships at sea in transit to or from North America. Chemicals were camouflaged in the containers and arrived undetected. Our distributors already have half their heroin, the other half is in transit across America and Europe. Street value is near $200 million U.S.," she informed.

"Thank you, Miss Chen, you may continue now," Li spoke and took a puff on the cigar.

"Oil drilling in the South China Sea is up as the price of oil continues to rise. Our British and American partners continue to be optimistic. New drill pipe and collars have arrived. The bits are en route and will arrive in a week or less," she said and was interrupted.

"Miss Chen," Li said.

"Yes, sir," she replied.

"Next time fly the bits in first. Don't ship them by marine transport from the U.S. Is that clear?" Li asked and looked her in the eye.

"Yes, sir. They will come by air next time," she replied nervously.

"Mr. Wen, you may continue with our smaller enterprises please," Li said and stood up and walked across the room to the windows again.

"Our counterfeit jeans factories have expanded to better meet demand. The orders for jeans in the $120 to $160 range skyrocketed last year. We have been able to match all the name brands right down to the stitching on the back pocket. Profits should reach thirty-five million dollars this year. We're no longer making purses, too much competition and Interpol was getting too close. A more thorough examination of our containers for purses and billfolds would have endangered our drug business in the United States.

"We have received new contracts on the dinosaur bones and elephant ivory coming from Tanzania. After we showed our client the pictures of the *Caudipteryx zoui,* he was willing to meet our new price of twenty million dollars if we included a breeding pair of pandas. Our two other clients are definitely interested in the containers full of loose bones and have committed $500,000 each. Our problem with the two British paleontologists has been resolved, sir," he said and twitched nervously in his seat.

"Yes, I'm listening," Sen Li said and turned to face Mr. Wen.

"We were able to get the two scientists, who made the discovery, back in China so they could meet an accidental fate and never be heard of again. This would keep our *Caudipteryx zoui* a company secret, so to speak. However, when we moved the bones this morning, we were unexpectedly confronted with the presence of a third British scientist."

"You were unexpectedly confronted?" Sen Li asked and walked closer.

"Yes, sir," he replied.

"Then your plan was inept and you are incompetent. Who was the third scientist?" Li demanded and puffed on his cigar.

"Mavis MacGregor, a British subject who now resides in America," Wen replied.

Sen Li spun on his heels and walked quickly to the window puffing furiously on his cigar.

"The Dr. Mavis MacGregor, wife of the zoologist Dr. Jack MacGregor?"

"Yes, sir," Wen said nervously.

"And why was Dr. MacGregor in our warehouse in the middle of the night?"

"She has an interest in the feathered dinosaur; therefore, the other Brits must have called her in Beijing. We have learned she flew to Shenyang in an American embassy aircraft. The pilot missed her at the rendezvous time and called the embassy. They've sent someone to Shenyang and alerted the People's Armed Police. We've learned that a Major Yufan Chen is now in Shenyang investigating her disappearance," he said and took a deep breath.

"I see. A simple plan to move rocks has now involved the police and the American embassy," Li stated, walking toward the table of consultants. He reached inside his suit coat and pulled out an automatic pistol and pulled back the gold-plated hammer. He pointed it at Wen's head. Suddenly he shifted his stance and pulled the trigger, aiming just over Miss Chen's right shoulder. She had a sudden urge to jump up as the bullet went through the chair and into the wall behind her.

"Miss Chen, you delayed my oil drilling by six days and cost me millions. As for you Mr. Wen, you'll not receive a bullet as Miss Chen nearly did, but your death will take several days and so will the death of every member of your family including your parents, your grandparents, the neighbors on both sides of your house, as well as the teachers of your children, if you do not solve this problem in three days. Am I clear about this?" Li commanded and holstered the gun inside his suit jacket.

"Very clear, sir," he replied.

"And for the rest of you, be aware that there is no retirement from this job. When you were added as associates, you were told it was a lifetime commitment, meaning your life," Li informed in between puffs of his cigar. "Finish your report about our natural resource business, Mr. Wen," Sen Li said.

"Yes, sir. We now have twenty-seven giant pandas in three wilderness locations in the Tibetan Highlands far away from government facilities. That's up from fourteen animals just one year ago. Our scientists are having great success with breeding and we have six clients waiting in Europe alone. There are now six red pandas in our facility in Xinjiang. Our connections in the government tell us that no one has discovered how we took them from the reserves in the wild or where our holding facilities are hidden. As proven by the Americans, a good breeding pair is worth millions in tourist money. We currently have four acquisition teams working across China under cover of the People's Liberation Army, learning where the panda researchers haven't conducted a bear census in the last two years. We can then go in covertly and take the bears without being noticed. There are, after all, over a hundred mountains that have an altitude of 16,000 feet or higher in Wolong alone. The wildlife agencies don't have our resources or the connections to the army. Everyone is paid well. Our acquisition teams could be twenty miles away and never be noticed by the hundreds of thousands of tourists that visit Wolong every year," Wen said and breathed deep.

"Your work may have redeemed you, Mr. Wen," Sen Li stated and headed for the door when he stopped and turned quickly.

"Miss Chen, I will match Mr. Wen's $50,000 dollar bonus for his job with our pandas and ivory if you can find my drilling bits by this time tomorrow. You will have all or nothing," Sen Li said and closed the door behind him.

"This past August in Egypt, we discussed the affect of large dams on tectonic plate movement. We suspect that there have been several incidents where the accumulation of massive amounts of water on top of geological strata that wasn't formed with the weight of water present, did in fact, cause a shift that resulted in an earthquake magnitude of four or better. Based on this data and the presence of fault zones upstream of Three Gorges, there is a likelihood of geological disturbance," Dr. Houlette said as the audience shook their heads in agreement or disagreement.

Jack sat quietly trying to focus on the lecture but was worried by the news that Mavis was late for her flight from Shenyang.

"Dr. Houlette," a Chinese scientist said as he stood up. "We have studied this problem and believe there will be no interference in fault zone activity because of the movement of water behind the dam and the release of the water for hydroelectric power. We feel you are using a false premise and faulty data to make your point."

"I see, but several geologists are using the same criteria

to come to the same conclusion," Houlette replied.

"Then all twelve are wrong," the Chinese scientist said, firmly standing his ground.

Jack fidgeted in his seat and got up and walked back to the foyer of the conference room. He took out his cell phone and dialed Sherri Biggs.

"This is Sherri Biggs. I am unavailable at this time. Please leave a message or call the embassy public relations office if this is an emergency. Thank you."

Jack walked over to the windows, looking out on the Three Gorges. He couldn't focus on the dam or his reason for being there because of Mavis. "Why hasn't she called in?" he thought and gritted his teeth. He thought about calling Chris but decided not to worry the kids. This had happened before. Mavis had given up her career as a paleontologist for him and their family and couldn't be blamed for the occasional adventure with her old buddies from England. She loved studying dinosaurs and what would it hurt if she took off for a few days?

"Dr. MacGregor," a young female Chinese scientist said. "We're ready for the round table discussion. Your participation would be greatly appreciated."

"Sure. No problem. I was just doing some thinking. Great view," Jack said.

"Yes, it is. To look at one of man's greatest engineering feats is, indeed, an inspiring moment. All of China is proud of this accomplishment," the young woman said, spewing forth propaganda as if Jack had pushed a button on her back. He could also see the pride on her face, so he thought she might be sincere.

"Let's go," Jack said and they walked back into the large hall where he would join Dr. Houlette and four other scientists for the next presentation.

The small boat cruised across Shanghai harbor with two men dressed in pants, shirts, and plain shoes and a woman in traditional Chinese attire. They gazed across the water at the over one hundred massive skyscrapers that jutted up from the surface of the earth as if a giant dragon had pushed its spiny back upward from the realms below. Soft, white clouds filled the sky and a cool wind drifted across the water.

"When did you hear about the shipment?" one of the men asked.

"Just yesterday. My contact told me Sen Li had a *Caudipteryx zoui* and much more in Shenyang. They knew the fossils were being shipped to a warehouse here in Shanghai in preparation for a sale," Zen Zong replied.

"Why didn't we hear before yesterday?" Shao Shen asked. He moved closer.

"It was a sudden move. Their client was wavering on the price."

"What's the price?"

"Li started at five million dollars and now it's up to twenty million. Seems the feathered dinosaur is in perfect condition and a one of a kind specimen. There are only two others like it and this one is the biggest and best."

"I see. Where are they taking it?"

"The trucks won't get here for two days. But my contact says there was an aircraft that left with three scientists on board and a separate cargo plane that was loaded full to the tail ramp. The trucks may be a decoy and contain only plain rocks."

"Three scientists? Who are they?" Shao Shen asked.

"This is where Sen Li has a big problem. They are British and one is the wife of Dr. Jack MacGregor."

"MacGregor, the zoologist, Sen Li, indeed, has a problem."

A cell phone rang and Zong answered it.

"Yes, a transport plane? Yes, I see. Thanks," Zong said and disconnected.

"I'm waiting," Shen said.

"That was my contact. The fossils are definitely being flown to Shanghai in a large transport plane. My early information was correct. It will be here in less than two hours."

"Then we must be prepared to move quickly. Get our people to the warehouse and eliminate any resistance there. When the feathered dinosaur arrives we will be there to receive it and move forward with our plan. We'll let Sen Li do all the work."

"What about MacGregor and the other two British scientists?

"They won't exist after another seventy-two hours. Sen Li and his family will take the blame for their deaths. After we take them, we'll keep them alive long enough to learn more about the fossils so we can sell them to our highest bidder. Tell our network to contact all the university buyers and paleontology stores worldwide, especially the wholesale buyers in London and Tucson. I wager that in three days we'll have the bidding up to Li's asking price. We'll throw in all the loose fossils for free if they buy the *Caudipteryx zoui.*"

"Good plan," Zong said. "We'll pretend we are there to rescue them and they will relax and tell us more. After we get the information we need, we'll dump their bodies at sea."

"Excellent idea," Shen commented. "We're nearly there. Take the Brits from the warehouse out to my yacht. Give them food, clean clothes, and make them feel warm.

We'll take the plane by force and move the fossils to a safe place at the same time."

"Commandeer the aircraft and fly it to one of our hangers in Kowloon," Zen Zong suggested.

"We'll see," Shen said and looked toward the approaching dock.

The small boat cruised up to the dock and two men caught the rope line that was tossed to them and tied the boat securely to the dock. The two men and one woman climbed a ladder up to the top of the wooden pier and walked to a waiting car. As the car drove away, the aircraft with Mavis and the two British paleontologists landed at the Shanghai airport.

9

Wolong Pandas

The three-hour drive up the mountains of the lower Tibetan Plateau was both tedious and tiring although the view was nothing short of spectacular. The MacGregor kids and Natalie were exhausted and fell asleep on the first long hill and slept the entire trip. Kayaking, the flight to Beijing, the flight back to Western China, and now the mountain ride in the van with the heater turned up high, all the while dressed in mountain gear, was enough to send all of them off to dreamland for hours.

The drive ended amidst a light snow as the van stopped at the end of the road. The minute the side door slid open and the fresh cold mountain air rushed in, everyone, except Heather, awakened and rubbed their eyes and yawned. There were four small buildings scattered in the forest with two ATVs and one snowmobile. The mountain outpost of the Wolong Reserve was a far cry from the modern high tech visitor center a hundred miles away. About a hundred yards away was a corral with four mules and six horses. A barn just big enough for the animals was attached to the corral. The primitive nature of the buildings brought a surprised look to the faces of all the kids.

"Did we go back in time?" R.O. asked as he bounded from the van.

"I wish you had gone back in time," Heather replied as she began to step down beside him.

A greeting party consisting of three Chinese scientists, two men and one woman all dressed in forest green shirts, pants, and coats walked toward them with big smiles across their faces.

"My name is Dr. Win Chi," one of the men said and reached out to shake hands with Chris.

"Chris MacGregor," Chris said and took his hand. "This is my friend Natalie Crosswhite from Oklahoma, my sister Heather, and my brother Ryan, we call him R.O."

All three Chinese bowed their heads and then the woman stepped forward.

"I am Dr. Hsu, the director of field research for the Wolong Panda Reserve," she said.

"Is this your entire staff?" asked Natalie.

"No," Dr. Hsu replied. "We have many more field staff who are scattered across the Reserve. The rest of the research staff is housed at the international visitor center where we greet over 100,000 visitors each year. There they do most of the behavioral studies in preparation for loaning out breeding pairs to zoos around the world. Out here, our work is all field biology and most rigorous."

"So there are only a dozen or so of you for an area the size of our state of Delaware?" Chris said.

"I don't know Delaware, but I assume it is a very large state," Hsu replied.

"It's small but comparatively, it's pretty big for that few scientists," Chris replied trying not to be rude.

"I vote we go to the tourist center," Heather said loudly but was ignored by everyone.

"You must be tired from your long journey from Beijing.

Come into our house and have some tea and refreshments. Afterwards we'll show you to your tent. You will need to rest in preparation for our three-day hike through the mountains to visit the pandas. We spotted three just eight miles from here last week," she said.

"Eight mile hike through the mountains?" Heather asked with a stressed look on her face.

"Yes, that's very close. Normally we have to hike for days and nearly twenty miles to find them. But the bamboo close to our camp is rich and sweet and the animals have migrated closer to us this season," Hsu answered with a smile.

"Lucky us," Heather said as she turned away.

"This is exciting," Natalie added.

Within minutes the kids had unloaded their gear and were walking toward a large tent that had a stovepipe protruding out the back of the tent with smoke flowing out. They stepped through the wobbly door that was attached to the canvas front. The tent had a full wooden floor with six small mattresses, a cooking stove that also served as the heater, and a latrine that was draped with curtains from the top of the tent to the floor.

"All the amenities of home," Natalie said as she walked around.

"Please drop your gear and follow me," Dr. Hsu said as the teenagers obeyed and followed her out of the tent and down a path to a wooden cabin. As they stepped inside, they were hit in the face with the stale aroma of cooking oil from the thousands of meals that had been prepared there. They all sat down on pillows around a knee-high table and cups of tea were poured in front of them. A tray of cookies was placed in the middle of the table. R.O. was the first to snatch one and plunge it into his mouth. Everyone else followed suit and began to drink the hot tea.

As the kids ate the cookies and drank the tea, one of the scientists stirred a large pot of soup on the stove.

"The soup will be ready in a few minutes," Dr. Hsu said.

"So this must be the appetizer?" Heather inquired.

"You may call it that. We call them our hospitality cookies," she replied. "I prefer not to eat them before a meal, too much sugar, but my guests never hesitate."

"We thank you regardless of how they are intended," Natalie said politely.

The soup was served in wooden bowls. As the kids ate quickly, the room grew quiet. The Chinese staff poured bowls of rice into their soup while their guests watched them use their chopsticks, dropping only a few grains of rice.

"That is so cool," R.O. said. He tried his chopsticks but spilled rice everywhere.

Chris and Natalie were getting proficient but Heather never tried them.

An hour passed while they talked and more soup was poured into their bowls. As their stomachs became full their eyes began to droop. Soon they were all walking back to their tent to get to bed early.

"I will wake you at four in the morning so we can get an early start on the first day. We can just about reach the pandas by dark tomorrow. Sleep well," Dr. Hsu said and left.

"O.K., spread out and pick a bed," Chris said.

Natalie dropped her pack on the back mattress. Heather got as far away from the latrine as possible. R.O. was the first on a bed, boots off and fast asleep with clothes on. All the kids settled down, as the cabin grew dark, each one turning off a lamp. Chris decided to leave the oil lamp burning on low and leaned back and instantly fell asleep with his head settled on his rolled up goose down parka.

Natalie watched his eyes close and got up and leaned over and kissed him. He opened his eyes and reached up and pulled her face back down and kissed her back.

"Sleep tight," she said and smiled.

"I will, thanks," Chris said.

Four o'clock came quickly, even though the kids had slept for nearly ten hours. Dr. Hsu was gentle with her wake-up call, simply walking around and talking softly.

"Good morning, MacGregors, we have a long day ahead of us. Move quickly and be sharp. That's what we learn in the People's Liberation Army," she said.

Heather mumbled something about Sergeant Hsu and rolled over and pulled her parka over her head. R.O. popped up and trotted to the latrine and pulled the drapes quickly. Natalie was next in line, followed by Chris. Heather waited until everyone was finished and shyly wandered over and took her turn. Taking care of business in the wilderness never bothered her because she was always alone. The small tent with her brothers was a different story entirely. Within twenty minutes the kids were dressed, packed, and standing outside the tent ready to go. Chris checked his watch and it read 3:50 a.m.

"Well, we're up and ready to go with ten minutes to spare," Chris noted as Dr. Hsu and two of her staff members walked toward them.

"Good morning everyone. Please follow me to my cabin for some morning tea and Bao Zi. I have people stationed along our path equipped with snacks, lunch, and dinner. Our first meal is cooking at this very moment."

"I honestly think I'll grow hair all over my face after drinking this tea. It's so strong but there is something sweet about it," Heather said and took another sip. "I like it. Can I have another cup?" Heather asked and lifted up the metal cup. After quickly drinking another cup, she joined the others outside. "O.K. I am ready to go," Heather said loudly and everyone turned toward her.

"Too much caffeine already, Heather?" Chris laughed.

"I'm ready to go big bro. Show me the bears," she said and hitched up her pack and snapped the clasps across her chest.

Dr. Hsu started on the path into the forest carrying her lantern. Two of her staff handed each of the kids a flashlight for the trail as they stepped in behind her. The light snow covered the path but the kids noticed the Chinese scientist moved quickly through the forest as if following a country road back home in Texas. In awe of their surroundings, the teens followed along without saying a word as the trail made a gradual climb up through the forest into the wilderness panda reserve. Even R.O. didn't have much to say and followed along behind Dr. Hsu. She rarely spoke, except to warn of impending danger such as logs across the trail, low hanging limbs, small streams, or large boulders.

It was three hours of silent hiking in the forests of the Tibetan Plateau before the tea hit and everyone needed a "nature break." After a few minutes of rest they continued for another hour before the smell of smoke drifted down the trail. Then they smelled food cooking. The aroma drifted through the dense, nearly frozen forest prompting everyone to acknowledge hunger. It was twenty more minutes before they reached the small camp set up by the two breakfast cooks.

"I'm starved," Heather was the first to say.

"Me too," followed Natalie.

R.O. didn't say a word but walked straight to the cooks and asked about eating. They didn't understand a word he said and then he motioned with his left arm like he was putting food in his mouth. They both laughed and nodded their heads. One of them opened a small portable oven from what seemed to be a permanent storage building built next to the trail for this type of event. Next to it was another large box full of cooking utensils, bowls, bundles of chopsticks, and sealed bags of rice. He handed a steaming bowl of rice to R.O. and bowed. R.O. took it and bowed and looked over to Chris who nodded as if saying he should eat it. R.O. decided to hand it to Chris.

"Thanks," Chris said and then put a wad of rice in his mouth with his fingers. The cooked nodded his head in agreement and slightly bowed again.

"You have honored his gift," Dr. Hsu said. "We have more Bao Zi, rice, and hot tea. Take an hour rest and fill yourselves up. It is seven thirty, we need to arrive at our next break station by noon," she said and helped herself to a cup of tea.

"Got it," Chris replied and took another bite of rice and the steamed meat-bread called Bao Zi. He then retrieved a cup of tea and washed down the rice. It burned his throat slightly and he hastily swallowed more rice.

Soon everyone was eating Bao Zi and drinking the strong tea.

"I never thought I would do this, but then again I never thought I would jump on a camel's back either," Heather added as she found a spot to sit on the plastic tarp that had been laid over the new fallen snow. "They think of everything. This is amazing."

"I agree, amazing and efficient," Natalie said as she swallowed part of some Bao Zi.

R.O. was on his third piece of Bao Zi when Chris handed him a cup of tea.

"Better drink up little brother. We need all the nutrition we can get at each major stop," Chris stated and sat down next to Natalie.

"There isn't any nutrition in hot tea," R.O. said and looked at the cup.

"Dark, herbal Chinese tea is famous for tons of vitamins, minerals, and a bunch of unknown phytonutrients which haven't been discovered yet," Chris informed and drank some tea.

"Phyto what?" R.O. asked.

"Stuff that is found in plants," Heather answered and smiled.

"Oh, I get it. Secret stuff," R.O. replied and gulped it down quickly and let out a belch.

"You are so gross," Heather said.

The guests and Dr. Hsu finished the breakfast break on time and were again on the trail up the mountainous path. About an hour into the next leg of the hike, Dr. Hsu stopped them and turned to speak.

"We can leave our lanterns here and retrieve them on the

way back. There is sufficient daylight and our last stop will have other lanterns for us to use," she said. "I think you call them flashlights."

"We call them lanterns when we dive in the ocean," Chris replied.

All of the kids set the lanterns in a large box that had been camouflaged by the forest. Dr. Hsu closed the lid and started back up the trail. A light snow began to fall.

"As you can see around you, there is an adequate supply of bamboo this season. Our friends, the pandas, do not hibernate because the supply of bamboo is adequate in all seasons. We were very worried because in years past the bamboo crops have failed and there has been a decline in the panda population," Dr. Hsu said.

"Did they die?" Heather asked.

"Yes, some of them died from starvation, and some females were unable to reproduce because of lack of nutrition. It was a very tragic time for us here at the Wolong Reserve. But we fear there were other causes," Dr. Hsu said. "Our regular census was unable to keep track of so few animals in such a large region of China."

"What were those, Doctor?" Natalie asked as she tightened the hood on her parka.

"Poaching," Dr. Hsu responded.

"Poaching?" Heather questioned.

"Yes. The giant panda is a much loved and revered animal all around the world and to capture a wild panda and transport it out of China to be sold to private collectors would bring lots of money and prestige," Dr. Hsu said.

"How long has this been going on?" Chris asked.

"Ever since the end of the Second World War and the emancipation of China by the People's Liberation Army," she replied in her factual and political tone. "In recent years more and more greedy entrepreneurs have emerged in China and with capitalism comes the challenge to make more profits. Pandas can be a source of such profits. They are a natural resource but also a national treasure. Our government wants them for our people to see and enjoy. But the government also realizes that for a short stay in a foreign zoo, two pandas can bring millions of dollars to the people of China with literally no investment. Unfortunately, others have learned that as well."

"But I heard that a zoo that has a mating pair has to meet all kinds of strict standards set by the United States and international wildlife agencies regarding endangered species. Meeting those standards eventually drives up the cost of keeping the bears to the point of becoming unprofitable," Chris said.

"You are correct. They do have to meet strict qualifications and for some it is too costly to have pandas visit," Dr. Hsu added. "However, we have our own rules in China."

"Are the poachers still active?" R.O. asked.

"Yes, they are. There are years when we have losses that can't be attributed to poor bamboo crops. Those are the suspicious ones. We only have 1,600 animals spread out across our reserves. Some estimate nearly 2,000. About 1,000 bears are in protected areas, the rest dwell in unprotected territory. There are over 150 bears in Wolong that we know of. However, with the price of pandas going up on the black market to well over a million dollars, poachers are bolder and more high-tech than ever before," Dr. Hsu responded.

"My father wanted us to learn from you first hand and not rely on any printed material," Chris spoke honestly.

"He is very insightful. We'll talk more as we travel," Dr. Hsu replied.

"I shouldn't have sat down," Natalie said as she stood. "Haven't kept up with my swimming and running in Stillwater like I should have."

"I warned you when I emailed you from Alaska," Chris said.

"I know. I'm toning up quickly and I did beg to come. I won't go home with a bad reputation for complaining. I do want to come back," Natalie said in her defense and pushed up against Chris, as the others began up the trail.

"You can come along anytime," Heather offered as she looked back over her shoulder.

"Thanks, Heather," Natalie replied.

"O.K., you've got my vote," Chris said and pulled her by the hand toward the rest of the party.

The second leg of the hike passed quickly and soon the aroma of food filled the air. The kids hit the camp in a rush and dropped their packs. They ate up the noodles, onions, beef, and chicken in a hurry and sat down on another plastic tarp to rest.

"We are getting way too spoiled," Chris said.

"Are you sad that we aren't eating MRE's and jerky and aren't hanging over a crevasse 200 feet deep," Heather responded with a smile.

"No, I think he would want us to starve all day before we had to climb the mountain without coats in sub-zero weather," Natalie added.

"Wait, wait. I've got it. He would want us to dodge meteors as they plunge from space and created wildfires all around us," R.O. chimed in and smiled at what he thought was the best scenario.

"That's weird," Heather replied. "But Chris would like that for sure."

"Actually, I would prefer that aliens snatched all of you up to the mother ship where you would disappear forever," Chris said and got up. "Shouldn't we be going, Dr. Hsu."

"Yes, we can get started on the last leg early if you prefer," she said and stood up and lifted her pack.

"Chris!" Natalie exclaimed and frowned.

"Way to go bro," Heather said with an equally rigid frown on her face.

"Payback's rough, isn't it," Chris said and filed in behind Dr. Hsu on the trail as she moved forward into the forest.

After they had hiked nearly eight hours and were deep into the forest home of the pandas, the group stopped. One of Dr. Hsu's scientists approached them coming down the trail.

After a long conversation, Dr. Hsu turned toward the kids.

"This is Cheng Chong, an expert in forestry resources. He helps us keep track of the bamboo growth. He says that the pandas we spotted last week have moved from our intended rendezvous to another location two miles north of here and possibly only a mile away. We need to turn toward the new destination at the bottom of this valley and follow a new trail, if we are to see them early in the morning," Dr. Hsu informed. "Chong notified our night camp director several hours ago and he has moved our camp."

The teenagers, beginning to drag from the fatigue of an all day hike, welcomed the downward slope of the new path and the hope of camp not far away. With renewed spirits, they made the new leg of the trek in good time, keeping pace with the fit Dr. Hsu.

"Why don't you use radios, Dr. Hsu?" R.O. asked.

"We do sometimes. But the mountain peaks in this area prevent clear reception and it's an unnecessary expense in batteries and replacements. Each of our new visitor camps have a satellite radio, but the field posts don't have them yet," she said.

Again, the aroma of cooking food reached their nostrils as the last light of day disappeared through the canopy of the forest. Heather was first into the small clearing of three tents and an outdoor cook-stove. She walked straight into the cooking area and motioned for food. The female staff member smiled and handed her a hot bowl of rice. Without even taking off her backpack, she shed the glove on her right hand and started stuffing her mouth. The bowl was gone in four big bites.

"Godzilla returns and just ate New York," R.O. laughed as he walked by her.

Heather smiled and poured a cup of tea and took a big gulp. She blew out the steaming hot mouthful all over R.O.'s parka by accident.

"Heather!" R.O. shouted.

"Boy, did she sucker you into that one," Chris said as he dropped his pack.

"O.K. Watch your back, Heather," R.O. stated and got a bowl of rice.

The cook and a female staff member of the reserve passed out bowls of Huo Guo, a dish of vegetables, bamboo shoots, meat, and mushrooms. Dr. Hsu showed the kids how to take the thin slices of raw meat with chopsticks and dip it into the boiling sauce cooking it quickly. It was then mixed with the other ingredients and eaten.

"This is a great meal. Not what I expected from a hike," Chris commented.

"What does Huo Guo mean?" Natalie asked.

"It means fire pot," Dr. Hsu answered and smiled. "We entertain many special people in the Wolong wilderness and are stocked with a variety of good food. You are our honored guests. And we know that your father can help our country in many ways," Dr. Hsu added and began to eat.

After about forty minutes of eating and talking, everyone left for the small tents. Natalie and Heather were in one, R.O. and Chris in the other. Dr. Hsu helped her staff pick up the dishes and store them in the forest boxes for another occasion. Soon the teens were asleep and dreaming of a wonderful day meeting their first giant panda.

10

The Brits

Nigel, Julian, and Mavis were herded through the hangar that stored crates full of fossils. Some were open with pallets of bones laying around in a disorganized manner. The three paleontologists couldn't see their surroundings or talk to each other. Hoods covered their faces and their mouths were taped shut. Once they were carefully placed in front of three metal folding chairs, they were pushed down until they were seated. One by one their hoods were taken off. Then the same man walked down the row and ripped the tape off their mouths.

"Who do you think you are? I'm an American citizen and these two men are subjects of the Queen. Do you want the entire global force of the United States and Great Britain breathing down your puny necks until they crush you like the insects you are?" Mavis shouted at them.

"Dr. MacGregor . . ." the man, who was wearing the suit started and was interrupted.

"Major Yufan Chen of the Armed Police Service of the Revolution or whatever it's called will discard you like trash. You won't . . ." she stopped as the man pressed a

Baretta 9mm pistol hard into her cheek. A trickle of blood slid down to her chin as the sharp edge of the barrel cut into her face. She winced from the pain.

"Dr. MacGregor, it would behoove you and your friends if you would shut up. Do I make myself clear?" he asked and pressed harder as he pulled back the trigger.

"Yes. You made your point quite clear," Mavis replied softly.

"We have been instructed by our superiors to escort you and your friends to a safe place," the man said as he holstered the gun under his coat.

"And that would be to the American or British embassy or consulate in whatever city we are, if you please," she said.

"Mavis, don't push these people," Nigel stated firmly.

"Your colleague offers good advice, Dr. MacGregor," the man commented.

Two more armed men walked into the hangar, bringing the total to five plus the man in the suit. One of the armed men spoke quickly and then looked down. Their captor turned red in the face and then looked toward the three British scientists.

"There has been a change in plans. We are going to put tape back on your mouths and hoods on your heads. If you cooperate, you'll be alive when we take them off again. If you resist, the last image you'll have is me placing the hood back over your head. Are we all in agreement to cooperate?" the man said abruptly, obviously irritated by the news he had just received.

"Yes. We will oblige," Nigel said. "Dr. MacGregor will be in compliance. Right, Mavis?" he asked and looked at her.

"Yes, for no other reason than the sake of my children," she answered as the tape was pulled across her mouth.

The three scientists slowly walked across the hanger to a waiting van. In minutes, they were maneuvering through the bustling traffic of Shanghai. It was a forty-five minute drive to the harbor. Once they reached the harbor the van pulled into a brick building on the docks and the three captives were unloaded. They were walked into the building where they were led down a flight of stairs to a water level dock. One by one they were handed over to three men who braced them as they stepped into a small boat. Their hoods were taken off.

"This is where we part, Dr. MacGregor. As long as you cooperate, your colleagues will stay alive. If you misbehave, your new hosts will kill them one by one in front of you. Am I clear?" the man in the suit said, ripping the tape from her mouth.

"Ouch. Yes. Very much so," Mavis replied as she sat down on a wooden crate in the middle of the boat, her lips swollen from the constant ripping of tape. Another guard pulled the tape off the mouths of Nigel and Julian.

The man spoke to the three men on the boat and then walked back to his car and got in. In another minute the car had left the warehouse and docks.

"Nigel," Mavis whispered. "Those fossils at the warehouse were not the same ones that we saw at Shenyang, were they?"

"No, they weren't. They were a different set. The rock looked more like the Mongolian formations we were digging at two years ago," Nigel replied.

"My thoughts exactly," Julian said and sat down next to him. "I think we've been handed off to a new set of kidnappers. My Chinese is rough but I could make out something about a trade and the bones."

Two men kept their rifles trained on them while the third put the boat motors in reverse and backed out of the dock into the harbor. The water was a little choppy because of the early evening traffic in the warehouse district. The canopy over the forward two-thirds of the boat kept the captives out of sight of the casual passersby as it cruised across the harbor.

Within minutes they began to approach a floating city of

over a thousand boats of varying sizes and designs. The boat slowed to five miles per hour and drifted through the middle of the boat city until they came to a large, old Chinese sailing ship called a junk. It was sixty-five feet long with the gunnels sitting six feet off the water line at midship. The sail was ribbed rather than having a canvas mainsail.

"Dr. MacGregor," one of the armed men spoke. "I'm going to take off your wrist manacles. You are then going to crawl up the ladder and step on board. If you stop or hesitate, I will kill both of your friends. Understand?"

"Yes, I understand," Mavis replied and looked at Nigel and Julian.

In a couple of minutes she was standing on the junk and her hands were again being handcuffed with metal police handcuffs in front of her. Nigel was next, followed by Julian.

"Welcome aboard," a female voice said from behind them.

The three Brits turned around and found a gorgeous woman standing there. She was five foot two inches tall with long, black hair down to her waist. Her exotic Chinese face was accented with eye shadow and long, black eyelashes. She wore a red, silk dress that revealed her curvy figure and red, high heel pumps. She looked out of place standing in the old junk.

"Doctors, you are now my property. My Tai-Pan has negotiated a trade for you but the deal has a few strings attached. You are free to stay alive on my boat for a few days, weeks, or months, depending upon the negotiations that are happening as we speak. We will, I mean, you will be at sea by daybreak and will be out of reach of any rescue efforts sent by either the Americans or the British," she said.

"Why are you keeping us?" Julian asked.

"Because you are valued objects of trade. There are many forces that have gained power in the new China. We now use gold, jade, precious gems, artifacts, natural resources, and people as a form of monetary exchange. All of these convert to another important form, American dollars," she stated.

"The more dollars we have the more power we have."

"But what would three paleontologists be worth? We study rocks and fossils," Nigel asked.

"Nothing. It's Dr. Mavis MacGregor, wife of Dr. Jack MacGregor, who has value. You must continue to maintain her cooperation with us. If you are dead, she has no reason to obey us. As a package, your value is quite sizeable. Besides, I like having another important woman around. I get lonely with all these men and their guns," she added and smiled.

"My husband is a zoologist. He studies endangered species and environmental problems. He's here just to study the Three Gorges Dam and that's it. What he says or thinks won't have one ounce of influence on the Chinese government," Mavis said.

"Yes, I know, but you underestimate your husband's value," the woman replied.

"Then, I don't understand. Why are you keeping us?" Mavis demanded.

"The three of you know too much about the fossils that we market around the world. The *Caudipteryx zoui* is a valuable piece of merchandise. But our scientists have found fragments of another fossil that may be of greater value. We need time to search the crates, in order to find the rest of it. But if that were the only reason, you'd be dead. We would simply take the fossils and look for the other pieces," the woman replied.

"There is another more important reason that we discovered only a few hours ago," she continued. "You were scheduled to die in the warehouse at the harbor by the hands of your original captors. Your bodies were going to be put in concrete and dropped into the sea, never to be found. However, our intelligence contacts across the globe came up with something we can use. So we made a deal with your captors who felt you were just an albatross to them. Geoffrey MacGregor," she said and smiled.

"Geoffrey. Oh my," Mavis said and forced a deep breath.

"Yes, now do you understand?" the woman asked.

"Who's Geoffrey MacGregor? Nigel asked Mavis.

"Geoffrey is Jack's Canadian cousin. He works for the Royal Canadian Mounted Police but is assigned to antiterrorism with MI6 and Scotland Yard," Mavis answered.

"Very good, Dr. MacGregor, or can I call you Mavis? My name is Jane Chung," the beautiful woman said.

"Geoffrey won't help you. He's a solid policeman," Mavis said.

"He will if your life's at stake, don't you think?" Jane asked.

"Never. He's a man of honor," Mavis responded.

"We'll see. He has access to information that would be useful to my colleagues. By the time we get out to sea, we'll have photos and some personal belongings, Mavis, that will convince him that we do have you. We do mean business, and he must cooperate. That will test his honor, don't you think?" Jane asked.

Mavis said nothing and just glared at her.

"Finally, something that will silence you. I had a feeling it would," Jane said. "Now, we'll take you below and get you into some comfortable clothes, feed you, and put you to bed. You'll feel better in the morning."

As they walked down the narrow steps to the lower deck, Mavis felt as if the wind had been knocked out of her. It was hot and the air had the pungent aroma of dead fish. Her head was spinning as she thought about the kids again and where Jack might be and how long it would be before they missed her. As she turned the final corner, she felt a needle prick in her arm and as she fell two men caught her and lifted her up. Nigel and Julian were also drugged and fell to the floor of the ship in a thud. Mavis' vision had begun to blur; the lights were spinning and she could barely make out the sound of the diesel motor starting before all went black.

Jack walked through the lobby of the hotel that housed

the scientists attending the Three Gorges Dam conference. Fearing that the world would gang up on them, the Chinese government had made a point only to invite one hundred scientists from various fields. Stacking the deck in their favor was a habit of theirs.

"Jack," Gary Houlette yelled out from across the restaurant.

"Hey, Gary," Jack replied and walked toward the tall, bearded scientist. "I enjoyed your presentation. Too bad the Chinese scientists never heard it."

"They were there. Oh yea, I get it. They'll never hear it or anything like it," Houlette responded. "Please join us? This is Professor Kim Do, an expert on the Mekong River Delta, and Dr. Cheryl Wolfe, she teaches plate tectonics at the University of Colorado. We just ordered our food. Come on, have a seat."

"Sure, I need a little company right now. I've got my family scattered all across China," Jack said as he sat down.

"Where are they?" Wolfe asked and drank some hot tea. "Would you like some tea? We have a fresh pot and extra cups."

"Yes. That would be great," Jack replied. He held the cup for Cheryl to pour and then took a sip. He set the cup down and continued talking.

"Well my kids, Chris, Heather, and Ryan and their friend Natalie are out west, visiting the Wolong Panda Reserve. My wife's a paleontologist and she met two of her British colleagues at Shenyang to look over some new fossils from Mongolia. And here I am. We just got in from Alaska a few days ago," Jack said.

"Yea, Jack and I go way back," Houlette said. "But we were together just last August in Egypt for the Aswan Dam conference. Darn shame about all that silt," the gray-bearded scientist said and took a drink from a bottle of water.

At that moment, two officers of the People's Armed Police walked through the restaurant and everyone turned toward them. They stopped next to Jack.

"Dr. MacGregor?" one of them asked.

"Yes, I'm Dr. MacGregor," Jack said.

"Major Chen has asked that we find you and take you to the communication center of the hotel so that he may speak to you," the officer said.

"Sure, I'll follow you," Jack said. He turned to the others at the table. "Better eat without me. I'm sure it's one of the kids calling. It was nice to meet you Professor Do, Dr. Wolfe. Take care Gary, we'll be in touch."

Jack followed the policemen through the restaurant and out into the lobby. They walked across the lobby of the new hotel and into a narrow corridor that ended at a metal door. One of the policemen went in first. As Jack stepped into the room he was faced with a large bank of video monitors, radio equipment, satellite earthlink equipment, and much more he didn't recognize.

"All of this for a little hotel?" Jack asked.

"It's for the protection of our esteemed guests," the officer replied. "Major Chen is waiting for you. Please use this headset." He handed it to Jack and stepped back. Jack put on the headset.

"This is Jack MacGregor," he said.

"Major Chen here. We have a situation in which we think that your wife and her two fellow scientists have been kidnapped," he said candidly and without emotion.

Jack felt a deep sigh leave his body and worked at catching his breath.

"When? By whom?" Jack asked. "Tell me all that you know."

"We know that they were taken at the building where the fossils were being kept. A thorough search of the warehouse district yielded no clues as of yet. The fossils are gone and so are the scientists. We have received no demands but we expect to any hour. Crimes like this do not happen in China. This is so rare I could almost call it impossible," Major Chen said.

"I guess not totally impossible," Jack said gaining his composure."Where are my children?" Jack asked.

"I have inquired on their safety and they are on the eastern slopes of the Tibetan plateau in the Wolong Panda Reserve. They're under the care of Dr. Hsu. She's a very capable scientist and loyal citizen of the government. My understanding is that your children and their friend are on the second day of a three-day hike. I suggest we not tell them of this at the moment, Dr. MacGregor."

"I agree. When can the kids be brought back to Beijing?" Jack asked.

"That won't be until the day after tomorrow. By then we may have all of this solved and your wife returned safely," Chen responded.

"I have only one question left, Major," Jack said.

"What is that?" Chen asked.

"Remember that sermon you gave me about how the safety of my family was your number one concern? With that said how can I be sure that when all of this is over, your head will roll?" Jack stated gritting his teeth.

"You have my deepest apology for this error. I will remedy it myself. A jet will be landing at Sandouping in ten minutes. You will be escorted to the plane and taken back to Beijing immediately," Chen said.

Jack took off the headset and threw it on the floor, effectively ending the conversation and startling the two officers and the three communication specialists. With Mavis missing, the kids out of reach, his nerves were more than frayed.

"Oh, Mavis," he whispered under his breath as he walked out to the lobby. To his surprise, his suitcase and shoulder satchel were waiting for him and being held by a hotel employee. He realized that several people knew what was going to happen before he did.

It was only a short ride to the airport and he arrived just as a Chinese government Dassault Falcon Jet was landing. Once on board he buckled in and leaned back. He tried to rest but couldn't. A female military officer offered him something to drink and eat. He didn't feel like it but knew he should if he was going to have his wits about him. He ate a stale sandwich and drank a bottle of water and a cup of hot tea. As he glanced out at the stars he knew it was two hours to Beijing and maybe an eternity to Mavis.

The constant thud of the diesel engine bounced around in Mavis MacGregor's mind as she struggled to open her eyes. She could hear everything around her as if it were being amplified one hundred times. She blinked hard and got one eye to stay open. Then she did it again and again and could see for a moment before both eyes shut.

"Wake up," she said and tried to force her eyes open with only limited luck.

She struggled a while before her eyes began to water and her eyelids stayed open long enough to dilate and view the room around her. She turned her head and saw Julian and Nigel on the floor next to her. They were still unconscious.

Testing her arms, she felt the steel manacles on her wrists but nothing on her ankles. She sat up slowly and felt light-headed. Leaning her head down so she wouldn't pass out, she pushed her back against the wall and stretched out her legs. She could barely reach Julian. She gave him a small kick in the arm and got a slight movement.

"Julian, it's Mavis. You're still alive. Open your eyes. I've got kidney pie and hot tea ready," she said and broke a smile for the first time in a while.

Without moving, Julian let out a grown and spoke.

"I'm Scottish, Mavis. I hate kidney pie. You know that," he said and opened his eyes. "That light is maddening."

"It's a tiny twenty-five watt bulb that looks like a light-house after you've had a dose of their drugs, Julian," Mavis replied. "Welcome back."

"What in the Queen's name are the two of you blubbering about? I've got a headache that would put an army to sleep," Nigel said and tried to roll over, only to hit his head on the wall. "Ouch."

"Easy, Nigel. It took me thirty minutes to wake up. Now we're all together again," Mavis said softly.

"I suppose our Chinese princess kept her word and took us out to sea," Julian said and sat up next to Mavis. "That thumping noise must be the diesel motor."

"I checked my watch and it's been four hours since we were drugged. That would make us about ninety kilometers out to sea or down the coast," Mavis said.

"You were always full of good news," Nigel said.

"I suggest we relax and hope for a little nourishment soon. That would take the cobwebs out of our heads, don't you think?" Julian asked.

There was noise on the outside of the door like a lock being turned by a key. The door swung open and a burly fellow carrying a tray of food walked in followed by a man holding an automatic rifle.

"Julian, you must be an oracle," Mavis commented as she tried to stand up.

"Stay down," the man with the rifle commanded.

The other man put the tray on the floor and backed out of the room.

"Miss Chung says you are to eat. If you eat all the food, then we can take you topside for fresh air. You will keep your manacles on in case you think it smart to jump over and try to swim to shore. That way you sink," he said in broken English.

"Thank you. Then we shall dine," Mavis replied and reached for the tray and unwrapped the paper bags. Ah, tuna sandwiches. How appropriate. Don't you think so Nigel? And you Julian, quaint isn't it?" she asked and looked up.

Annoyed, the armed man left and they could hear the door being relocked. Without much talk, the three scientists began to eat the sandwiches and drink the bottled water.

"Very tasty, I have to admit," Nigel said with his mouth full.

"I agree," Julian added.

"It should be noted that such praise is coming from two bachelors," Mavis said. "The sandwiches will keep us alive and not much else. I wonder what my children are eating. I wonder if they even know I'm gone. I wonder if Jack even knows yet."

"Someone will find us, Mavis," Julian said. "Well, we at least hope they do."

11

Panda Bandits

It was nearly seven in the morning before Dr. Hsu walked to the tents and awakened the teenagers. They had slept for over nine hours; the long hike into the reserve had taken its toll. The down sleeping bags and small heaters in each tent had kept them toasty. Dr. Hsu, accustomed to the shock the hike brought to many of her guests, let them sleep late to be ready for a fun day of finding and watching pandas.

"Wow, do I feel better," R.O. said, as he was the first to crawl out of the tents and stand up. He fished a fresh shirt out of his pack, changed, and stuffed the dirty one inside. He sat down again and put on a fresh pair of socks and pulled out the hiking belt he had left in the pack the day before. He checked his lighter, flashlight, multi-use knife, compass, and a PayDay candy bar that he had bought at the hotel in Beijing. He opened it and took a big bite.

"Hey, no fair," Natalie said as she came out of her tent. "Give me a bite and I won't tell." She smiled and winked at him throwing all her charm into the moment.

"O.K., just a small one," R.O. said and handed it over.

Natalie bit off nearly half the candy bar.

"Hey, I said just a small bite," R.O. complained.

"What's all the noise?" Chris said as he emerged from the tent.

"Aw, nothing," R.O. answered and hid the candy bar.

"Natalie?" Chris said as he watched her start to giggle with her mouth full of the candy bar. He crawled over toward her and put his face up to her face and sniffed.

"PayDay. Where is it?" Chris asked sternly and turned to R.O.

"Right here," R.O. said reluctantly and handed it to him. Chris took a big bite.

"Hey, that's mine," R.O. whined and reached out for the candy.

Chris passed it off to Heather who had just come out of the tent.

"Candy. Real candy. Thanks Chris," Heather said and put the last part of the PayDay in her mouth. "Umm, that is so good."

"Thank R.O.," Chris and Natalie said together and started laughing.

"You all really make me mad," R.O. said and got up and walked toward the cooking area.

Within a few minutes, all the kids had on fresh shirts and socks and were lined up for their morning dose of rice and tea.

"I don't know if I'll ever go to another Chinese restaurant," Heather said as she took her bowl of rice, a piece of Bao Zi, and tea to a large fallen tree and sat down.

"My feelings exactly," Natalie added and sat down next to her.

"Now quit the belly aching. You know you like Chinese food," Chris said and took a bite.

"Just won't look the same," Heather replied.

"You didn't feel that way yesterday when you were stuffing down the rice," R.O. said as he walked up. "I'm all done."

"We leave in five minutes," Dr. Hsu said.

"Well, we'll have to see when we get home what it's like and decide then," Chris said.

Ten minutes later they were all on the trail headed further down into the valley. It was an easy walk compared to the climb the day before.

"How do the pandas eat the bamboo?" R.O. asked Dr. Hsu who was walking in front of him.

"Their wrists bend like an opposable thumb, giving them something to grip with as they eat the bamboo," she answered.

"I thought bears were omnivores," R.O. said.

"Yes, they are. Most bears eat meat and plants. They have the digestive system of a true carnivore. But the giant panda exists almost entirely on bamboo," she replied.

"That's really cool," R.O. said.

"Stop," Dr. Hsu whispered. "I think I hear something ahead."

The hiking party stopped and became quiet. Dr. Hsu walked onward on the trail and then stepped off into the snow-covered forest. She was gone for five minutes and then returned with a huge smile on her face.

"Our bears are just ahead about two hundred yards. We'll leave the trail and double around to the west. No talking and when I give the motion to crouch down do so without making the slightest noise," she said. "Let's go."

The kids were now giddy with excitement and forgot their sore legs and backs. They moved through the thick forest stepping over broken branches and fallen limbs, careful to make as little noise as possible. Dr. Hsu was ten yards ahead of them with her walking stick probing the snow covered leaf bed of the forest floor. She suddenly motioned for all of them to get down. They did so instantly. Then they heard a puffing noise as if something was breathing hard and trying to run.

The giant panda burst through the brush on a run and darted right by them without even looking their way. From only five feet away, the kids were overwhelmed with the sight of the running panda. Dr. Hsu came over to them.

"Strange. That was very strange. He was running faster than normal and seemed very anxious. Normally they trot down the trail smelling for the scent mark of a female. This male was on the run. He had been frightened," she said.

"What of?" Chris asked.

"I don't know," Dr. Hsu replied. "Maybe he sensed our presence. Let's move back to the path."

The group walked through the thick forest back to the path and began following it down to the valley, which took about ten minutes. They walked for another hour before Dr. Hsu motioned for them to crouch again. They did so, hoping another panda was nearby. They all sat motionless and quiet for ten minutes before a rustling noise could be heard ahead about one hundred yards.

"Follow me quietly," Dr. Hsu said and moved in that direction.

The teenagers followed her closely and the distance was covered quickly. They could see some movement at the base of a tree and moved toward it. As they got closer, it was obvious what it was.

"Oh my," Natalie said first.

"A trapped panda," R.O. said.

Dr. Hsu pulled tree branches off the top of a portable cage and revealed a healthy female panda bear. Her eyes were bright and she wasn't the least bit agitated.

"How beautiful," Heather said as Dr. Hsu walked around the cage and checked it carefully, looking for more traps. She then looked up to the trees and stared skyward for a couple of minutes.

"Be careful for human traps, kids. Look up and beware of what might come down from the trees to kill you," she stated and everyone looked up and stared throughout the tree canopy.

"Wow, this is scary," Heather said and bumped into Chris who was looking upward.

"I'll let the bear go in about thirty seconds; she'll charge forward and run up the trail, so stand back and be ready," Dr. Hsu said.

She yanked hard on the lever that controlled the hatch on the front of the cage. The female panda sat still for a second and then burst forward into the forest. She ran about twenty feet and stopped and looked back at the kids. Then she began running up the trail and out of sight.

"I'm afraid we have active poachers in the reserve. It's been many years since they've had the courage to enter," Dr. Ling said. "But Wolong is huge. The mountains are tall and the valleys carry on for miles and miles. We would need an army brigade to patrol it for poachers. Tourists only get to see our research animals and beautiful visitor's center. The real Wolong is all around you."

"Won't they get punished if they get caught?" Heather asked.

"Yes, the government punishes them harshly," Dr. Hsu replied and the group fell quiet.

"In short, they disappear," R.O. said and looked around. "Are there any more pandas around here?"

"Yes, nearly two hundred but they're scattered all over the mountains. Let's continue up the trail to see if there are any other trapped bears," Dr. Hsu said. "Keep your eyes and ears alert. We may not be the only humans out here today."

The group had walked for another hour when they all agreed to take a break and munch on some bread that the staff had given them at breakfast. Each also pulled out a bottle of water and took a drink. Chris made sure they stayed hydrated.

"The panda was beautiful," Natalie said and jerked to her right as a cracking noise reverberated through the forest.

"What was that?" R.O. asked.

"It was a gunshot," Dr. Hsu responded.

"Were they aiming at us?" Chris asked and looked around.

"No. I doubt it. We would've been hit if they had been," Dr. Hsu said.

All the kids put their packs back on and stood close to Dr. Hsu who was formulating their options. Then there was the echo of rifle fire down the trail again.

"That was close," Chris said. "I guess about two hundred yards, maybe a quarter of a mile."

"That's my estimate too," Dr. Hsu added. "I served in the People's Liberation Army in the infantry. I have a good sense for gunfire direction and sound. We can't leave until we find out what it was. All of you stay here. I want to go down the trail to investigate further. If I'm not back in one hour, return to the base camp. You are a day and half out. You know where the break stops are. Just gauge your time so you're not on the trail after dark and get too cold."

Without another word she disappeared down the trail.

"O.K. guys, take a rest. We may need it," Chris said.

Not a word was spoken for thirty minutes as the kids began to worry for Dr. Hsu. Then suddenly three more gunshots could be heard in rapid-fire succession.

"That's it. We're headed back in ten minutes if Dr. Hsu doesn't show up," Chris informed.

Just as they were getting up, Dr. Hsu appeared on the trail slightly bent over as she walked. When she reached the kids, she fell to the ground. Chris and Natalie got to her first and turned her over onto her back. Chris's hand had blood all over it.

"She's been shot," he exclaimed.

Natalie and Chris started searching for the wound and found it on her left side just above her hip. She was unconscious.

"What are we going to do?" Natalie asked. Heather and R.O. just stared at the blood soaked shirt and coat.

"It'll take us four days to carry her out. If I go for help and walk all night, I can save time. But if I take the wrong path and get lost, we all could die. Let me think," Chris said. "Find her cell phone. Maybe she's got a radio."

R.O. and Heather tore her small pack apart and found neither.

"Nothing Chris," Heather said.

"We've only got one choice. We need to find out how the poachers got here. They had to have a way in here and a way out. There's no way they're going to carry that big panda all the way to Chengdu," Chris said. "They've got an exit plan and we're going to find it and use it. Natalie, you stay with Heather, R.O., and Dr. Hsu. Keep pressure on the wound or she'll bleed to death. I'm going down the trail to see what I can find," Chris said and took off his pack. He pulled out his trail knife and attached it to his belt. He also attached a flashlight and a thin spool of wire. He placed two packets of dried trail mix in his coat pocket and put on his gloves.

"Be back before you know it. Keep her warm," he said and took off in a jog down the trail.

After nearly a hundred yards, he slowed to a walk. He kept the pace brisk but always tried to listen for signs that man was nearby. After a quarter mile, he began to hear some commotion and voices. He crouched down on the trail and tried to listen. He could hear what sounded like metal cages being moved around and the growling of a panda. He inched forward and could see movement through the forest. In order to move faster and make less noise, he decided to stay on the trail. He dropped down to his hands and knees. He moved slowly when suddenly he felt a human hand on his shoulder. He froze in place.

"Don't move, kid," the voice said in a whisper.

"I'm not armed," Chris whispered back.

"Be quiet. Listen carefully. We're the good guys. Those people out there are the bad guys. Got it?" the voice stated in plain English.

"Got it," Chris whispered back and dropped to his belly on the trail.

"Slowly roll over and look at us," the voice whispered.

Chris turned over slowly and looked up into the faces of two people. They were wearing camouflage and their faces were painted from ear-to-ear and chin-to-hair.

"Commandos?" Chris asked.

"You could say that. Who was that lady who got shot?" the man whispered.

"Did you shoot her?" Chris asked.

"No, but we saw who did it. Armed poachers. Well supplied and organized," the man responded.

"Who are you? You're Americans?" Chris whispered.

"That's complicated," the man replied. "For now, we're the good guys and you can help us."

"How? I've got to find a way out of here to take Dr. Hsu to a doctor. She could be bleeding to death," Chris whispered.

"First, trust us. Second, take this. The second person reached over the shoulder of the man facing Chris and held out a .41 caliber Desert Eagle semi-automatic pistol.

"Take it," the second voice, a female commanded. "You're going to need it when we charge the poachers."

"Charge the poachers?" Chris questioned.

"Yes. Now listen. We're going to let you get back on your knees. You'll go straight down the trail until you can see them. There are five of them. They have two bears trapped in cages. They have an ATV that we think will take them to their way out. We haven't found their exit. They could have an aircraft or trucks, we don't know yet," the male voice whispered. "We're going to close on both sides. If they try to come up the trail, you lay a barrage of fire into them and drive them back to us. Kill them if you have to. They will kill you in a second and not think twice about it. Got it?"

"Yes. Kill them if I have to," Chris said.

"We'll leave you two extra clips. That equals twenty-four rounds. Don't worry about hitting them, but it'll be a good thing if you do. Now get up."

Chris rolled back over and got up on his knees and could see the two people better. They were armed with AK-47s, two side arms, and some flash-grenades. Suddenly a second female commando crept up behind them and spoke to them in Chinese. The male spoke back in Chinese and turned to Chris.

"She says we've got to go now. Remember, turn them

back to us if they come this way," he said and the three commandos quickly moved into the forest and disappeared.

Chris looked down at the big gun in his left hand and knew it wasn't a dream. He checked the gun and chambered a round quickly recognizing that it was single action. He released the safety and edged his way over behind a large spruce. He felt a vibration on the tree as he touched the tree trunk and quickly looked up as Dr. Hsu had warned. A medium-sized panda was suspended twenty feet above him, looking down at him.

"I wish I were up there with you," Chris said and braced for what was going to happen.

Then he heard voices followed by gunfire, lots of it.

He heard an ATV being fired up and then it stopped. Then there was the noise of men running. His heart rate began to increase when he realized they were running toward him. Two men appeared through the forest on the path brandishing automatic rifles. He pointed and pulled the trigger three times. The bullets ricocheted off tree trunks and limbs, and the men opened fire in his direction. The trunk of the spruce was hit several times. When there was a momentary break, Chris fired five more rounds their way. He was met again by the fire of automatic weapons. The bullets splintered tree limbs and branches all around him, covering him with small pieces of wood. Chris popped out the empty clip and it dropped to the ground. He pushed in the full clip, chambered the first round, and pulled the trigger two more times not really aiming at anything, just letting them know he was loaded and ready.

Another barrage of automatic rifle fire was sent his way before the poacher's turned and ran back toward their camp. There they found the commandos waiting for them. Shouting could be heard as well as several rounds from an AK-47. Then there was silence.

A few minutes later a voice rang out through the forest.

"Hey, kid. It's clear. We've got them all," the man's voice said.

Chris slowly got up and then heard footsteps running up behind him. He raised the gun and swung around quickly.

"Don't shoot!" Heather shouted.

"What the heck are you doing?" Chris asked. "I could have killed you."

"Where'd you get the gun?" Heather responded her eyes widened in surprise.

"Answer me first, now," Chris yelled.

"Dr. Hsu is getting worse," Heather said. "She's lost a lot of blood, and she's very cold."

"I'll explain about the gun later. Go back and tell them you found me, and I'll be up there to get Dr. Hsu in a few minutes," Chris replied.

"Roger," Heather said and took off in a run.

Chris jogged down the path and entered a small clearing where the three commandos had four poachers spread eagle on the ground with their hands being tied. One of the poachers lay dead next to the ATV.

"Good job, kid," said a tall man with dark hair and deep creases in his cheeks. "I'm David Bloom, ATF, United States."

"ATF? What are you guys doing deep in China?" Chris asked.

"We're on loan to the Chinese to teach them how to control poachers and the movement of contraband. You know, a good neighbor diplomacy type thing. This is my partner. She's actually a bear specialist with U.S. Fish and Wildlife Service," Bloom said.

A tall blond dressed in camouflage and covered in face paint walked up.

"You were the other one on the trail," Chris stated.

"Yes, I was. Can I have my gun back?" she replied and put her hand out.

"Sure," Chris said and handed her the pistol. He reached into his pocket and pulled out the remaining eight shot clip.

"Good shooting," she said. "You drove them right back to us. They thought we had a dozen people out here."

"Thanks. But I've got to use that ATV to get Dr. Hsu and bring her down here. We've got to use the poachers' trucks to take her out of here," Chris said. "They do have trucks, don't they?"

"Sorry, no trucks. They flew in. Yen Hwa Yu, our Chinese partner, told me they've got a Chinese army helicopter about a quarter mile down the valley in a small clearing," Bloom said.

"Helicopter. That's perfect. I'll be back in a minute," Chris said and hopped on the ATV and drove away on the narrow path to rescue the injured scientist.

Breaking branches and rocks, he made it to the teenagers in just a few minutes.

Natalie and Chris picked up Dr. Hsu and laid her across the back of the ATV. Heather crawled up next to her to steady her. R.O. got up front with Chris and Natalie. Chris hurriedly drove them all back down the path toward the clearing. When he had reached the others, he came to a stop.

"I've had some medic training in the army. Let me look at her," the female commando said.

As she was examining her, R.O. leaned close to her face.

"Ginna?" he asked.

The woman looked up and smiled.

"What if I said Regina?" she replied.

"Ginna Bloom from Alaska. We just saw you there," R.O. said as she continued to examine Dr. Hsu.

"She's not doing so well," Ginna said. "David, got any ideas?"

"Remember, I can fly helicopters," Chris said. "I'm going to fly us out of here."

All three adults just looked at each other.

"You think you can do that, son?" asked David Bloom.

"You better believe it and we better get going now," Chris said and started up the ATV.

"We're going to release these two bears and we'll be right behind you on the other ATV," Ginna said as Chris drove away. "Our friend with the China Wildlife Service will stay behind to watch the poachers until they're picked up."

The trip to the clearing was only five minutes on the ATV. As they stopped next to the vintage military version of the Bell 412 painted with military colors, the kids carried Dr. Hsu over to the open side door and lay her on the floor of the passenger area and began throwing out animal traps and equipment the poachers had brought with them. Chris stepped up between the two front seats and looked at the instrument panel.

"Oh no, Chinese," Chris said.

"What's Chinese?" Natalie asked and sat down next to him.

The other ATV arrived and the two agents dismounted and ran up to the helicopter.

"Why isn't she turning over?" David asked as he bounded into the cabin.

"The instruments are all in Chinese," Natalie said.

"That's no problem. I can read it and speak it. Hop up and let me sit next to him," David said as Natalie moved to the back.

In a few minutes, Chris and David had flipped all the right switches and the big rotary blade was turning and gaining revs.

"Close the door," David said and Ginna pulled it shut.

Everyone found a seatbelt and buckled in. Dr. Hsu was wedged between their legs on the floor and barely breathing. There was a sudden lift and a bounce as Chris learned the feel of the helicopter, which was nearly twice as large as the ones he trained on while in Italy. Chris gripped the collective firmly in his left hand and continued to push forward. The aircraft gained altitude. He pushed the cyclic forward with his right hand and the helicopter began to move through the sky. Pushing hard with his left foot the helicopter spun around until the compass read southeast and Chris eased off.

They were now airborne and climbing, moving forward across the clearing. Once Chris had cleared the forest canopy he took in a deep breath. They were headed to Chengdu. He increased the speed and flew to one thousand feet. It was a gray winter day and the snow had stopped. The sun was beginning to peak through the clouds. He thought it was best to stay at one thousand and fly through the valleys to reach the main road to Chengdu. There were too many mountain peaks to avoid and a low ceiling.

"Ginna, what are you doing here?" R.O. asked.

"I could ask you the same thing," she said.

"I asked first," R.O. replied.

"I work for the U.S. Fish and Wildlife Service. I was in Alaska trying to track the illegal trade in animal products. I had been actively pursuing the poaching problem in the national parks as well as some pretty nasty bad guys. Then my husband David called and said he needed help in training the Chinese in anti-poaching techniques. The Chinese don't want to admit they have a problem, but they did decide they wanted to stop poaching instead of just killing poachers. I came over to help him. We don't always walk into an active poaching situation. Two days ago, the Chinese team got a tip that poachers were moving into the west side of Wolong. We had to prove it was happening before they would commit the army to the area. Since it was winter, we didn't think the Chinese would have guests in the reserve," answered Ginna.

"How about you?" she asked.

"Well, you know who my dad is; I told you that in Alaska. He's here helping just like you but with the environmental concerns of the big dam project. We were on a three day hike through Wolong when Dr. Hsu caught a bullet," R.O. said trying to sound adult.

"Well, looks like your brother is doing a great job getting her to safety.

"Yea, Chris can do just about anything," R.O. stated with pride on his face.

The one-hour flight to Chengdu passed quickly and Chris circled the Bell 412 around the airport, watching for crowded airspace. He set her down near the main terminal. Two police jeeps drove up to the helicopter immediately. Since there had been no radio communication and it had landed in an unauthorized place, the aircraft was deemed suspicious.

ATF agent David Bloom stepped from the side of the helicopter with his arms in the air. After quickly explaining everything to the excited Chinese policemen who had drawn their weapons, an ambulance was sent out to take Dr. Hsu to the hospital. As the ambulance was driving away, the four kids and the Blooms stood next to the helicopter.

"Great job, Chris. Ever want to be an ATF agent, let me know," David said.

"Maybe. After college," Chris replied.

"And after he talks to me about it," Natalie said and squeezed his arm.

"How about me?" R.O. asked.

"When you grow taller and are big enough to shoot either my Colt .45 or my Desert Eagle," Ginna replied.

"So who's Regina?" Heather asked.

"She's my cousin on my mother's side. Our mothers named us like that because they thought it was cute," Ginna said. "Regina's husband is an airline pilot and flies his routes for two weeks a month and lives in the outpost the other two weeks. She grew up in South Africa where her father was a diamond mine expert."

"Why didn't you tell me all that before?" R.O. asked.

"I was undercover, remember," responded Ginna.

"That's pretty cool," Heather said.

"Way cool," R.O. replied.

About that time another police vehicle drove up to the helicopter and an officer with the People's Armed Police got out and walked over to the kids.

"Chris MacGregor?" the officer asked.

"Yes, that's me," Chris said.

"I have a call for you from Major Chen," he said and handed Chris the cell phone.

"Hello, Major, this is Chris."

"Chris, I have some news for you that I want you to think about. Listen to me carefully. Your mother has been kidnapped and your father is on his way to Beijing at this moment. We are working on the case with all of our resources and you can be confident we will find her and bring her to safety very soon," the Major said.

Chris was stunned into silence. He swallowed hard and spoke.

"Where can I reach my dad?" Chris asked.

"Your father will contact us as soon as he lands," Chen replied.

"Thank you," Chris said and hung up.

"O.K. guys listen to me," he said solemnly.

"Mom's gone missing. Major Chen thinks she's been kidnapped," he informed.

Heather gasped and burst into tears and R.O. put his hands to his eyes and his mouth turned down quickly. Natalie leaned over and put her arms around Chris.

"What can we do to help?" the Blooms asked.

"Help me find her," Chris replied and looked them straight in their eyes.

"Whatever it takes," David Bloom replied as he ejected the partially used clip from his pistol and pushed in a fresh one. "Whatever it takes!"

12

South China Sea

---◯---

The door to the tiny room in the ship's belly swung open and fresh air poured in. Mavis, Julian, and Nigel had fallen asleep and didn't hear the door open.

"Get up," the guard barked rudely and poked Nigel with his rifle.

"I'm getting up, thank you," Nigel mumbled.

"Give us a moment," Mavis said and struggled to get to her feet with her hands still manacled.

"Shut up," the guard responded.

When they were all standing, the guard motioned with his gun for them to leave the room. Another guard was waiting in the narrow hallway and pointed his gun at their faces as they walked by. The first guard led them to the narrow stairway that took them topside. With each step closer to the top, fresh air entered their lungs and rejuvenated them. Once they were on deck, the night sky seemed endless. The stars jumped toward them from outer space. The prisoners couldn't help but notice as they walked out from under the large canvas canopy over the stairs and cabin entrance that Jane Chung was sitting in a rattan chair padded with silk pillows.

"Good evening," she said as she smoked on a long brown cigarette.

No one said a word in response.

"Did our drugs dampen your spirits, Dr. MacGregor?" she asked.

"I thought you weren't going to come along for the cruise," Mavis responded.

"I changed my mind. My men can be a little brutal sometimes and I couldn't afford not to have your cooperation. You should be pleased I am here," Chung said.

"Overwhelmed," Mavis answered.

"No need to be rude, Dr. MacGregor. We've already made contact with Geoffrey in London and have his first response," she said. "What? You have nothing to say? How unusual for you, Mavis."

"I will let my husband and his cousin speak for me," Mavis quickly replied.

"I'm sure you will," Chung said and walked over and unlocked the manacles on Mavis' wrists.

"Thank you," Mavis said a little puzzled.

"Very good then. Geoffrey doesn't quite believe you're in danger," Chung said and then spoke to one of her men in Chinese. He walked over and produced a satellite telephone. Chung dialed a number and waited. About a minute passed before she spoke.

"Hello, Mr. MacGregor. I have Mavis here with me. Would you like to speak to her? Very good," Chung said. "Please, Dr. MacGregor, and be polite."

"Hello," Mavis said.

"This is Geoffrey. Mavis, what's this all about," Geoffrey said.

"I'm the guest of some Chinese thugs who want you to do a favor for them or they said they'll kill me, Julian, and Nigel," Mavis said and looked up at Chung.

"When they first called, they faxed me a picture of you and the two guys asleep on the floor of some room. I didn't know what to make of it. I tried to call Jack, but I couldn't track him down. What do they want?" Geoffrey asked.

"I haven't a clue," Mavis said when suddenly Miss Chung walked over to Mavis. She pulled a small gun from behind her and grabbed Mavis' free hand. In one swift movement she held up Mavis' free hand and pulled the trigger. The bullet went through her hand.

"Are you insane?" Mavis screamed and dropped the telephone to the deck as the pain followed the sudden shock of seeing a hole shot in her hand. With her good hand she gripped the bleeding left hand. "You're insane."

"I only put a bullet through the skin between your thumb and index finger," Chung said and leaned down and picked up the telephone. She handed it back to Mavis, who now had tears falling in sheets down her cheeks.

"Take it and talk to him now or the next bullet will be in Julian's brain. It's a small caliber. He will die slowly," she demanded.

Mavis let go of her left hand and the pain vibrated up her arm. She took the phone and put it to her face. Blood dripped to the deck.

"Geoffrey," she whimpered.

"Louder," Chung yelled.

"Geoffery," Mavis said.

"Mavis, what happened? Are you all right?" he asked.

"She shot me in my left hand. Missed the bones. It's just a flesh wound. I think she's trying to tell me something, Geoffrey," Mavis said and gently tried to open and close her wounded hand. The bleeding had slowed to a few heavy drops.

"Keep your wits about you and watch for us, Mavis," Geoffrey stated.

Chung yanked the telephone out of Mavis' hand and brought it up to her face.

"Mr. MacGregor, I could just have easily killed Mavis or one of her friends. Do you understand?" Chung asked.

"Yes. Clearly," Geoffrey replied.

"Someone in London will contact you and arrange a meeting place. Do not tell anyone that we have contacted you. We will need your assistance with a few matters within Scotland Yard. If you resist, Dr. MacGregor will be killed and her body dropped overboard. Our man will contact you at 10:00 a.m. London time," Chung said and switched off the telephone.

She turned to one of the armed men and spoke in Chinese. The man put down his rifle and walked over behind Julian. He wrapped his arms around him and began dragging him toward the gunwale.

"What are you doing?" Julian protested.

"Stop, I won't cooperate again," Mavis yelled.

The big guard lifted Julian up to the gunwale and dropped him over the side into the sea.

"You can't do that. You can't," Mavis yelled and ran toward the side of the ship and in one jump went over the rail and into the black ocean.

Chung started yelling orders frantically to all the men who now were grabbing life rings and ropes. Another flipped a switch on the side of the main cabin and floodlights instantly showered the ship and the ocean, for about fifty yards around it, in light. Mavis could be seen reaching with her free hands toward Julian who was struggling to stay afloat with his hands still bound. She got to him and pulled him to the surface and began kicking.

"I've got you, Julian. Don't struggle. Just kick. Come on, kick," Mavis said as Julian began moving his legs frantically to stay afloat.

"Thanks, Mave," Julian said and coughed out a mouthful of seawater.

Mavis heard a splash behind her and turned to see Nigel struggling to keep his head above the water. She began to pull Julian toward Nigel as she reached out with her wounded hand, tears pouring out of her eyes. She finally latched onto Nigel's flailing hands with her wounded hand, grimaced, and let out a small yell. The seawater burned the open wound.

"Which one will you let drown, Dr. MacGregor?" Miss Chung called out and laughed.

"Nigel, relax. Just kick. I've got you," Mavis said, trying to calm him down.

"Nigel, do it. She's got us," Julian yelled out.

"I know. I'm trying. I'm trying," Nigel said as he would kick and sink down to his eyes and kick again.

"We're going to make it. Hang on to me. Let me swim to keep us up," Mavis said. "Oh my, Jack, where are you?"

The Falcon Jet landed at the military base outside Beijing. The American embassy's Cadillac Denali drove across the tarmac escorted by a car belonging to the People's Armed Police. As soon as Jack had stepped from the jet, Dr. Sherri Biggs stepped from the Denali.

"Dr. MacGregor, how are you?" Dr. Biggs asked.

"I don't know yet. My wife is missing. I haven't talked to my kids in two days. I don't even know where they are. You tell me, Dr. Biggs," Jack replied sternly. "I'm sorry. I don't mean to be rude."

"I understand completely," Dr. Biggs said. "I received a call from Major Chen who filled me in on the investigation," she said as they settled into the car. "The warehouse where the fossils were being kept by a private company has been totally vacated. Even the large fossil that Mavis had gone to see is missing. There is no evidence to suggest how the fossils were transported or where. For all practical purposes, everything and everyone has vanished."

"I'm stunned. This is a nation that watches everything. How can that happen?" Jack demanded.

"It's a new China, a hybrid of old communists and new capitalists. Hidden in between is a layer of organized crime. Crime syndicates built out of ancient families, with a Tai-Pan and warlords, are difficult for the new Chinese government to fight without ruthlessly killing everyone. Unfortunately for you, we think Mavis walked into a transaction between two of these families involved in the illegal dinosaur bone trade," she said.

"Then I need to talk to these families," Jack said.

"Which one? There are thousands large and small. Right now Major Chen said we need to sit tight and wait until a request surfaces," Dr. Biggs stated.

"A ransom?" Jack asked.

"Not exactly. They will want something more than money. Now that they have the wife of a well-known scientist who was promised a safe stay in China, they have leverage with the government. Hurting Mavis would ruin their chance to manipulate the government. I assure you the Chinese government will do everything in their power to bring your wife home safely and punish her captors," she replied.

"O.K. What do I do now?" Jack asked.

"I suggest you get your kids back here as soon as possible," she replied.

"Where are they now?" Jack asked.

"Major Chen's office told me that they are in Chengdu at the airport. It's just about dark there," she answered.

"At the airport? They're supposed to be in the mountains at the Wolong Panda Reserve," Jack said.

"I was informed that there was a change in plans and the kids were flown to the airport in an army helicopter. They are fine and can be reached by telephone when we get back to the embassy," Dr. Biggs stated.

"Good. At least they had a good distraction while all of this was going on. I'll be relieved once I talk to them," Jack said.

"How much longer can you stay afloat, Mavis?" Chung yelled out.

"We'll float together or we'll die together and you and your friends can go to hell," Mavis yelled back.

"Good for you ole' girl," Nigel said and spit out more seawater.

"At least the current is warm here," Julian joked. "Cold water would have been a bit too much."

"Quit talking. Breathe deep and kick," Mavis said.

Mavis felt her foot touch something and she yanked it back quickly.

"What's that?" she screamed. "I hope it's not a shark."

"What's what? Did you spot something?" Nigel asked anxiously.

"My foot just touched something. Wait, there it is again. A rope of some kind," answered Mavis.

"It's their sea anchor," Julian said. "Try to wrap your legs around it. That would hold us in place."

"I'm trying. There it is. Got it. Now, let's try to relax a bit more and I will steer us down current of the ship," Mavis said. Her arms were beginning to ache. "Gentlemen, I've got to get a rest soon or we'll be chasing the *Titanic*."

"Three more Englishmen on the *Titanic* is not a good thought," Nigel quipped as he felt for the anchor line. "I'm on it. Steady as she goes."

"Two English and a Scot, if you don't mind," Julian offered.

"O.K. Then it's one English, one Scot, and an American," Mavis said and forced a smile.

In the distance a boat motor could be heard. The sound was growing louder all the time. Out of the darkness a red cigarette speedboat appeared and docked alongside the older Chinese junk. It was an odd contrast of antique and modern sea-going vessels. A man in a turquoise, silk shirt climbed from the forty-five-foot cigarette boat into the ship. Mavis, Nigel, and Julian, now somewhat relaxed and floating with their feet on the sea anchor line, watched quietly from fifty feet away.

The man looked out and spotted them in the water and started yelling at Jane Chung. She began yelling back and suddenly pointed her little gun in the face of the man. A shot rang out from the cigarette boat as one of the crewmen fired a small carbine rifle at Chung. She dropped dead on the deck.

The man yelled orders to the crew of the ship and soon life ropes were being thrown toward the floating paleontologists. Then one of the men on the junk dove overboard and swam toward them. He reached out and grabbed Nigel and swam with him toward the ship. Mavis took one of the ropes and held on.

"Julian, hang onto my waist," Mavis said.

Within ten minutes, the wet scientists were standing on board. The man in the silk shirt barked more orders and the manacles were taken off of Julian and Nigel.

"My extreme apologies, Dr. MacGregor. This will not happen again while you are in my custody. Let me introduce myself. I am Xu Fe. I have orders to transport the three of you back to Shanghai," he said and bowed.

"Shanghai, so that's where we were," Nigel stated still rubbing his wrists.

"Yes, a wonderful city. You will now be my guests there until the negotiations with Geoffrey MacGregor are complete. At that time, you will be released," he said.

"Sounds simple, but I'm always concerned about easy solutions to complex problems," Mavis said.

Xu Fe barked orders to the crew and Mavis, Nigel, and Julian were led off the ship, stepping around the body of Jane Chung, and down into the comfort of the luxury speedboat. They each found a soft seat and were given a fresh bottle of water, which they downed vigorously, washing the salt from their mouths. Mavis was given a towel to wrap around her bleeding hand.

As the cigarette boat was pulling away from the ship, one of the crewmen tossed a small package over the gunwale. The driver of the cigarette boat pushed the throttle forward and the boat leaped away from the ship in a run. Seconds later an explosion ripped into the hull of the Chinese ship, tearing a massive hole. It began to sink.

Mavis, Nigel, and Julian watched the burning ship for miles until it was only a speck on the horizon.

The cigarette boat flew across the water with the four-member crew keeping watch on its satellite instruments and radar in order to avoid a collision with another boat or ship. As the lights of Shanghai began to appear, the captain of the boat began to throttle back to avoid attention. Soon it pulled to a stop against a 150-foot yacht in Shanghai harbor, about a mile from the shore.

"Dr. MacGregor, please come aboard," the man in the turquoise shirt said and climbed up the ladder.

Mavis carefully followed him upward, having to grab each rung with her right hand and balance with the injured one. They walked along the deck outside the main cabin until they stepped into the stateroom. Mavis was amazed at the leather furniture, mahogany and teak wood tables, crystal light fixtures, and thick rugs. The air conditioning gave her a sudden chill.

"Are these still the bad guys?" Nigel asked as he came in behind her.

"On a scale of one to ten they're a seven. Jane Chung was a ten. But we're still prisoners," Julian replied. "I think there's been another switch. The language is sketchy, but I can tell that these are new kidnappers or maybe the ones that grabbed us first."

Mavis walked over to a bar and opened a small refrigerator. Inside she found a soft drink and pulled it out. Unscrewing the cap, she took a big swig.

"Caffeine. Finally," she exclaimed and tried to smile but the hand that was holding the plastic lid was crusted over with dried blood, some of which had washed off in the sea, and was still throbbing ferociously.

"I'll have someone bring you dry clothes. Sorry, but they will be plain and will probably not fit very well. We will feed you and then you may stay in this room to sleep, read, watch satellite television, or whatever you wish. There's a bathroom through that door," he said and pointed.

"Thank you," Julian said. The others nodded.

The man disappeared through another door and the guards were left standing outside the room.

"I found some crackers," Mavis said and ripped open a package with her teeth and started munching.

"My turn," Julian said, tearing open another package.

"What a change of events. One minute we're about to become shark bait and in the next we're being treated like Arabian princes," Nigel commented.

"That's what worries me," Mavis stated and walked across the soft rug and looked out at the lights of Shanghai. "Suddenly I feel very tired."

The two male scientists walked over to her and stood on each side of her.

"We don't know how this will play out, Mavis, but Nigel and I owe you our lives," Julian said.

"At least we get to live long enough to tell you we love you for what you did out there. Valor above valor, Mavis," Nigel said. "If I were the King, you would be knighted."

"Here's to Sir Mavis," Julian cheered and raised his bottle of soda.

"Here, here," Nigel added and raised his too.

Mavis started to speak but put her bloody hand to her mouth. Tears escaped her eyes. She leaned on Nigel's shoulder and began to cry.

Followed by David and Ginna Bloom, Chris, Natalie, Heather, and R.O. entered the small airport terminal as a squadron of the People's Armed Police surrounded them and began asking questions in broken English. Before she was taken into surgery at the local hospital, Dr. Hsu had regained consciousness just long enough to explain what had happened at Wolong. The kids wandered away from the Blooms and found a small restaurant that catered primarily to tourists at the airport. Their eyes lit up as they read the menu mounted on the wall next to the cashier. The menu had Western and Chinese cuisine listed next to each other.

"Cheeseburger works for me," Natalie said first.

The tiny lady behind the register wrote down the order in Chinese characters.

"I also want French fries and a coke," Natalie continued.

"Same here," R.O. said.

"Ditto," added Heather.

The little lady looked up with a puzzled look.

"She wants the same thing," Chris said. "Better just make it four cheeseburgers and four French fries."

A policewoman walked up from behind them and ordered for them in Chinese. The little lady at the counter laughed and wrote down the order correctly.

"Thanks," Chris said. "Are you our escort?"

"Yes, that is a polite way to put it," she answered and sat down at a table near the kids.

Approximately fifteen minutes later, their food was brought out to them on a big tray. Not long after, it was all gone.

"I could eat another one," Heather said.

"Man, it's been awhile since we ate that good," R.O. said.

"Just two days, little brother," Chris replied and ate the last fry. "And it was a Thanksgiving dinner at that."

David and Ginna Bloom walked in still dressed in their camouflage and carrying their guns.

"Are they going to let you remain armed?" Chris asked as David sat down. Ginna went over to the counter and ordered food. R.O. ran up behind her and added a hamburger to her order.

"For now. When we were out in the field, a Chinese officer with their wildlife service would keep our weapons until we were away from the population at large and then pass them out to us. That was Yen Hwa Yu, whom we left with the poachers. These police don't know quite what to do. We showed them our papers, and now they're worried about asking for them without a dozen or so officers present. So I imagine they are calling their superiors to learn the protocol. We'll probably just surrender them in a bit, so they don't get up tight. Your Dr. Hsu saved us a lot of grief. We'd be in a jail right now waiting for the U.S. Government to respond to a diplomatic inquiry if she hadn't explained everything," David said as Ginna sat down.

"What about you guys?" David asked.

"Well you know about the news of our mom. She's missing up northeast near Mongolia with two of her dinosaur buddies from England," Chris answered. Sadness returned to all the kids' faces. "We haven't heard from our dad yet. We know he's in Beijing by now. Wish he'd had stayed in Sandouping, which is only an hour from here by air. Now, he's back in Beijing. I don't know how much more flying we can take in those government transports."

The little Chinese lady brought the food to the Blooms. R.O. grabbed his hamburger and started gnawing on it. All the kids began picking at the French fries.

"Why don't we call dad?" R.O. asked.

"And just how are we supposed to do that?" Heather replied sarcastically.

"With a cell phone," R.O. said and began to dig around in his pack. He soon produced a small cell phone.

"What's that?" Chris inquired.

"It's the phone Mom gave me to take with us to Wolong. She said the embassy gave it to her and since she didn't need it, we should take it," R.O. said. "Since no one was using it, I was going to take it apart. I hadn't had time to start yet."

"Why didn't you tell us? We could have used it to get out of Wolong," Chris demanded a bit enraged and moved toward R.O.

"I forgot," R.O. said as Chris snatched the phone out of his hand and reached out to shove him back in his chair.

Chris retrieved a card from his billfold, punched in some numbers, and heard the phone ringing.

"This is Jack."

"Dad, Chris. Any word?" Chris asked anxiously.

"Not yet, son. Major Chen and Dr. Biggs assured me that everything is going to be okay. They're telling me that Mom and her friends got caught in an argument between two crime families over dinosaur bones," Jack answered, trying to simplify the details for Chris's benefit.

"That sounds better, but abduction is still abduction," Chris replied. "Heather wants to talk to you, hang on."

"Hi, Dad, we miss you. When can we see you?" Heather asked.

"I don't know, honey. It's getting dark and civilian aviation doesn't travel as often in China as in the United States. I'll have to arrange a flight for you back to Beijing. I'll ask Major Chen if he can help," Jack replied.

"Not another military flight, dad. Those are miserable," Heather said.

"I'm sorry. We'll do the best we can do. Is Ryan there?" Jack asked.

"Just a second," Heather responded and handed him the phone.

"Hi, Dad. Where are you?" R.O. asked.

"At the American embassy in Beijing. How are you doing, fella?" Jack asked.

"Great, Dad. We saw lots of pandas," R.O. answered back.

"That's wonderful," Jack replied.

"Yeah, the poachers had trapped them and we were letting them go. Then we met up with two commandos who gave Chris a gun and they had a big shootout in the forest," R.O. said with a smile of excitement.

"Wait, this is no time for exaggeration son," Jack stated sternly.

Chris yanked the phone away from R.O.

"Dad. There were some poachers but it's no big deal now. We'll talk about it tomorrow," Chris said.

"That's a good idea, son. Call me tomorrow and maybe by then we'll have figured out a plane ride of some kind," Jack said. "Later, dude."

Chris smiled knowing his dad never talked like that. "Take care, Dad."

"You idiot. When will your mouth ever learn to clamp shut?" Chris fussed and glared at R.O. who shrank down in his chair. "Dad's got too much on his mind right now to think about all that we've been through."

"Mom would assign more homework for talking to me like that," R.O. shot back.

"Instead of going back to Beijing, why don't I ask that policewoman over there to watch you for a few days here in Chengdu?" Chris said and glanced toward the officer.

"O.K. I get it," R.O. responded and looked away.

"Let's all get a room at the inn across the street. We'll think better with some rest," David Bloom suggested and stood up. The People's Armed Police officer stood up at the same time. "I think I make her nervous." He reached down to his holster and the woman stepped back. Using only a finger and a thumb he lifted the pistol from the holster and placed it on the table. Ginna did the same. The policewoman spoke into a radio. Two officers walked through the door and across to where the guns had been put down. They picked them up quickly and left the room.

"That was easy enough. I'm beat," David Bloom commented.

"Come on kids. Let's all get rooms. We've got to contact our superiors and see what's next. I'm afraid having you here has complicated our little operation," Ginna informed.

"What about your partner at the poacher's camp?" Chris asked.

"Trust me; we would just be in the way. She's a very tough customer and she loves those pandas. I would be more concerned about the poachers. She's regular army when she's not tracking pandas and poachers. I wouldn't want to mess with her," Ginna replied.

The Blooms and the teens left the small terminal and walked across the four-lane street to the inn. An hour later, they had all showered and were tucked in bed for the night.

Jack had been given a room at the embassy and was lying wide-awake in bed. It would be two more hours before he drifted to sleep.

Mavis, Nigel, and Julian were scattered across the large stateroom on couches and pillows. Mavis had built a small nest in a corner with about a dozen silk pillows and was curled up with a blanket across her. She had wrapped her left hand in a linen napkin after pouring a pint of Scotch whiskey on it that she had found under the bar. Nigel and Julian had held her hand under the stream as she screamed from the burning of the alcohol. Worn-out from the exhaustive night, she nuzzled into a pillow and fell asleep.

13

Gray Skies over China

It was six o'clock in the morning and the traffic was already congested on Jordan Road. People were pushing their way to the bus stop when a tugboat blew its loud horn and the blaring noise shrieked across the water from Kowloon to Hong Kong. Hong Kong was a city that never slept and was known to keep her citizens in a perpetual state of sleep deprivation, much like some major cities in the United States and Western Europe. A city bus cut the corner and two tires rolled over the curb just missing a young girl who was setting up her flower station for the day. She barely noticed as the bus spewed carbon monoxide fumes and dust all over her. Instead, she buried her face in a bouquet of carnations and breathed deeply, masking all the smells of the city waking up.

Right behind the bus, a middle-aged man pulling a rickshaw came with a single passenger. The passenger was dressed in a white suit and therefore seemed out of place at this time of the morning. The rickshaw sped along at four miles per hour, which suited the driver and the passenger just fine. It came to a stop at the terminal of the Star Ferry.

The man got out and paid the driver, who pulled his rig over the curb into a park next to the terminal to wait the man's return.

The man in the white suit was robust and pink in the cheeks. His white hair hung below the brim of the straw white hat that sported a black silk band around the crown. He walked toward the terminal and then at the last moment took a set of stairs that led him down to the water's edge below the pier above him. Waiting for him there was a Chinese man dressed in the traditional high collar and button down front. When the white-suited man walked up, he bowed.

"Good morning, Mr. Alexander," Wen Chen said.

"Good morning, Mr. Chen. The harbor is already hopping for such a time of day," he said.

"Yes, it is, sir," Chen replied. "Did you bring the envelope?"

"Yes, Mr. Chen. I certainly did. Her Majesty's Secret Service would never forget about one of her most loyal agents," he answered.

"You know I'm not an agent, Mr. Alexander. I am just a business associate," Chen said.

"And a very good one you are, Mr. Chen," Alexander said.

The Chinese man opened the white envelope and counted the thick wad of £100 notes.

"A very nice way to start the day, wouldn't you say, Mr. Chen?" the Englishman commented.

"A very nice way, sir," responded Chen.

"Now let's have it," the Englishman said and stepped closer to the smaller Chinese man.

"Your cargo is still at sea near Shanghai. It should be transferred to a civilian cargo aircraft today. It will rendezvous with the fossils in Guangzhou, at the Ling-Ming pharmaceutical company. Disguised as a shipment of medicine, it will cross the New Territories and enter Hong Kong in two days maybe even by tomorrow," Chen said.

"Where will they take the cargo once in Hong Kong?" Alexander asked.

"I don't know," Chen replied.

"You don't know? My dear fellow, your river of money is about to dry up if I don't get the answer I'm paying for. Am I clear?" Alexander asked.

"I may have heard where they are taking it," Chen responded and looked up into the face of the Englishman. "I have a cousin whose family would like to move to England. They are from Xi'an and have made their way to Hong Kong."

"I see. Your timing is right, Mr. Chen. You held out for the big prize with the big carrot. Tell your cousin to walk in the front gate of the British consulate. Have him present this card," Alexander said and took a card from his coat pocket. "It says that he and his crew are new housekeeping employees and it is signed by the ambassador. Have them carry only what can fit into their pockets and a lunch sack . . . and they must wear work clothes. If they have any material wealth bring it to my office next week and I will see that it gets to them."

"Thank you, sir. Thank you very much," Chen said.

"Now. The rest of my information please," Alexander ordered.

"The cargo will be taken to the Apex building on Nathan Road, just across from the Peninsula Hotel," Chen said.

"I know the building. It's getting a facelift, I believe. It's the one with all the bamboo scaffolding all over it, isn't it? Can't even see the building for the wood poles." Alexander said.

"Yes, that's correct, sir. You've been most generous," Chen answered.

"You've earned it, Mr. Chen," Alexander replied. "It's time to say good day."

The Englishman began climbing the steps back up to street level and stopped to look back towards the Chinese man. He was already gone. With the Republic of China controlling Hong Kong, espionage was once again a tricky business.

An hour later, Alexander was in his office at the British

consulate. He picked up a secure telephone line to Scotland
Yard and MI6.

"Hello, Mr. Alexander. I'll get Mr. MacGregor for you,"
the female voice answered.

"Hello, John, what's the news?" Geoffrey MacGregor
asked anxiously.

"News is that the cargo will be here in two days and in
one piece. We have the rendezvous point and it should be
under easy surveillance before the arrival time. I've already
got two people headed there. By nightfall there will be over
a dozen," John Alexander replied and sipped a cup of his
favorite Indian tea.

"Geoffrey, may I ask how your cousin's wife, a good
British subject, came to marry a Yank?" John said smugly.

"Long story, John," Geoffrey said. "I wish I could get
there, but it would take almost two days, and I wouldn't be
worth much when I arrived."

"Have no fear. MI6 Hong Kong is at your service. We
haven't had to snatch anyone for a few weeks but we're still
in good practice," John responded and sipped more tea.
"England has gained a new family of five in the trade, so
there is always some good that comes out of these things."

"Just be sure you get her and her two British pals back,"
Geoffrey said.

"Wouldn't dare think of leaving our best and brightest
behind, Geoffrey. Need to run, a full day ahead is waiting,"
John stated.

"Good-bye, John. Thanks," Geoffrey said and hung up.

He looked at the bank of clocks on the wall opposite his
desk and noted that it was 7:10 a.m. in Hong Kong. Suddenly
he felt fatigued knowing it was 12:10 in the morning in
London. He took a drink from his coffee mug and swallowed
hard. It had become cold.

A young woman dressed in a fashionable, business suit
walked into the room where Geoffrey and ten other analysts shared offices, computers, maps, and a host of related

equipment. He was the last one on post at the time.

"Here's the latest from the kidnappers, Mr. MacGregor," she informed and put the file in front of him. "The requests don't make much sense."

Geoffrey picked up the file and read through it.

"They want a list of all of our agents in China? These guys are amateurs. They're just a bunch of thugs who want to go big time in one day. Get my cousin Jack on the phone. He's at the American embassy in Beijing," Geoffrey said.

Two minutes later, Jack answered the telephone.

"Hello," Jack said sleepily.

"Sorry to wake you up," Geoffrey said.

"That's alright. I just dosed off. Been awake all night anyway. What's going on?" Jack asked.

"I heard from the kidnappers again. Jack, now listen to me. I've been doing this for quite a while and I've got to tell you that these guys are a bunch of amateurs. They are most likely rival families that have operatives in several types of organized crime, one of them fossil smuggling, and Mavis and her buddies walked into a bad scene. Once they found out that they accidentally snagged a celebrity, they got a big head and decided to try to step into the big time. What they want from us I couldn't give the president of the United States," Geoffrey stated and let out a sigh.

"I see. That's bad," Jack replied.

"Well, it could be. Don't get too down about it. When they realize that they have nothing to bargain with or for, they'll have to let them go. I can't believe the Chinese government wouldn't track them down and lock them and all their relatives away for a hundred years for pulling a stunt like this," Geoffrey said.

"Yeah, I agree. But when you push a wild dog into a corner, they tend to come out fighting," Jack added.

"That's the other option. Now, for the good news, we know where she's going to be day after tomorrow. I'm going to string them along from London and we'll give them some information that will make them feel important. Once they've got Mavis, Nigel, and Julian in place our people at MI6 will step in. You can't share this with the Chinese authorities. They might move in ahead of us and spoil it," Geoffrey said.

"I agree. They were supposed to be our protection service in the first place," Jack replied.

"Where are the kids?" Geoffrey asked.

"They're in Chengdu near the panda reserve. I'm trying to find them a flight back to Beijing, but I'm not having much luck," Jack answered.

"Well, hang in there. We're doing all we can. Call me on the direct line I gave you and only from an embassy safe phone. I checked before you answered and your room has a protected line," Geoffrey stated.

"I will. Thanks. We're planning on being in London in five months. Mavis wants to see her parents and take the kids on a castle tour," Jack said.

"She'll be here and so will all of you. Good bye," Geoffrey said and hung up the telephone.

Jack got out of bed and walked into the bathroom and splashed cold water on his face. He looked in the mirror and noticed a two-day growth in his beard. He decided he would shave. He ran some hot water and slathered foaming gel on his face. He wanted to feel normal and to look normal when the kids got there. He didn't have a clue what the day had yet to bring.

The sun was just rising when Chris MacGregor walked out of the hotel and breathed in the cold, November air. There was a light snow falling, but it was melting as soon as it hit the ground. He walked over to the airport terminal and stopped at the information desk. There were no direct flights to Beijing. The nice lady explained in broken English that she could get them all to Beijing if they were willing to fly south to Kunming, change planes, and then fly to Xi'an.

There another flight could take them to Beijing the next morning. As he was walking back to the hotel he thought the military plane didn't seem like such a bad idea. The telephone in his pocket rang.

"Chris," Jack said.

"Hi, Dad. Any news?" Chris replied.

"Only that some good people are working on this. Mom should be back soon. That's all I can say," answered Jack.

"Great," Chris smiled as the chill of the morning got to him and goose bumps ran across his neck.

"I want you to let your crew sleep in and stay at the hotel. I feel better knowing you're in one place and not moving across China. This place is so darn big and with millions of people, well, just stay there," Jack said.

"Will do, Dad," Chris replied.

"By the way, how did you get Mom's phone?" Jack asked.

"R.O. had it in his backpack. He said Mom gave it to him at the embassy before she left. She said she didn't need it and we should have it. I didn't know about it until we got back from Wolong," Chris responded.

"Well, give him a hug for me for remembering. I hate to talk to you through the police," Jack said. "I will call you back later today or sooner if we receive any news. I love you, son."

"I love you too, Dad," Chris said and heard the line disconnect.

Mavis MacGregor rolled over on her injured hand and nearly sat straight up from the jolt of pain. Her wounded hand began bleeding through the linen napkin. She struggled to her feet, feeling every muscle and tendon in her arms and legs, and the throbbing in her hand reverberated up her arm to her head. She walked across the room and noticed that the large yacht was moving. She looked out the window and saw they were along the coastline and Shanghai was no longer in sight. Nigel was snoring on the couch and Julian was asleep on the floor wrapped in a blanket. She walked over to the bar and found a cabinet with tea bags and cups.

"I need coffee," she said out loud.

Looking further she found a box of instant coffee bags. She opened the box and put one packet in a cup; then she filled it with water from the tap and put it in the microwave for ninety seconds. When the timer dinged she removed the cup and smelled the aroma.

"Fix me a cup, won't you?" Nigel asked, sitting up on the couch.

"Will do," Mavis replied and took him her cup.

"It's hot. Good," Nigel said.

She got back to the microwave just as the other cup was ready. Julian was still asleep. She retrieved the hot cup of coffee and walked over to the couch. She sat down next to Nigel and they sipped the instant coffee together.

"How's your hand?" Nigel asked.

"It hurts," Mavis replied. "But what can I do? I'll just have to deal with it."

"We would have never guessed we'd be in the South China Sea together that first year of graduate school at Cambridge, would we, Mave?" Nigel asked.

"No, we were still so naive about science and the world," Mavis answered.

"Jack was perfect for you. I wouldn't have been able to tame you," Nigel added and sipped the hot coffee.

"Do you hear that?" Mavis asked.

"I do. It's an aircraft. Must be amphibian," Nigel said and got up and walked over to the big window on the port side. There it is."

"They're coming to get us, Nigel, but I bet it's not the good guys," Mavis said and walked over next to him.

They leaned over and woke Julian and gave him the rest of their coffee. Soon they all watched as the yacht slowed to a full stop and the large amphibian aircraft came alongside. Two of the yacht's crew members lowered a Zodiac rubber raft into the water and then set a small motor on the transom. The Zodiac zipped over to the plane and picked up a man who was waiting at the expansive open window over the wing.

"We better go to the bathroom and be ready," Mavis said and walked across the room.

Five minutes later they were standing together as the outside door opened and a man they had never seen before walked into the lush quarters.

"Good morning. I'll be your host for the day. You will be advised to do as you are asked or the consequences will be severe. But I assume you have already been threatened many times? Is that not so?" the man asked.

"Yes. We know the drill quite well," Mavis replied and held up her hand with the bloody bandage. You wouldn't happen to have an aspirin, would you?"

"I think I can find one once we're on the aircraft," he answered back.

Two guards walked in and aimed automatic pistols at them and the three scientists followed the man out the door. They walked down the side platform to a ladder. Mavis tried to go first but couldn't take the pressure on her hand.

"Nigel, you first, and push on my bottom as I go down to steady me on the ladder. But be polite," Mavis smiled.

"Always a gentleman, Dr. MacGregor," Nigel replied.

"I'm ready to get into the air," Julian said and waved bye to the guards on the upper deck. "We could have been such great friends, if I had the guns in my hands."

A few minutes later they were sitting in the Russian-made Be-103 amphibian, watching the yacht pull away for a return voyage to Shanghai. The side window was secured and a man with a gun sat down behind them. The engines of the Beriev turned over and the six-foot propellers began to rotate. The big amphibian became a swift moving boat and glided across the ocean waves, reaching its take-off speed before it gently lifted into the air.

Chris walked into the hotel lobby only to meet David Bloom coming out.

"I've been looking for you, Chris," David said. The China Wildlife Conservation Association wants Ginna and me to go back to Wolong and pick up their agent and bring the poachers back here. Seems the provincial government won't have a helicopter or a pilot available for another two days, and they don't want their agent out there alone for that long."

"From what you said, I think I would worry about the poachers more than the agent," Chris added.

"You're right," David replied.

"I'll tell everyone to hang at the hotel for a couple of hours," Chris said and walked toward the stairs.

When Chris reached the helicopter there were only two People's Armed Police officers sitting in a car watching the Bell 412. David Bloom had secured the fuel truck and was having fuel pumped into the helicopter. Moving the fuel truck away from the helicopter, he talked to the two policemen and gave them a copy of his new orders from the Wildlife Division of the Sichuan Provisional Forestry Department, the regional branch of the China Wildlife Conservation Association. Bloom stepped inside the massive army helicopter and closed the side door.

Chris was busy flipping switches and checking gauges, when David fastened his seat belt.

"You caught on quick," David said.

"It was easy, once I saw what each toggle did. Then I could remember the characters by shape," Chris said.

Five more minutes passed and then the Bell 412 lifted off. After circling the small airport, Chris pointed the helicopter northeast toward Wolong. David pulled out a couple of maps and soon they were oriented back to the pandas' mountain home. An hour passed before they spotted the clearing on the edge of an escarpment and the smoke from a campfire.

"There it is," David said into the mouthpiece of his headset.

Chris began an approach and softly set down the big air-craft in the clearing with only a few bounces.

"Man, you're good," David said.

Chris smiled.

"Yea, I wish. This baby is huge."

Yen Hwa Yu walked up to the helicopter with an AK-47 slung over her shoulder. The rifle looked huge slung across her five foot three petite frame.

"You finally came back," she said to David.

"Had to shower, shave, eat, and get a good night's rest first," David replied.

"Must be rough," Yu added.

"Where are the poachers?" Chris asked and looked around.

"They tried to escape so I killed them all," the agent said calmly.

"You what?" Chris asked.

"Just kidding, follow me," Yu laughed.

David, Yen Hwa, and Chris walked across the clearing into the forest next to the campfire. There they could see the three poachers tied at the neck and ankles to three different trees.

"Wow," Chris exclaimed.

"They don't complain and they don't try to escape this way," Yen Hwa said. "I built a campfire around them so they wouldn't totally freeze last night."

"Let's get them in the chopper," David ordered. "Chris, go around the camp and pick up all the loose weapons."

"I've got them stacked over there," Yu stated and point-ed to the pile of weapons.

"Sure, no problem," Chris replied.

In the pile were automatic assault rifles, pistols, shot-guns, machetes, and several bags of ammunition. Chris felt like a mercenary from a third world country as he emerged from the trees with all the guns over his shoul-ders, stuffed in his belt, and dragging from his hands. He laid them gently in the back cabin of the helicopter next to where the tied-up poachers were being stacked like cord-wood. The rank odor of the captives grabbed his attention.

"How can I fly the helicopter with those guys smelling like that?" he asked as David walked up.

"I guess we could leave them out here to die," Yen Hwa responded, walking up. "That would be my choice. But we need to know who pays their way. These guys are the small fish."

"We'll leave the side door open and hope they don't freeze, I guess," David said and tossed one of the poachers on top of another who let out a muffled yell through the duct tape over his mouth.

"I get it," Chris commented and walked to the pilot's seat.

As David secured the side door, the rotary blade began to turn. When everyone, except the poachers, was buckled in, Chris adjusted the collective and the cyclic and the helicopter lifted off the ground. Making a sharp turn around the clearing and gaining altitude, Chris spotted a black-and-white panda perched high in a tree. He smiled and knew the pandas would be a little safer as they flew away. The flight back to Chengdu took only an hour and the helicopter sat down just as another light snow began. The People's Armed Police service brought a truck and hauled the poachers away.

Chris took out the cell phone and dialed the embassy.

"Hello," Jack answered.

"Dad, I've got to tell you that I've been flying a Chinese Army Bell 412," Chris blurted out and held his breath.

"Good job, son. But why?" Jack asked.

"We were at Wolong and one of the scientists was hurt and needed to be flown to Chengdu. I was the only one there who was capable of flying it. It's just an older and larger version of Jennifer January's Bell Jet Ranger. I knew I could do it, so I said I would help," Chris replied.

"I'm proud of you, Chris." Jack said. "Why don't they let you fly your brother, sister, and Natalie back to Beijing?" Jack questioned.

"I'll ask, if that's O.K. with you?" Chris said.

"Sure, son. Just be careful and know what your limits are," Jack answered back. "And stay in close touch."

"Roger, Dad. And thanks," Chris said and turned to David.

"Do y'all have any plans today or tomorrow?" Chris asked David.

David looked Chris in the eye and then smiled.

"Son, you're not thinking what I'm thinking?" David asked.

David turned and spoke to Yen Hwa Yu in Chinese whose face now sported a grin from ear to ear and began laughing.

"She says it would be fun to check out some of the other panda reserves to the east. We can fuel at civilian airports with her army clearance. By my estimate, we can reach the eastern coast in two days or less. We'll need to pace ourselves so you don't get too tired," David said.

"No need to hurry," Chris responded. "It'll keep us busy until we hear more about my mom."

"Good idea. I'll go get your crew and Ginna. You two stay in the chopper so the airport doesn't come haul it to a hangar for the army to pick up," David said.

"What about all of these weapons?" Chris asked.

David turned to the agent and told her to cull out the good and stow them away on board and to toss the others out on to the tarmac to satisfy the police when they came back.

Twenty minutes later, R.O. bounded up into the helicopter.

"Is it true, we're going for another ride?" he asked Chris.

"That's a roger," Chris replied.

Natalie leaned over the front seat and swung around into Chris's face and kissed him.

"Good morning," she said.

"Good morning back. Get buckled up," Chris said and smiled back at her.

Ginna Bloom was the last to climb aboard. She was still dressed in her camos because their gear was in another base camp on the other side of Wolong. It could be seen that she was a natural blonde, now that her face paint was gone and the grime washed out of her hair.

Chris adjusted all the instruments and the blades began turning. In a few minutes, the big helicopter was again airborne and flying toward Chungking.

"Let's keep her pointed southeast, away from the winter," Yen Hwa Yu said.

"I agree with that," Heather responded through her headset microphone, keying so everyone could hear her comment.

R.O. was glued to the window as Chris began to gain altitude.

"Which dial operates surface and air radar?" Chris asked.

David leaned over and read the Chinese characters and flipped two toggle switches. Two eight-inch monitors flickered on and the small radar antennae on the top of the helicopter cabin began to turn.

"We've got eyes," Chris said with a grin. "That'll keep us away from any tall peaks or aircraft that head our way."

"Stay above three thousand and it's clear all the way," Yen Hwa said. "And call me Tracy. The tall peaks are all to the west. We've only got a couple to the southeast."

"Great, thanks, Tracy," Chris replied. "Where did you get that name?"

"From some friends in America. I've been twice to visit them in Florida and they come back to China when they can."

Natalie, Ginna, Heather, and R.O. settled in on top of all the duffle bags and backpacks that they had brought on board for their adventure east.

Chris, David, and Tracy concentrated on the all the dials and gauges and flew the aircraft to the southeast at 140 mph, just below the cloud ceiling. They watched the occasional flake of snow bounce off the front windshield. Chris looked out at the vast countryside and held on firmly to the controls with both hands, keeping positive pressure with both feet to maintain the helicopter tracking in the right direction. He tried to focus on flying but his thoughts kept turning toward his mother. He knew she would be proud to see him flying like this. In his heart, he wished he was going to rescue her, but today it was just a fantasy. Perhaps tomorrow it would be a different story.

14

Bell 412

Chris held tight to the controls of the helicopter as it cruised easily with a tail wind from the Tibetan Highlands. The aircraft had seen better days but the hydraulics were smooth and the motor hummed along as if it had just left the factory. Agent Bloom studied the maps that he had found and consulted with Tracy about the safest path. Tracy would answer the occasional radio inquiry about a Chinese army helicopter in a certain region, but when she would respond with her standard panda protection story, the caller was satisfied and they easily moved from one province to the next.

"That was uneventful considering the size of the airport," Chris said.

"Yes, Chungking can be a challenging airport to get in and out of," Tracy answered back. "It's home to one of eight regional military bases in China. We're fortunate that the People's Liberation Army had a fuel depot and that they accepted my credentials."

"Yes, but they were curious about all the Westerners you were transporting," David added.

"What's next?" Chris asked.

"Looks like a peak of 8,600 feet at 160 degrees SSE. We need to stay east at 120 degrees and 4,000 feet altitude to avoid these mountain peaks. There are some tall ones out there to the south and southeast but nothing like the ones we left behind us. Next fuel stop is Ch'ang-sha," David replied.

Ginna leaned over his shoulder.

"Have y'all decided what we're doing and where we're going? I think our liaison back in Beijing would like to know how the anti-poaching training is progressing," she said.

"No worry. He's my cousin," Tracy said.

"Why didn't you tell us that before?" Ginna asked with a frown on her face.

"I think you might worry about telling me everything and being, as you say, straight with me," Tracy said.

"I understand," David replied. "I think we need to get these kids east instead of north and back to Beijing right now. It's a great ride for them and will take their mind off all the stuff that's going on. We'll stop somewhere along the way and put them on a military flight to Beijing. Then we'll go back to Wolong and finish our job. In the meantime, we get to explore China and have fun, and Chris gets to log some time behind the wheel or cyclic or whatever he called it," David said.

"Sounds good to me," Ginna replied. I'll tell these three back here so they can relax and enjoy the scenery.

Chris banked the Bell 412 to slide into the 120 degree coordinate and brought it up to 4,000 feet. With each hour he grew more comfortable in the pilot's seat. His trainers in Italy had been impressed with his ability to learn each move quickly. He knew how to "strap on the helicopter and become part of it," as Gieuseppi had told him. David's knowledge of Chinese made him the perfect co-pilot.

The sun began to peak through the clouds, and the brown patchwork of fields below became more defined as they mixed with the occasional rough terrain and river system.

R.O. pressed his face against a window and his mouth turned down in a sad expression as he once again thought about his mother.

"What do the satellites tell us?" Geoffrey MacGregor asked as he leaned over the British Naval lieutenant's left shoulder.

"We've got some pictures coming in. The American CIA loaned us one of their birds that run up the east coast of China. We targeted all the smaller vessels leaving Shanghai harbor," the brunette said.

"How many are we talking about?" Geoffrey asked.

"About 3,500 give or take a few dozen," she replied.

"Well, scrap that idea," Geoffrey answered back.

"No, sir, not now, because we also got a reading of an amphibious aircraft that landed next to a yacht. Both the amphibian and the yacht are rare breeds in China, sir," she said and smiled.

"What could you see?" Geoffrey asked.

"It's coming up now, sir," she said and pointed to the fifty-two inch monitor on the wall. "Here's the yacht, and then in this shot you see the amphibian landing and moving next to the boat. It looks like a Russian-made Beriev Amphibian. They are easily spotted because of the big twin props that sit on top of the fuselage just back of the wings. We found twenty-two registered in China from Manchuria to Hong Kong. Another boat is leaving the yacht in this frame, and as we go frame to frame to frame we can definitely see three people being taken from the boat to the aircraft."

"Why is the last frame black?" Geoffrey asked.

"That's when the American bird turned off, I suppose, sir. The CIA wouldn't tell us," she answered.

"Well, that's a hit if you ask me. We haven't gotten any other reports about foreign nationals being kidnapped or traded have we?" Geoffrey asked.

"Just the standard numbers out of the Middle East, Colombia, Ecuador, Philippines, and Central Africa. Even

Central America is quiet. Nothing in China," she replied.

"Good, thanks, Lieutenant," Geoffrey said and walked into the next room where nearly a dozen analysts were busy at their stations.

"What's the word?" a voice from behind him asked.

Geoffrey turned around and found Admiral Gregg Koehn, director of International Security and MI6, standing there.

"Hello, sir. Didn't know you were in on this," Geoffrey responded.

"MacGregor, I'm in on everything. Especially if it personally involves one of my people, and even though you're Royal Canadian Mounted Police on loan, you're one of my commonwealth people," Koehn said.

"Well, thank you, sir. Ground intelligence had the three scientists snatched in Shenyang, flown to Shanghai, transported to a boat at sea, and then on an amphibian aircraft to points unknown," Geoffrey said. "The CIA satellite snapped an actual photo of the three of them boarding the last aircraft."

"What about the fossils?" Koehn asked.

"That's the unusual part, sir," Geoffrey said. "We haven't received any confirmed intelligence from the Chinese army that a large transport moved the fossils across China to the far south. But we do know that there's a cache of fossils in a warehouse in Shanghai that isn't moving and it was there before all of this started. So there are more fossils out there than the Chinese Academy of Geological Sciences can account for or attach to a specific dig site."

"So are they counterfeiting dinosaur bones now?" Koehn asked.

"We don't know, but our three paleontologists walked into a deal gone bad between two warring families who may not only be involved in illegal dinosaur bone trading but a dozen other organized crime activities across China. I think their government is clean on this one and probably doesn't know as much as we do about it right now," Geoffrey replied.

"Who are the families involved?" Koehn asked.

"The only one we can identify in the dinosaur black market is Lee Jring Wong. She is the matriarch of a very old and large family. Her family has controlled certain markets in the Pearl River Delta for five hundred years," Geoffrey answered. "We just don't know enough to put a name on the other warring faction."

"Well, we better soon. It looks like our three people have been passed off twice now. I'm afraid another trade will mean a less favorable deal for the bargainers and possibly violence," Koehn said.

"That's where the demands from me come into play," Geoffrey stated.

"Did you set up a dummy list you can feed them when they contact you?" Koehn asked.

"Yes. It's ready to go, but we haven't heard anything yet," Geoffrey responded.

"Could be that the last trade hasn't been reported up the pipeline to the crime families' heads. That may not go well," Koehn said.

"That's what I'm worried about," he looked at his watch. "I need to contact my cousin again and keep him from worrying," Geoffrey announced.

"We get paid for that, he doesn't," Admiral Koehn said.

"Yes, and he's got three kids scattered across China on some field trip about pandas," Geoffrey responded.

"It's best they're kept busy. Keep me posted," Koehn said and walked away.

The Beriev Amphibian taxied up the ramp in the secluded harbor one hundred miles south of Shanghai. A twin-engine prop driven Beech King Air 200 sat waiting, as the prisoners were off-loaded and walked over to the other aircraft.

"Musical chairs again," Nigel said and was immediately poked in the ribs with the barrel of a rifle.

"Shut up!" the man said.

The exchange took exactly six minutes, and the King Air was moving down the runway and gliding into the air. There were no buildings or aircraft around, just the Beriev and the King Air.

Mavis watched as two men in suits engaged in an intense conversation. Her hand throbbed and no one had produced the promised aspirin. She knew they had been lying all the while. One of the men took out his cell phone and attempted to make a call when the other man slapped it from his hand. It landed one row forward of Mavis under a seat. Their argument continued.

"Miss, miss," Mavis said and waived to the female who was assigned to watch her.

"Yes," she said as she walked up to Mavis.

"I need to use the facilities," the Chinese woman looked puzzled. "Bathroom. I need to . . ."

"Yes, I know," she interrupted and reached down and unlocked her manacles from the seat.

Mavis stood up, nearly bumping her head on the low ceiling, and turned toward the front and took two steps.

"No, No. It is this way," the Chinese woman said.

Mavis was now standing over the cell phone. Julian and Nigel were already asleep. Mavis took one step and then fell down.

"Ouch," she said as she stood up shaking her wounded hand.

"You must be more careful," the Chinese woman said.

"This aisle is too narrow," Mavis said and smiled.

She followed her to the bathroom that was located at the rear. She reached out with her injured hand and gritted her teeth as she painfully grabbed the door and closed it. A small tear escaped her left eye. Once inside, she locked the door slowly and quietly sat down. Her knees were touching the door, and she started breathing deeply in an effort to gain her composure in the small enclosure. She opened the cell phone, which had been hidden in her other hand. It was labeled in

Chinese characters but she knew all cell phones worked alike. She thought for a minute and then dialed the number to the phone that the embassy had given her. There was no service.

"Darn it," Mavis whispered to herself. The engines droned loudly, and she felt safe enough to talk.

She waited and tried again and the screen lit up with the connected number. She put it to her ear and waited.

Chris felt the vibration in his pants pocket and looked down.

"Must be Dad calling," he said to David and he fished it out in a hurry.

"Hey, Dad," he answered.

There was silence on the other end.

"Dad, you there?" he asked.

"Chris, Chris, this is your mother," Mavis said softly.

"You'll have to talk louder, Dad. I can't hear you over the noise of the helicopter," Chris replied.

"Chris, please. Listen to me," Mavis pleaded, her voiced beginning to break.

"Natalie, take this phone and talk to Dad. I can't hear him up here," Chris said.

"Sure, babe," Natalie said and took the phone.

"Hi, Dr. MacGregor," Natalie said.

"Natalie, this is Mavis," Mavis said.

"Mavis, oh my gosh. Where are you?" Natalie yelled into the phone.

Everyone around her stopped what they were doing and stared at her. Chris swiftly turned around in his seat.

"Natalie, I don't have long. I'm in an airplane. We left Shanghai and are being flown south. The fields are becoming greener the longer we fly. Nigel and Julian are with me. Notify Major Chen. Tell him to trace the phone I'm using. It belongs to one of the . . ."

Suddenly she was interrupted as the door was kicked in on top of her. One of the men ripped the door to the side, yanked her out, and grabbed the cell phone. Without saying a word to her, he swung his right fist in her direction and punched her on her left cheekbone. She felt no pain as she immediately fell to the floor unconscious.

"Mavis, Mavis," Natalie shouted and looked at Chris. "The line went dead."

"Come up here. What did she say?" Chris asked.

"She said they had left Shanghai and were in an airplane being flown south. Something about the fields getting greener and greener the longer they flew," Natalie said.

"Give me the phone, we've got to call Dad," Chris said.

He dialed the number to the embassy and in two transfers Jack MacGregor picked up the phone.

"Jack MacGregor," he said.

"Dad, this is Chris. We just talked to Mom," Chris said excitedly.

"You what?" Jack asked incredulously. "When? How?" Jack added.

"She called us from a cell phone that she may have stolen. She said they were flying south from Shanghai and the fields were greener and greener the farther they flew," Chris replied.

"I've got to inform Major Chen and my cousin Geoffrey," Jack said.

"Geoffrey? What's he got to do with this?" Chris asked.

"He's helping out. That's all I can say," Jack answered. "Where are you?

"I'm flying the helicopter southeast toward the coast. Heather, Ryan, and Natalie are in the back. We're fine. We've got three armed escorts so don't worry about us," Chris responded.

"I'm all worried out, son," Jack said. "Can't think of anyone else but your mother. You take care of your end. I trust you. I've taught you everything you need to do, now's the time to be the man I know you can be."

"Thanks, Dad, you can count on me," Chris said with a lump in his throat.

"I better hang up and make my calls. I love you. Tell Heather and R.O. I love them and give Natalie a hug for me. Bye," Jack said and hung up.

Chris sat in silence just watching the beautiful Chinese countryside as he flew along at four thousand feet.

"What's the vector of an airplane flying southwest of Shanghai?" Chris asked.

"There's only one major city in that direction," Tracy replied. "Hong Kong."

"Then that's where we're going. Run us a vector to Hong Kong with fuel stops along the way," Chris ordered.

"That's 800 miles from our next fuel stop," David said. "And based on this map we've got some five and six thousand foot peaks along the way. This chopper doesn't carry oxygen for high flying and it would get too cold."

Tracy chimed in. "But I know this country. My ancestors are from Hunan Province. There are two major river valleys we can fly. We'll never have to fly over one thousand feet. It will add two or three more hours to the trip but we'll get there by tomorrow afternoon. We can land for the night at my ancestral home at Ying-te on the Pei River. My family will be very happy to see me and will welcome you as guests. I know the local PLA commander. He won't touch the helicopter," Tracy said smiling.

"That's a plan," David said.

Ginna and all the kids had been listening carefully.

"Then to Hong Kong we go," Chris exclaimed. "Hang on Mom, we're on our way!"

15

Tai-Pan

Another uneventful day had passed for Jack MacGregor. He awoke with the alarm and sat up quickly. Seven hours of sleep had barely made up for forty-eight hours of sleep deprivation, but he sensed he felt better as he reached for the phone beside his bed. He dialed the embassy operator.

"Dr. Biggs, please," he said.

As he waited, he noticed that his clothes and luggage from the hotel had been brought over to the embassy. Then he looked across the room and saw eight more bags and suitcases, which represented the MacGregor family luggage for the trip to China. It was not the sight he wanted to see and quickly swung around and sighed.

"Dr. Biggs," the voice said on the other end of the call.

"This is Jack. Any word yet?" he asked and stood up reaching the maximum length of the telephone cord.

"Nothing on our end. Our CIA officer is being very mum about it, and the FBI isn't saying much either," Dr. Biggs replied.

"Well, that's not helpful. I guess I'll have to call London again," Jack said. "Can you tell the operator to give me a secure line?"

"No problem, Dr. MacGregor. If I hear something, I'll let you know right away," Sherri Biggs said and hung up.

A few seconds later, Jack's telephone rang.

"Dr. MacGregor?" the operator asked.

"Yes," he replied.

"When you hear the dial tone, just dial your number and you'll be secure," she said.

"Thank you," Jack replied and sat back down on the bed.

Fifteen seconds later a loud dial tone blared into his ear. Startled, he pulled the handset away and began dialing Geoffrey MacGregor at Scotland Yard. The satellite connection was amazingly fast and in thirty seconds he was talking to the switchboard at Scotland Yard.

"MacGregor," Geoffrey said as he answered the phone.

"Geoffrey, this is Jack."

"Jack, I was going to call you in a bit but I had to have a shower and some coffee," Geoffrey said.

"Sorry, Geoffrey," Jack said.

"Hey, no problem, cousin. I live just across the street in a suite at the St. Ermin's. It's a nice, old hotel with lots of English charm except now an Italian company runs it and the staff speak Italian. That's one of my weaker languages," Geoffrey said trying to make Jack feel relaxed.

"Any word?" Jack asked.

"Matter of fact, yes," Geoffrey replied.

Jack's heart started beating faster. He felt tightness in his chest.

"MI6 has narrowed it down to two different Tai-Pans who could be holding Mavis and her friends. Seems there's been a lot of dinosaur bone marketing the last forty-eight hours. It's not a normal commodity like diamonds, oil, or even food. We practically never hear of it, this is all new. There aren't a lot of buyers, so we turned our eyes toward art collectors and people who invest in intangibles. We got a hit when one of our agent's informants stepped up to collect a nice finder's fee. Jack, you still there?" Geoffrey asked.

"Yes, go on," Jack replied. "Tai-Pan, you mean foreign businesses?"

"Yes. Two companies that date back over two hundred years and have dealt with the West since China was opened after the Boxer Rebellion in the early twentieth century. Well, seems that these are two businesses that have been making offers to foreign agents to sell dinosaur fossils on the black market. No legitimate auction house like Sotheby's would touch something like this. But what's puzzling is that the amounts aren't that much out of line with normal fossil markets. The only way they could make a big profit is if the fossils are frauds," Geoffrey said.

"Counterfeit bones?" Jack asked.

"Yeah, looks like it," Geoffrey replied.

"Mavis would spot that in a heartbeat and so should have Nigel and Julian. I don't buy it, Geoffrey. Those three are some of the best paleontologists in the world. Nigel Wells and Julian Hilliard would never have pulled Mavis into a trap like this. For goodness sakes, Nigel was Mavis's old flame, and I don't think he ever got over her marrying me and following me back to Texas. He wouldn't risk her life for a second," Jack said.

"That's the puzzling part, Jack. We can't make anything of it. We know the Tai-Pans are associated with Ku Jong Wu whose family runs textiles and banking in Hong Kong and a Sen Li whose family has hotels and container ships. Then there's Lee Jring Wong. Her interests are quite large. All of them have financial statements in the eight figures. Doesn't make sense they're in the rock business," Geoffrey replied. "There's got to be more to it. I'm not one for conspiracy theories, but this seems more and more like one."

"Do they have any mainland ties?" Jack asked.

"Oh sure. Since the return of Hong Kong to Chinese rule two years ago everyone has ties to the People's Republic of China. I'm sure they're now paying more in corruption money than they ever paid in tariffs," Geoffrey responded.

"Is the military involved in any of this, I mean, these Tai-Pans?" Jack asked.

"The military is the government of China, Jack. They go to great lengths to tell you that a civilian government oversees the military, but if the military doesn't support the civilian government, then there's no government," Geoffrey said.

"They haven't changed much," Jack replied. "Then we need to investigate these two Tai-Pans and see what washes out."

"Ahead of you there, Jack. We've got teams looking into the Tai-Pan's businesses in the PRC and Hong Kong. We know that Mavis was taken in the northeast and flown south. We're unsure of the stops along the way but our intelligence has told us that she will be in Hong Kong later today or tomorrow. We don't know what bargaining chip they're going to use to try to get me to tell them information that I don't even know," Geoffrey said.

"Then what's going to happen when they call back and they're not given the ransom they want?" Jack asked, his heart beating faster.

"I don't know, Jack. We're doing all we can do. MI6 is operating on foreign soil when they're in Hong Kong. It no longer belongs to Britannia. It's all under Chinese control now. It's only an island, but there are six million people in Hong Kong and we're looking for three," Geoffrey informed.

"I just pray we can get to them in time," Jack said.

"We will. I can't tell you how or when but we'll find them," Geoffrey said. I'll call you back when I get up," Geoffrey said.

"Thanks, Geoffrey," Jack said.

"Bye," Geoffrey replied and hung up.

"Bye," Jack said and hung up the telephone. He didn't feel much better than before he had made the call.

Mavis awoke only to find herself secured to her seat with duct tape across her chest. The morning sun peeked into her widow as the aircraft cruised along at seventeen thousand feet. Her jaw was aching terribly and her vision was impaired in her left eye. She kept blinking and realized her eyelids were swollen. She instinctively tried to touch her face but couldn't move her arms.

"Mavis, Mavis," Nigel said from two seats in front of her as he heard Mavis struggle in her chair. He too had been taped to the seat. "Are you alright?"

"I'm a mess, Nigel. My head, my face, my hand are killing me. My neck hurts terribly," she said and started to cry softly.

"No talk," one of the men said and walked over to them. "I tape your mouths next."

The pain in Mavis' body told her to stop talking.

"We won't talk," Mavis said slowly and made eye contact with the man. As she blinked another tear escaped her left eye.

He nodded and walked back to his seat. She glanced out the window and squinted at the morning sun.

"When did it become morning? Wasn't it near dark when I got hit?" she whispered.

"We landed. We sat in the hangar for hours. I think you have a concussion," Nigel replied. "You gave us a fright. You've been out cold for eight or ten hours. I lost count. They looked confused about what to do until they got a phone call and new people arrived and took over," he stated.

The guard rose out of his seat and stopped in front of Nigel and took out a roll of tape. He quickly tore off a gray piece and stuck it on Nigel's mouth. He went to Mavis and started to do the same.

"Please, I can't breathe. I've had a concussion. Do you want me to die? What would be my value then?" she asked, her left eye still tearing.

"Leave it off," said the voice of a woman behind her. "She can't talk to him anymore and the red haired English has been asleep."

"He's Scottish," Mavis corrected.

"All beat up and in pieces and you still have the energy to correct me," the woman said as she stepped around so Mavis could see her.

Mavis looked up and tried to focus through the throbbing headache. She blinked several times before she got a clear image.

"Dr. Fong Cheng. I saw you die," Mavis said quickly.

"No, Dr. MacGregor, you merely saw me change employers," Cheng replied. "I knew my time was limited after I corroborated the discovery of the *Caudipteryx zoui*. It's amazing what a Kevlar vest and a couple of theatrical devices can do. I was most grateful that Mr. Chang didn't shoot me in the head."

"That would have been a nasty surprise, I suppose," Mavis retorted, returning to her British composure and ignoring her pain. "So now you have a new employer who has given you a tidy sum of money to deliver our feathered girl?" Mavis questioned.

"Yes. Ten percent of twenty million is a good commission, don't you agree?" Dr. Cheng responded.

"Yes, I believe a girl could be kept in shoes and hand bags for quite some time with two million dollars," Mavis replied. "I underestimated your bargaining power, Dr. Cheng. Then if I may ask, why do you need the three of us? We're merely laboratory rats who like to crawl around rock piles for our jollies." Mavis blinked again rather hard to get the tears to move down her face so she could focus her eyes better.

Fong Cheng took a silk handkerchief from her coat pocket, leaned over, and dabbed Mavis' eyes softly.

"A professional courtesy," Cheng said.

"Thank you. It is appreciated," Mavis replied.

"We need you because my Tai-Pan feels that your husband's cousin may eventually turn out to be a good contact for us. We don't intend on trading you for anything. We want to keep you as a bargaining chip for quite some time.

My superiors thought they could extract some information from Geoffrey MacGregor, Royal Canadian Mounted Police on assignment with Scotland Yard. However, Mr. MacGregor's reluctance to cooperate convinced us that keeping you for a year or two would be better. You see, Dr. MacGregor, the Chinese don't understand the concept of instant satisfaction. We prefer delayed gratification. We don't think in terms of days, months, or years. We believe in decades and centuries and that's why we continue to exist, grow, and conquer," Dr. Cheng said.

"I see. So now I'm your prisoner till I'm gray and wrinkled," Mavis said.

"Don't despair, Dr. MacGregor. We can always find your kids and bring them to see you . . . and stay," Cheng stated.

Mavis breathed in and gritted her teeth so that she could hold back the verbal tirade she wanted to launch. "Hold your tongue. Your time will come," she thought to herself. She felt the airplane bank to the starboard side and the landing gear drop. It was a relief knowing that soon she would be out of the chair and moving her arms again. She glanced down and could now see that her injured hand was blue and swollen, the obvious signs of an infection.

"Not good," she whispered as Fong Cheng walked away.

The Bell 412 cruised along at one thousand feet, just high enough to clear the mountain range near the New Territories slightly north of Kowloon. The night in Ying-te with Tracy's family of sixty was like a giant festival since Tracy only returned once or twice each year. The food was delicious but Chris never lost focus on his mother for a second. Heather cried twice, and R.O. was generally morose and inattentive to the details all around him. Everyone was ready to load back into the chopper and complete the last leg of the impromptu journey.

"I've plotted our approach to Kowloon across the western

edge of the New Territories," David Bloom said and pointed to a map.

"That's good," Tracy responded. "The army base there will let us land. I can get clearance on the radio as we get closer."

"Won't they take us into custody?" Chris asked.

"No, I don't think so. All we have to do is call your friend, Major Chen, and he can tell them to let you go," Tracy replied.

"No, you don't understand. Major Chen would have us locked up until a police guard could escort us back to Beijing, and that's where we don't want to go," Chris answered back.

Suddenly an alarm on the console went off and a high-pitched, beeping noise resounded through the cabin.

"What's that?" David asked.

"It's this gauge. Read the characters for me," Chris demanded urgently.

"It says hydraulic fluid," Tracy fired back.

"What's the measurement? Is it in pounds per square inch or what?" Chris hurriedly asked.

"Can't tell," David replied.

Then unexpectedly a second alarm sounded and a red light on another instrument began flashing.

"That reads compression of something," Tracy deciphered.

"What something?" Chris yelled back.

"I don't know. It's an aeronautical term. I don't recognize it. I'm a wildlife biologist," Tracy responded.

"This isn't good. I could lose the ability to tilt the rotor any second. The pedals might freeze and we would go into a spiral and start to spin violently. We've got to land now," Chris announced.

"I agree," David said and started looking at the map. "O.K. Dead ahead is the Sham Chun River, the northern border to the New Territories. That puts us in more favorable hands if we're picked up."

"How will you explain all the guns in the back?" Ginna asked as she leaned over his shoulder.

"Dump them out now," Tracy yelled. "Keep only the side-arms. We can toss them later if we have to."

Ginna and Natalie opened the storage boxes and told Heather and R.O. to stay fastened in. Tracy moved to the side door and opened it and a rush of wind blew her backwards. She held on to a hand strap as Natalie handed her the rifles and automatic weapons one at a time. Soon they were all out the door and flying like missiles to the ground below.

"No pedals. I just lost the pedals," Chris shouted. "We're going to start spinning. Wait, they're back. I'm setting it down while we've got a chance."

"It's all marshland so now's a good place," David called. "Everybody buckle in tight."

The Bell 412 swung around to catch the wind coming off the ocean, allowing Chris to lift the nose of the chopper in order to glide to a landing.

"One hundred feet, ninety feet, eighty, seventy, sixty," David shouted.

"No pedals. They're gone for good. Hang on," Chris bellowed as the helicopter began to turn slowly and then pick up speed. He promptly pulled back on the collective to feather the propeller on the rotary shaft while pushing the cyclic forward to keep the tail out of the marsh and to avoid flipping over.

"Twenty feet, hang on everybody," David yelled.

Heather put her hands over her face while R.O. couldn't stop watching Chris. Natalie closed her eyes.

Suddenly there was a splashing noise and water surged up around the aircraft as the feet of the helicopter penetrated the bog of the marsh and stuck.

"Turn off everything, quick," Chris ordered as he and David started flipping switches and toggles. The whining noise began to stop as the rotary blade made its last few revolutions. The console was totally dark and the cabin was eerily quiet now that the alarms had stopped.

"Let's get out. There could always be a fire," David said. "Everybody out. Get your packs and let's go."

Tracy and Ginna flung the side door back open and hopped out into knee-deep water and marsh grass.

"It's warm here," Heather noted as she splashed into the water and ran away from the helicopter.

"It's the tropics," Ginna said and helped R.O. out the door with his pack.

Natalie was next, followed by Tracy, Chris, and David.

"According to the map, there's a highway 1.2 miles away at 120 degrees southeast," David said.

"We have to walk over a mile in this swamp?" Heather asked.

Chris turned around and looked her in the face.

"Sorry," she said. "I know why we're here."

They trudged through the murky water in single file to avoid stepping into holes or tripping over barriers. Ginna held her pistol high, watching for the venomous snakes that Tracy had warned about and R.O. couldn't wait to see. After nearly a mile, Tracy stepped out of the line and faced them all.

"I guess it's time to welcome you to the New Territories. If I can get to a phone, I have a cousin who lives in Tai Po. He could come get us. He owns a bait business," Tracy said.

"Why don't you use this phone," Chris answered and reached into his pocket. Just as his fingers touched it, it began to ring.

16

25.5° N, 114.7° E

Chris pushed the green button on the cell phone and held it up to his face. Every one froze in their tracks.

"Chris MacGregor here," he answered.

"Mr. MacGregor, this is Major Chen. I've been informed that you have borrowed property that belongs to the People's Liberation Army. Is that not correct?" he asked.

"Borrowed is a good word," Chris commented as David moved closer.

"I must congratulate you; your flying skills are more superior that we had first guessed. Our air defense forces didn't detect you until late yesterday, south of Sandouping. Then they lost you again. Very skillful maneuvering, I must admit. Obviously you didn't want to be located, but now I have found you," Major Chen said.

"If you have, then tell me where I am?" Chris asked.

"You are in the New Territories," Major Chen replied.

"Then the bird must have some triggering device that went off when we crossed the border," Chris assumed.

"Very good assumption, Mr. MacGregor. There is a detail of the People's Armed Police en route to secure your safety. Please wait for them at the highway so that you may be safely returned to your father's care while we look for your mother."

"No, my mother is in Hong Kong. Weren't you told that she called me? I talked to her and she must be in Hong Kong. Major, why aren't you here?" Chris demanded becoming agitated.

"Mr. MacGregor, my officers will meet you shortly. They will escort you safely to me. I am in Kowloon and await your arrival," he said and hung up.

Chris turned to everyone and looked around and then across the marsh.

"Major Chen, obviously. There are police who are going to pick us up on the road and take us to Kowloon where he's waiting. I don't think it's good," Chris informed.

"Hurry, let me have your phone," Tracy said and reached out for it. After a one minute conversation in Chinese, she turned to David.

"We need to move. If the police capture us, it could mean trouble. Better to be picked up at the British or American consulate or even the wildlife service. My cousin will meet us at the road in fifteen minutes. I estimate it is twenty or twenty-five minutes to the police headquarters for this region," Tracy said.

"Let's double time it, kids," Ginna said and started running through the swamp which was now only a few inches deep.

"Let's go," Chris added and fell in behind her.

The quarter mile jog to the road was tiring. The teenagers had not yet acclimated to the humidity and heat. Still dressed for the cold Tibetan highlands, they began to shed their layers of clothes as they ran through the grassy swamp.

"I love this coat, but it's getting wet and very heavy," Heather acknowledged.

"Take it off and drop it," Chris responded.

"It's down and brand new," Heather replied.

"I'll buy you a new one," Chris said beginning to pant as he ran.

"Gotcha," Heather rejoiced and tossed it to the side.

"My boots are full of water," R.O. said.

"Cut the complaining you guys," Chris said.

For the last two hundred yards everyone was at a near sprint. R.O. arrived at the highway just as a truck full of lettuce sped by on the left side of the road.

"They drive like in England," R.O. commented and leaned over and put his hands on his knees to catch his breath.

Tracy was next, followed by Chris, Natalie, and David. Ginna and Heather were last and walked up to the group on the side of the road. Everyone was panting and wishing they had a bottle of water.

R.O. sat down in the grass as a series of cars drove by. A Datsun truck drove up and honked once. It was a rusted yellow with wooden side panels on the bed. Tracy's cousin engaged the emergency brake and hopped out and started talking in a rushed tone to Tracy.

"Everyone get in the back. Hurry," Tracy said.

The group crept up into the back of the truck one by one while David pulled up the back panel.

"Pull the tarp over and lie down," Tracy stated.

"It smells like fish," Natalie said.

"He's in the bait business," Tracy reminded her.

Soon they were all lying down and Tracy covered them with a smelly tarp.

"I'm holding my breath," Natalie mumbled.

"Me too," R.O. joined in.

The trip to Tai Po took only twenty-five minutes. Exhausted from flying, Chris fell asleep.

"Oh my, he's exhausted," Tracy said.

"He deserves a power nap. He's worked hard the past two days," Ginna replied, pushing up the tarp to look at them.

Everyone was equally tired and hungry from the jog through the marsh. The old truck came to a squeaky halt and they heard the door on the driver's side open and slam shut. David began to peel back the tarp when Tracy appeared and pulled it off.

"Fresh air," Ginna said and the kids all had a comment.

Chris awoke when the door slammed.

"Did I go to sleep?" he asked Natalie.

"Yup. For about twenty minutes. Feel better?" she asked.

"I do, a little," Chris replied and stepped off the back of the truck onto the ground.

"My cousin tells me he has some rice and fish if you are hungry. I think we should eat before we decide what we do next," Tracy said.

David and Ginna walked up to Chris and Natalie.

"Have you thought about what you want to do next?" David asked Chris.

"I don't know for sure, but I've been thinking about calling my dad's cousin Geoffrey in London or maybe our friend Trader Jim in Alaska," Chris answered back.

"What can Jim do?" Heather asked as she walked up.

"He was in intelligence work before he bought the big trading post and hotel on Kodiak Island," Chris responded.

"I didn't know that," R.O. said.

"It was all super secret and Dad said he never talks about it," Chris added.

Chris walked away from the group and dialed several numbers on the small phone. Since it was an embassy telephone, it was equipped with international dialing capabilities. It rang several times.

"Jim Gailey," the voice said.

"Jim, this is Chris MacGregor."

"Chris, I didn't think I would hear from you guys for a while. How are the MacGregors in China? We sure miss you in Alaska," Jim said as he looked out his big office window, viewing the beautiful snow covered mountain range across Kodiak Island.

"Jim, I don't have much time, Mom has been kidnapped by two crime families in China. It has to do with black market dinosaur bones or panda poaching or something. We're not for sure. Do you have any contacts in American intelligence that can help us?"

Chris asked.

"I do. Where are you now?" Jim asked.

"We're at a bait shop near Kowloon," Chris replied.

"O.K. Keep your phone active and don't hang up. I'll be gone for a few minutes and then I'll get back on the line.

"Roger," Chris said and sat down in a wooden chair and stared at all the eyes on him.

Jim Gailey got up from his desk and walked across his expansive office to a wall that was decorated with seventeen wild animal trophies. Reaching up to a mounted head of a big horn sheep, he delicately twisted one of the horns. Part of the wall began to move forward and he stepped back. The opening was large enough for him to walk through. He entered into another much smaller room, which was equipped with wall-to-wall computers, radio sets, radar screens, and one fifty-two-inch monitor. He sat down in front of the radio equipment, and as he was typing information on the computer, the wall closed. Within seconds a beeping noise was emitted from the radio set. Jim keyed in the code for the radio scrambler and hit enter.

"Kodiak station here, code 1005-1110, over," Jim said into the mouthpiece.

"Hey, Jim, what's up?" the voice answered.

"Need some help. A friend, Dr. Mavis MacGregor, has been kidnapped in China. I need to see if I can get some information about the incident. What do you have?" Jim asked.

"Be back in sixty seconds," the voice replied.

There was exactly a sixty-second delay before the voice spoke again.

"Scotland Yard and MI6 are heading up this one. Three Brits involved. There's an intel squad on two Tai-Pans in Hong Kong. They think they know the rendezvous point for the Brits and the Tai-Pans. Looks like a trade or something.

That's all I could get. The American side of this has been pretty much blocked. But I can tell you this much, our man on the street says someone in the Chinese government is helping the kidnappers. That's the only tip they would give me. You know, the old 'I owe you one' didn't work," the voice informed. "Scotland Yard has warned the company to stay out of it from the get-go."

"Well, if that's all you can get," Jim said.

"Anything on the South Korean fishing fleet movement through your waters?" the voice asked.

"Not much. They've been into port twice with a pretty good catch. No foreign nationals left ashore. They paid in U.S. currency for supplies and fuel," Jim said. "It's a shame we have to keep track of allies like this."

"I know, but the saying is true, keep your friends close and your enemies closer," the voice said. "That's where you come in; watch anything that floats by Kodiak Island. We don't know who our friends are any more. Got to go."

"Thanks, I'll check in tomorrow with more details on the fleet," Jim stated and turned off the radio.

He opened the wall and walked back to his desk and picked up the phone.

"Chris," Jim said.

"I'm here," Chris replied.

"Make your way to the British consulate. Try to find their MI6 chief of station. That's your best hope for getting close to the men who took your mother. They know more than I would have time to tell you," Jim said. "Tell your dad I'm thinking about all of you and be careful, son. These people are killers."

"That's what I'm afraid of," Chris said. "Thanks, Jim, goodbye."

"Goodbye, Chris."

Jim walked back into his secret room and sat down at a computer terminal. After he punched in several words and numbers, a map of Kowloon-Hong Kong appeared on the screen with a flashing arrow at 25.5° N, 114.7° E. He then typed in the cell phone number and pressed the return key. The trace had worked and the coordinates were sent to CIA headquarters in Langley, Virginia.

"Tai Po on Tai Poi bay. Hang in there, Chris. I'm trying to send you some help," Jim said out loud.

A few seconds later another screen appeared with the words "received" in the middle. Knowing that was all he could do, he shut down the computers and walked back into his big trading post and sat down. He gazed out the window with a frown on his face.

Chris informed everyone what CIA agent Jim Gaily had said and what his fears were.

"Chris, we're walking on thin ice now. If Ginna and I are arrested by the army, we could be charged with espionage. We're going to have to stay with Tracy and report with her to the army base. She can cover for our trip south and the crashed helicopter, after that our hands are tied," David said.

Tracy nodded in agreement.

"I understand. Just get Tracy's cousin to loan us his truck or have him take us into Hong Kong. From there we can make it to the British consulate on our own," Chris suggested.

"That's no problem. He can probably take you to the train station at Sha Tin. It's a short ride to Victoria Harbor. There you can catch the Star Ferry across to Hong Kong or you can stay on the train and cross the Harbor. The first stop is Harcourt Station. Get off there and find your way to the Consulate General. It's on the corner of Supreme Court Road and Justice Drive," Tracy said.

"How do you know all of this?" Heather asked with an amazed look on her face.

"My first army post was in Kowloon. I know the area well," Tracy replied.

"We better get going," Chris stated as he stepped forward and gave Tracy a hug. "We couldn't have done it without you. We'll forever owe you."

"I will come see you in Texas some day. Be safe."

She reached down the front of her fatigues and withdrew a circular piece of jade hanging on a gold chain. She carefully pulled it over her head and leaned forward and placed it over Chris's head.

"This will bring you luck and keep the good spirits with you," she said.

Chris hugged her again.

"Thank you, Yen Hwa Yu," Chris said.

Likewise, David and Ginna said their farewells, complementing Chris again for his helicopter piloting.

"You really helped us out in Wolong, Chris," David said.

The kids hugged Tracy, David, and Ginna and got back in the smelly truck. The ride was bumpy in the old Datsun, but they soon arrived at the train station. Tracy's cousin couldn't speak English, so he just waved goodbye and pointed to the station.

"Chris, do you know how to do this?" Heather asked as they walked up to the station with dozens of other people, all Chinese.

"No, but we'll figure it out," Chris replied.

As they approached the ticket window, Chris checked his billfold for cash and realized he only had American money. He noticed a well-dressed lady pay for her ticket with a credit card and laid his on the counter when she had finished. He held up four fingers and said "Harcourt Station." The older lady behind the caged window never spoke and pushed the button for four tickets. The machine spit out four tickets as if they were attending a Saturday movie matinee back home in Dallas.

"Hey, that was cool," R.O. commented as they walked away.

"Now, we have to find the right train," Natalie said.

"I think they all go to Hong Kong and then circle back," Chris said. "Like the tube in London. You just get off and on when you want, if you have the right ticket."

The next train roared into the station and slowed to a halt. Everyone quickly jumped aboard, and the doors began to close.

"What are you doing?" Heather asked R.O., who was looking up as he jumped on.

"I'm waiting for the recording that says 'Mind the Gap,'" he responded.

"That's in London, silly," Natalie laughed.

"Oh yeah," R.O. said and reddened a little.

The train moved out of the station and began to head south for Hong Kong.

The duct tape was removed from the mouths of Mavis, Nigel, and Julian and their arms were freed just as the plane stopped on the tarmac.

"Thank you," Mavis said and immediately reached up to her swollen face. She wanted to close her mouth but her teeth and jaw hurt too much. "Oh my," she thought as she tried to rub her swollen hand. "You've got a nice infection going there."

"Get up," the guard ordered and waved an automatic rifle in her face.

The three scientists were herded through the aisle of the aircraft and down a stair-ramp to a waiting van. They all were stiff from not being allowed to move for several hours. Mavis squinted when the sun hit her eyes. She reached for the van's handrail but couldn't grip it with her swollen hand. Changing hands, she stepped in sideways and sat down next to Julian. The side door was closed, and they were surprised that they weren't blindfolded or manacled again. Mavis looked out at the spectacular view of the high-rise buildings that lined Victoria Harbor and at all the earth moving equipment that was there trying to reclaim land from the sea.

"Jack would hate to see this," she whispered. "So much ecological ruin for simply more concrete and steel."

"You are a woman of strength," Julian stated. "To think

of such a high calling as saving the environment at a time like this shows your own level of personal security and integrity. Very admirable, Mavis."

"Thanks, Julian. Just a thought that crossed my mind," Mavis responded.

"No talk or I hit," a voice from behind them said.

They just nodded and stopped talking.

As the train whisked across Victoria Harbor, Chris looked out at the masses of buildings and people.

"You're out there somewhere, Mom, and we're going to find you. Somehow, we're going to do it," Chris said softly.

Natalie heard him and took his right hand and pushed up against him.

"We will," she said.

17

Hong Kong

A small "cherry picker" crane unloaded one large crate after the next from the trucks that filled the warehouse. After it had unloaded thirty-seven crates, each the size of a Mini Cooper, the crane's tracks began to move, and it positioned itself beside a rail car that was being opened like a can of sardines by the overhead crane. Four men hooked up cables to the ton of rock in the container and it began to lift. Slowly at first and then gaining speed, it lifted the *Caudipteryx zoui* and its associated rock layers carefully from the truck and onto a steel platform to be properly packed for shipment overseas. Once the chains and cable had been moved back, all of the foam packing was removed to double-check for damage and to prepare it for the private auction that would soon occur. Dozens of men began scurrying around unpacking crates and setting out fossils on long display tables as if there were going to be a convention of fossil lovers and buyers.

"Tai-Pan," a worker said to a man in a black, silk suit and yellow tie.

"Yes," Sen Li replied.

"The work is nearly complete. "What are your orders?" the anxious man asked.

"Tell your people to go home and not to come back until tomorrow at dawn," Sen Li said.

"Very good, sir," the man said and bowed deeply before running to the others and telling them the new orders.

Within minutes everyone had left and the warehouse became quiet. Sen Li was the only person there. A ship's horn vibrated through the steel building from across the harbor. He walked over to the *Caudipteryx zoui* and touched it with his right hand. The garage door on the east side of the warehouse began to open and a black Mercedes drove in and stopped at the feathered dinosaur fossil. Two white vans followed it. Two men got out of the Mercedes and joined Sen Li next to the rare fossil.

Four men got out of each van. The side doors were opened and sitting in each vehicle was a metal cage with a giant panda inside.

"Ku Jong Wu. It's good to see you," Sen Li said. "Our trade with Chang seemed to take a turn for the worse. "Did you get the MacGregor woman back?"

"Yes, Chang was most disagreeable. We had to kill several of his operatives and destroy a junk, but we secured Dr. MacGregor and her British colleagues. We should have never made the trade in the first place," responded Ku Jong Wu.

"I agree," Li replied. "But there was no way to know of her connection to Geoffrey MacGregor and Scotland Yard. Once we learned that valuable bit of information, we had to get her back. My men arrived just in time; she was floating in the South China Sea."

"She was in the sea? Chang is an idiot. He doesn't deserve to run his family business," Wu said. "We will have to eliminate Chang soon and absorb his assets into ours. The time has come. Chang would have never integrated well into our secret society. He is not worthy to wear the *sign of the dragon*."

"So when does the auction begin?" Sen Li asked.

"Tonight, at ten. While we are waiting I will bring the three Brits to you to learn what they know," Ku Jong Wu said and looked at his watch. "In fact they should be here any minute. I am also waiting for a shipment of elephant ivory from Tanzania and Kenya."

"I thought the East African nations had confiscated all of the available ivory," Li said.

"Our contacts have been storing it in safe places in Dar es Salaam and Mombasa. Gold still speaks loudly around the world," Wu said and smiled.

A few minutes later another white delivery van came through the garage door. It drove up to the black Mercedes and stopped. Two men opened the side doors and reached for Mavis, Nigel, and Julian. Nigel grabbed Mavis and braced her for her exit from the van. Julian stepped out last. There was no tape, no black bags, and no steel manacles. The three Brits were weak and had been punished into submission. Mavis walked over to the feathered dinosaur fossil and stood in front of Sen Li. She lifted her blood-dried hand and touched the feathered dinosaur fossil.

"A magnificent animal, wasn't she?" Mavis asked.

"Yes, and she still is. She represents so much more than you know. As the ancestor of our sacred dragons, the Tienlong, she is a symbol of power. Dr. MacGregor, Westerners don't understand that when I exchange her for money or gold, I'm not making a simple business transaction; I'm entering into a life-long relationship with another Tai-Pan. Our fossilized dragon is our bond. No one will come between us, and our houses will grow forever," Sen Li said.

"You're right, I don't understand," Mavis replied. "And those beautiful animals in the cages?" She asked looking at the wide-eyed giant pandas. "Are you going to sell them too?"

"But alas, Dr. MacGregor, free enterprise says that these animals, dead or alive, will reside with the highest bidder," Ku Jong Wu responded.

"That's very sad, "Mavis answered back.

"So what shall I exchange you for?" Sen Li asked and looked straight into her bruised face and black eye.

"I'm not worth much, but I wouldn't call twenty million for the prize dinosaur cheap. You know she's really not worth more than eight or ten million. But I'm just a paleontologist who likes rocks. What do I know?" Mavis retorted.

"Yes, eight or ten to the normal public. But my clients have special talents and special needs and twenty million is simply the cost of a piece of real estate to them," Wu said.

"Would you mind if I looked over *your* collection before we are shuffled off to another boat, airplane, or warehouse?"

"Not at all," he replied. "Help yourselves. All three of you are invited."

Nigel was the first to reach the row of tables. He carefully picked up a fossil that had been broken into three pieces.

"Those imbeciles," Nigel said.

"I agree," Julian added as he walked up. "I don't know how the buyers are going to appreciate anything if it is all in pieces?"

"It could be because half of them are forgeries, don't you think?" Mavis asked as she arrived at the table.

"They're very good if they are forgeries, Mave," Nigel replied.

"I see where you're going with this, Mavis," Julian said. "They shop all the broken and damaged goods and then bring out the few fossils that survived, which are forgeries and immediately get a higher price."

"A nice little bait-and-switch routine. However, someday an expert will reveal they bought just rocks," Nigel said and set a fossil down on the table.

"I doubt it. They want to keep it for themselves and so experts are never called. Just like art forgeries and private collectors. Real pieces go underground for decades until the collector dies and the family sells the work only to find out it was a forgery," Mavis said and picked up another piece. "My gosh, they've got enough parts here for a dozen animals. Nigel, did you discover any of these?" Mavis asked.

"I recognize a few pieces. The Chinese company supervised us closely where they could and controlled the pieces from the field all the way back to the warehouses. The Chinese university scientists and the geology ministry people were very good and quite respectable, but they were kept on projects out west looking for Cretaceous era birds and such. I think the government has clean hands on these. It's the private contractors who couldn't be trusted. While we were in Mongolia, we flew the pieces to London to be safe," he said.

"Julian, look at this," Mavis whispered and held a rock in her hand.

"My gosh, Mavis. Don't tell me that's what I am actually looking at," Julian said.

"Julian, ole' boy, you are looking at flight feathers," Nigel said with a wide grin on his face.

"Flight feathers," Mavis said and started picking up fossils from all over the table. "Dozens of flight feathers."

"They didn't come from Mongolia or Manchuria. The rock is different. Reminds me of western China, Xinjiang Province maybe," Nigel said.

"Nigel, I'm beside myself. This could be a major discovery. None of the Chinese dinosaurs could fly," Mavis exclaimed. "Until now!"

"Until now," Julian said. "We need a few months to go over every piece in this warehouse. We need to find their origin. Then we need to catalog and start putting the puzzle together. We may have a flying dinosaur right here in front of us."

"I'm getting sick to my stomach just thinking about it," Mavis replied. "What a discovery and here we are prisoners who may not be alive by midnight. I miss my family."

The sobering thought caused all the scientists to lay the fossils back on the tables and turn to look at each other.

"Your time is up," Sen Li said. "Please come back to the van. You're taking another ride."

"This is it, Harcourt Station," Natalie said.

The four teenagers stepped from the train with the masses of people arriving for a day's work on Hong Kong Island. The kids still dressed in the outdoor gear they were wearing in Wolong, immediately stepped into the shadows of the tall buildings and looked around at all the busy people.

"Chris, I know we've got to keep moving, but sooner or later Major Chen is going to have an alert out for us with pictures and descriptions. Wearing these clothes will only increase the prospects of getting picked up. We really stand out," Natalie said.

"I agree, Chris," Heather followed.

"Alright. We stop at the first clothing store and buy new clothes," Chris responded.

"I could use a bath, too," Heather added, pushing her grimy blonde hair behind her ears. "My hair is nasty, even for my scrunchie."

"O.K. One hour, that's all the time we'll take. Just one hour," Chris said.

Natalie and Heather gave each other a high-five and smiled.

"I'm fine the way I am," R.O. said.

"No, you smell like fish, too," Natalie replied.

"Let me grab this cab and we'll see," Chris said.

A taxi pulled to the curb and the group piled in.

"Take us to a place where we can buy clothes and take showers," Chris said slowly.

"I know about fifty such places," the cab driver joked in perfect English and pulled away from the curb. "You guys are smelling up my taxi."

Ten minutes later, the kids were delivered to the front of a high-rise shopping mall.

"Inside you will find bath houses, shops, restaurants, banks, it's all there," the cab driver said.

Chris took out his emergency roll of American money and paid the cab driver.

"Clothes first, then baths. We meet back here in one hour," Chris said. "R.O.'s with me."

"Roger, big bro," Heather replied with a smile on her face.

Natalie waved at him and then spoke.

"Scrub hard, you really smell bad," she laughed and smiled.

"Point taken," Chris replied as the girls walked away. "O.K., let's go find those showers."

One hour later Chris was sitting on a bench next to a fountain when Natalie and Heather walked up in new clothes that were neatly pressed.

"How did that happen?" R.O. asked.

"And all that in sixty minutes?" Chris asked.

"Chris, we took a quick shower and put on these clothes as fast as we could," Heather said.

"And all for just fifty dollars each," Natalie added quietly.

"That's a bargain?" Chris asked. "How'd you pay for it?"

"Your credit card," replied Heather.

"How'd you get that?" Chris demanded as he stood up.

"Just kidding. I used mine," Natalie said and smiled.

"I'll get some money from dad and pay Natalie back later," Heather said.

"Now, let's get back to work," Chris stated and his telephone rang.

"Chris here," he answered.

"Mr. MacGregor, I'm very disappointed that you didn't wait for us on the road to Tai Po. We could have you on your way to see you father at this very moment," Major Chen said.

"But that's the point, Major. My mother is not in Beijing. She's got to be in Hong Kong. Don't you see that?" Chris questioned.

"All I see, Mr. MacGregor, is a foolish young man trying to do advanced police work. Stay where you are and I'll have a car pick you up in three minutes," Major Chen voiced.

Chris immediately turned off the phone.

"He was tracking us with the phone. I'd dump it but it's the only number mom has. We've got to get moving. At least we blend in with the tourists now," Chris said.

"Except for R.O.'s smelly back pack. Does a lot of good to get a new shirt and new jeans and keep the old back pack," Heather said and jerked it from his shoulder.

R.O. pulled back and it ripped in half, spilling the contents onto the sidewalk. Out came an old Dallas Cowboys T-shirt, the motor from the hotel blender, several assorted rocks, another half-eaten PayDay candy bar, and an old stuffed sock. R.O. frantically started grabbing for his precious belongings when Chris picked up the stuffed sock and held it out in front of him. R.O. stood paralyzed, holding nearly everything that had fallen with the electric cord reaching to the ground.

Chris carefully tilted the sock over and slowly poured the contents into his right hand. As the head of the small gold Buddha hit the sun, bright shards of light filled the air and bounced all around the kids.

"Oh my, gosh," Heather said. "You took the Buddha."

"We're dead," said Natalie.

"I, I, went back and got it as you all climbed on the stage and into the tunnel. I thought I could use it. It had been there for thousands of years, and nobody wanted it anymore. I didn't think anyone would mind," R.O. said in his defense.

Chris carefully slid the Buddha back into the sock and out of sight and knelt down in front of R.O.

"You did good, little buddy. I'm going to use this chunk of gold to buy our mother back," Chris proclaimed.

R.O. jumped forward and put his arms around Chris's neck. Heather started crying again and Natalie hugged her.

"O.K., let's get some food, and then I need to try to contact organized crime leaders on Hong Kong Island. We'll start at the British Consulate General. How about Chinese food?"

"No," everyone cried in unison as they wiped their tears.

One hour later they walked into the new, shiny British Consulate General building and up to the information desk.

"May I help you?" the young lady asked in a British accent.

"She sounds just like Mom," R.O. said to Heather.

"My name is Chris MacGregor. My second cousin is Geoffrey MacGregor and he works for Scotland Yard. I want to talk to someone with MI6. It's a national emergency."

The young lady looked up at him and then at the other kids and spoke into her headset.

"Mr. Alexander, this is the operator. I have a Mr. Chris MacGregor standing in front of me with his brother and sisters," she said.

"He's here now?" Alexander asked.

"Yes, sir. Just three feet from me," she answered.

"Tell him I am coming to him now," Alexander said and hung up.

He leapt from his chair and hurried to his outer office to call for security personnel.

"Sergeant, notify security that there are four kids at the front desk. Don't move on them unless they try to leave. If they try, arrest them and hold them for me. I'm on my way down," Alexander barked. In the old building, he thought, he could just walk down the hall, but now he had to change elevators and run across the building, just one more wish to be 007.

The white van drove through the basement-level parking garage and pulled up to the elevator doors. Mavis, Nigel, and Julian were guided to the elevator. Sen Li followed right behind in his Mercedes and stepped out. He retrieved a key from his pocket and put it in the key slot and turned it to the right. The elevator doors opened and they all stepped inside. One man still held a gun in plain sight, aimed at Mavis' stomach. The elevator began to rise and the ride to the nineteenth floor of the Apex building went smooth and quickly. The doors opened and Mavis was nudged with the gun. As she, Nigel, and Julian stepped out, another elevator door opened. Ku Jong Wu entered the room followed by a man whom Mavis couldn't see. She turned to be sure her friends were still with her, always fearing they would be separated. Then she heard his voice.

"Dr. MacGregor, you should have listened to me in Beijing," the man said.

She turned and her jaw dropped, jolting her face with more pain. She felt ill all over.

"Major Chen," she stuttered and swallowed. After breathing in deep she continued. "I assume you haven't come to rescue us."

"Good guess, Dr. MacGregor," Chen said and walked up to her.

"What started as an innocent trip to be with your friends turned out to be quite the spider's web for you, Mavis, if I may," he said. "You have unfortunately become the unwitting pawn in a struggle between two ancient and great families in China."

He circled around her.

"One family does the little things like smuggle drugs and contraband of all sorts to America, while the other has its eyes on the control of China and domination of the East."

"Alliances," Mavis said.

"You catch on fast or my partners talk too much," Chen said.

"Partners. I thought you were the boss, or what's the word, Tai-Pan?" Mavis asked.

"Tai-Pan, I am. It's my birthright and it was stolen from my grandfather by the Changs, and I intend to take it back and all of China with it," Chen said. "My family is heir to a great tradition, Dr. MacGregor. Royal blood flows through my veins and the Tienlong watch over my family," Chen responded.

"The celestial or heavenly dragon?" Mavis asked slowly.

"What Westerners dismiss as folklore and mythology because of their ignorance, Chinese revere as holy and sacred," Chen replied. "It is by this sign that we will again control China." Chen pulled up his sleeve and revealed a tattoo of a circle with the five claws of the celestial dragon wrapped around it. "The *sign of the dragon.*"

"I see. Then why don't you take the dinosaurs, the contraband, the drugs, and just let us go. I'm an American citizen and they're British. We're all scientists. We have no interest in your politics," she insisted.

"Unfortunately you have become a bargaining chip for information that we need from the British. They must think we are amateurs because we asked for some intelligence that would be impossible to acquire from just anyone. But you see, we started there and then we intend to ask for less, but what we ask for will be strategic to our cause in Beijing," Chen said and stopped in front of her.

"Beijing. You don't think you can overthrow the government, do you? You must be insane," Mavis questioned.

Chen moved close to her.

"I'm not insane, Doctor. My network within the government includes several officers in charge of the People's Armed Police, People's Liberation Army, and three civilian ministries. No one would have expected a lowly major to lead this coup d'état. With half the Tai-Pans in Hong Kong on my side, we will control the economy of China. We will gain power and never fire a shot, except into the heads of certain people, of course," he informed and walked away from her.

"And how do we help you? We're an accident. We should have never been in the equation," she asked.

"You will earn us a new ally. We will coerce the United States and Great Britain to simply look the other way. For the safe return of the wife of a famous scientist and a whole team of world-renowned scientists, the Americans and British won't have to negotiate a thing. They don't want to help Communist China anyway. They would welcome new leadership in Beijing," Chen answered. "They will think the businessmen of China are behind this change of government. They will hold press conferences hailing it as the new China. Then one year later after they have lowered their defenses, written new treaties, given us loans, and ships and aircraft, they will learn who is in control. Then it will be too late. Our military will be greater, their's weaker. China will negotiate from power. We will emerge as the new world power with nuclear weapons to back us up and an economic alliance with the West that can't be broken."

"What? Trading one dictatorship for another?" Mavis asked.

"Mavis," Julian interrupted.

"You make your friends nervous, Doctor. I now see why you are so bruised and bloody," Chen added. "Take them to the holding room. Give them some water but no food."

"But what if America and England tell you to go to hell," Mavis yelled as she was being led away.

"Then, Dr. MacGregor, you will go there ahead of me, at eight tomorrow morning. Sleep tight." Chen fired back and smiled.

Chen walked over to Sen Li and Ku Jong Wu. "Gentlemen, we are hours away from the beginning of a new era." Chen said. "This century will belong to China."

18

Secret Intelligence Service
MI6

Chris, Natalie, Heather, and R.O. wandered around the expansive lobby of the British Consulate General of Hong Kong as if they were waiting for a number to be called at a fast food restaurant. For having traveled over a thousand miles in two days in the Bell 412, they seemed little worse for wear with their new clothes. Chris had found a safari vest like the one he wore in Africa, which was sitting inside his luggage at the American embassy in Beijing.

R.O.'s T-shirt sported a colorful dragon that was magically dancing on a cloud. After spotting a *year of the dragon chart* in the shop, a salesperson had explained that his birthday coincided with the year of the Earth dragon, 1988. He had not stopped talking about it. Chris was now carrying the sacred Buddha in a new backpack that he had bought and slung over one shoulder and across his chest. He had also purchased a pair of Zeiss binoculars and a red cap.

John Alexander exited the elevator as fast as he could and scurried across the marble floor to where the kids were standing. They turned and watched as the middle-aged man hurriedly walked toward them. They noticed that his white suit seemed out of season and that he was constantly tugging at his belt to pull up his pants.

"John Alexander," he said as he reached them.

"Chris MacGregor. This is my friend Natalie Crosswhite, my sister Heather, and my brother Ryan," Chris said. "We call him R.O."

"It's indeed a pleasure to meet the family of Jack and Mavis MacGregor. Please come with me and I'll get some refreshments for you," Mr. Alexander said.

"That would be good. We haven't eaten today," Chris said.

"Then let me call ahead so that things will be in preparation," Mr. Alexander replied and pulled out his cell phone. "Alexander here. Please set a table of food for our four guests. Yes, the Albert Room will do nicely."

"Let's be off. Our new building is like a small city," he said.

"It's beautiful. The angle with the perimeter in glass is absolutely amazing," Natalie commented. "Forty-five degrees is it?"

"Exactly. Very good Miss Crosswhite," he said. "This way please."

A few minutes later they were walking into a room where a cart covered with a white sheet had just been dropped off. It looked more like a living room than an office. The carpet was a deep, plush burgundy and a portrait of Prince Albert dressed in his military uniform hung on the wall. Mr. Alexander walked over and lifted the sheet. There was sliced roast beef, ham, and chicken all neatly stacked and arranged. Three loaves of different kinds of breads were there along with jars of mustard, mayonnaise, horseradish, and jam. Another tray was covered with pickles, olives, baby carrots, lettuce, and bright red, sliced tomatoes.

"I've ordered some ice water, American soda, and tea for you to drink," he added.

"I'm impressed," Heather said.

"Don't forget, this is Her Majesty's Secret Service," Mr. Alexander said with pride in his voice.

Mr. Alexander sat down and everyone began to prepare a sandwich. A man dressed in kitchen attire pushed in a cart full of drinks, and after he had left, Chris walked over next to Mr. Alexander.

"I want to talk to my dad's cousin, Geoffrey MacGregor. I believe he has some information that will lead us to my mother and her friends," Chris said.

"My dear boy, SIS is in on it more than you can imagine. We know where they will be at exactly ten o'clock tonight. We have intelligence assets in the competing Tai-Pans' organizations and on the street. We have eyes in the sky following the movement of several key players. Your father's cousin is monitoring numerous other sources of communication from Scotland Yard in London," Mr. Alexander said from the comfortable leather chair.

"So you know where she will be?" Chris asked.

"Of course we do. I may look like someone's grandfather, and I am, but we are a lean and mean operation, to use some of your American vernacular," Mr. Alexander responded.

"I see. Of course, you couldn't tell me where she is, could you?" Chris asked losing his appetite and setting the plate of food down on the seat of a chair.

"I could since you aren't leaving this building until she is free. But it's best not to bother you with the details. You will see her soon enough," Mr. Alexander replied.

"But how will you know they will let her go? I mean, they're criminals and that makes them liars," Chris asked and moved closer.

Mr. Alexander got up and straightened his white jacket and black tie. He walked over to the refreshment cart and picked up a bottle of water and opened it. After a long swig he screwed the lid back on and turned to Chris.

"Most everyone that I deal with outside of this building is a liar, Mr. MacGregor. However, there is a certain honor among informants and people like myself. There has to be a certain level of trust. If what I am told doesn't happen, then the informant knows that he or she won't get my money. Money is what they want. They care for no one but themselves," Mr. Alexander answered back.

"So where is she?" Chris persisted.

"Come with me," Mr. Alexander said. "Kids, Chris and I are going to take a walk. You simply relax, turn on the television, and eat lots of the Queen's food. We'll be back before you know it."

"Can I come?" R.O. asked.

"No. Why don't you go send Drew an e-mail. You haven't done that this trip. Is that computer O.K. to use?" Chris asked.

"Most definitely. It's here for guests to communicate with whomever they choose," replied Mr. Alexander.

Chris followed Mr. Alexander out into the near sterile hallway and through several connectors until they reached a room that required a security check. After producing a key card, palm print check, and voice analysis, Chris followed Mr. Alexander into the darkened room that was full of flat panel computer monitors and three eighty-inch plasma monitors.

"This is one of our satellite monitoring rooms, Chris," Mr. Alexander informed.

Chris was speechless. Mr. Alexander led him over to one of the eighty-inch monitors.

"Lieutenant. Would you play the tape of the airport transfer of Dr. MacGregor and her friends, please," he commanded politely.

Within seconds, the screen was activated and came alive with three people walking from a Beech King Air and stepping into a white van. The screen then cut to a scene showing the white van pulling into a warehouse on the wharf on the east side of Hong Kong. Chris noticed a shiny glass building just across the inlet next to the warehouse. The white van drove through a garage door that opened as it approached.

"Was that my mom?" Chris asked.

"Yes, it was. Our intelligence has told us that at ten o'clock tonight a private auction will be held in that warehouse to sell dinosaur bones, one in particular being a rare and complete feathered dinosaur," Mr. Alexander answered back. "We've also been tracking illegal ivory from East Africa through India to Hong Kong for six months. The Indians tipped us off. Our analysts suggest that it's all part of funding a new crime family."

"That's why she went to Shenyang, I'm sure. She had given up all of that for our family," voiced Chris.

"And it's obvious to me that it was well worth it," Alexander said.

"How will you get them out?" Chris asked and looked back at the replay of the film.

"We have highly trained specialists who are planning the rescue at this moment. Within two hours they will penetrate the warehouse and lay in waiting for the meeting. We will extract your mother and her friends and then drop the hammer on the people who are there. We can't arrest them because we don't control Hong Kong any longer. But we can inflict some casualties that will take them months or even years to repair and replace," he said.

"Sounds efficient. Is there any way I can talk to Geoffrey?" Chris asked.

"Well, let me see . . . it's about two in the morning. He'll probably be off duty by now but we can try," Mr. Alexander said.

"Lieutenant, please take care of Mr. MacGregor's call and then usher him back to me in the Albert Room. Thank you. Chris, see you in a moment," he said and walked out of the room.

The naval officer dialed a number without taking off her headset and then turned to Chris.

"Mr. Geoffrey MacGregor is on the line. Please use the green headset over there and I'll connect you," she said.

"Thanks," Chris said and walked over to another console and put on the headset.

"Chris," Geoffrey said.

"Hi, Geoffrey," Chris replied.

"How are you holding up?" Geoffrey asked.

"We're doing good. I'm just really anxious about all of this. Have you talked to Dad?" Chris asked.

"Yes, about five hours ago. I've been grabbing little naps until we get your mom home," Geoffrey replied.

"Do you think I should call him?" Chris asked.

"No, the People's Armed Police have kept him informed of your whereabouts. He was pretty freaked when he found out you flew a helicopter across China. Man, you are something else. I don't know many secret agents that could have pulled that off," Geoffrey boasted trying to keep Chris distracted about his mother.

"I couldn't have done it without Tracy and David," Chris said.

"Tracy and David. Who are they?" Geoffrey asked.

"Tracy is Yen Hwa Yu, a Chinese wildlife biologist, and David Bloom is a former secret service agent under the vice president," Chris said.

"I'm impressed. You travel in tall company, Chris. I can see how you made it to Hong Kong in an army helicopter. You know you are destined to come work with me some-day in London at Scotland Yard," Geoffrey said.

"That would be nice. Geoffrey . . . " Chris said changing the subject. "Do you think they're going to get Mom out alive?"

There was a pause, too long for Chris.

"Chris . . ."

"No, you paused too long. What are you keeping from me, Geoffrey?" Chris asked.

"I'm not hiding anything from you. There are so many little details about all of this and it would just burden you even more. Trust me, we're doing everything possible to get your mother back," Geoffrey responded.

"O.K., I'll trust you. Please keep me informed," Chris said.

"You got it. Take care of your brother and sister. They need you right now," Geoffrey said.

"I will. Goodbye," Chris replied.

Geoffrey MacGregor hung up.

"Lieutenant, could I see the film of my mother again?" Chris asked politely. "I haven't seen her in a week or so."

"I can't see what harm that could do," she said and then looked back at Chris a second time. "How old are you, if I may ask?"

"Eighteen," Chris replied.

"I see," the young female lieutenant said raising her eyebrows. "Here's the film coming up now."

As the film ran from beginning to end, Chris studied it carefully, memorizing every single detail.

"Thank you," he said.

"You're welcome, Mr. MacGregor," she said and smiled as he left.

A young ensign was waiting outside the door for Chris as he stepped through.

"I'm your escort to the Albert Room," she said.

"Thank you," Chris replied.

Back in the Albert Room with the rest of the kids, his mind began formulating an escape plan.

"Please get Dr. MacGregor and bring her to me," Ku Jong Wu said to one of his men as he stepped out of the Mercedes. He made his way up to the nineteenth floor and entered into a luxurious suite.

Four minutes later, a man was practically dragging Mavis across the floor. She could barely stand up when she reached Mr. Wu.

"Dr. MacGregor, you look ill," he commented.

"I have an infection in my hand and I think it has spread to the rest of my body," she said weakly.

She was sweating with a fever and looked pale. The

bruises on her face had darkened, and her hand was continuing to swell. Her fingers were unable to bend.

"Dr. MacGregor, I am taking your colleagues back to the warehouse. My partner will stay for the sale tonight and your friends will be asked to render professional opinions, knowing that if they fail to support my fossils as authentic, you will be killed. Is that clear?" he asked.

"I'm sure they will be helpful," Mavis replied, blinking her eyes several times.

"Put them in the car," he said to his men.

"I need an antibiotic. I'm worthless to you dead," Mavis forcefully pleaded.

"In twelve hours it won't matter anyway," Wu answered back.

"Lock her back up," Wu ordered and walked to the elevator.

Chris drank another bottle of water and downed a piece of roast beef. He knew he was going to need his strength.

"R.O., may I look in your backpack?" Chris asked and picked up his and walked over to Ryan's.

"Sure. Don't bother me, I found some games," R.O. replied from the computer station. "And Drew says hey."

"Say hey back," Chris said and started digging.

He transferred a small flashlight, a hiking utility belt, field knife, and cigarette lighter to his pack. He retrieved the gold Buddha and then zipped up the back pack. He walked over to Natalie and sat down.

"Natalie. I'm going out for awhile," Chris said.

"Not without me, you aren't," she responded barely whispering.

"I've got to go find Mom. I talked to Geoffrey and she might not make it through this tonight," he said.

"If you go, I'm going too. Heather's almost asleep and Ryan's occupied. We should walk out now," she said.

"Let's go," Chris whispered back to her.

"Hey, Ryan, we're going out to the fountain to talk," Chris said.

"O.K.," Ryan answered back and kept on playing the game.

Chris and Natalie left the Albert Room and walked down the hall toward the elevator. When they got to the elevator they realized there weren't any buttons, only keyholes and slots for card keys.

"What now?" Natalie asked just as the doors opened.

Chris stepped in and pretended he had just put something in his pocket. The two people in the elevator barely noticed over the stacks of files they were holding. He pushed the button for the lobby and when the doors opened they stepped out casually and confidently, talking about getting a bite to eat.

"Those files are about to drive me crazy," Natalie mentioned as she walked by the new receptionist.

"I'll help you tomorrow after I finish my case load," Chris said, playing along.

As they stepped out of the building, two British marines looked them over carefully. Chris and Natalie just smiled and held hands tightly. Once they turned the corner and were out of sight, they began to run and didn't stop for nearly two blocks.

"We've got to get to a computer," Chris said.

"Look, there, a Qantas Airways' office. I bet they have one," Natalie pointed out.

In a few minutes, they were inside the office.

"May I help you?" the young lady asked with an Australian accent.

"Do you have a computer we can use? I'm looking for a virtual tour of Hong Kong before I book our flight back to Sydney and then to Hamilton, New Zealand," responded Chris.

"We have a complimentary one, and then I can help you with your tickets," she said.

"Great, thanks," Natalie replied.

For the next thirty minutes Chris searched every virtual tour of Hong Kong and Kowloon with no luck. He leaned back in the chair and could barely speak. His heart was in his throat.

"I can't find it," he said quietly.

"Excuse me, we're closing. Can I help you with your tickets now?" the young lady asked.

"No, we're leaving," Chris answered back and stood up.

"If you're looking for a tour of the city, I have some beautiful brochures you may have," she said and walked over and handed them to Natalie.

"Thanks," Natalie said.

"Americans?" she asked.

"Yes," Natalie acknowledged.

"Come see me tomorrow for your bookings. I open at nine in the morning," she said and escorted them to the door.

"She was very nice," Natalie commented and opened her new purse to put the tour brochures inside.

Chris was looking at the sidewalk when out of the corner of his eye the cover of one of the brochures caught his attention.

"Let me see that," he said and yanked it from her hand.

"You nearly gave me a paper cut," Natalie fussed.

"This is it," Chris exclaimed and pointed to the cover showing the architecture of the beautiful glass building on the wharf.

"Taxi," he yelled at three passing taxis. The last one stopped.

"Take us here," he said and pointed to the picture.

The cab driver nodded and put it in gear and drove away from the curb. Twelve minutes later he was pulling up in front of the beautiful glass opera house and theater.

After paying the driver in American dollars, they hurried over to the rail overlooking the harbor. Chris came to an abrupt halt.

"There it is. That's the warehouse where she's at," Chris said.

"It's still early, Chris. What time was the auction you were telling me about?" Natalie asked.

"Ten. Right at ten," Chris replied. "But if Geoffrey's right, then MI6 teams should be arriving any minute or are already here. I want to get closer."

"But what can we do?" Natalie asked.

"I'm thinking about that," Chris responded and took her hand and began to walk normally. They walked around to the end of the wharf near a flower garden.

When they had covered half the distance, Chris led Natalie into the garden among a stand of trees. He opened his pack and took out the Zeiss binoculars. He started scanning the area around the warehouse and couldn't see any activity except for some repairmen replacing a rail along the opposing wharf. Then he noticed a tour boat puttering along in the small inlet.

"They're here. MI6 is out there. I spotted two places and I'm sure there are more," he said.

As he was scanning the building, the side garage door opened and a black Mercedes exited.

"Someone is coming out and they're turning onto this street. I've got to get closer. Stay here," he stated and gave Natalie his pack and took off running through the garden between the beautiful beds of flowers, neatly trimmed bushes, and trees. He finally reached the edge of the garden next to the street just as the Mercedes drove by. He focused the binoculars on the moving car.

"Steady, hold it, wait for the car to catch up to the field, got it," he said as he memorized the tag number.

He said it to himself several times until he found Natalie.

"I got it," Chris said.

"Why? Isn't MI6 going to take care of it?" Natalie asked as he sat down on the bench.

"No, not according to Geoffrey. I could sense that he didn't know if Mom would survive an assault on the warehouse tonight. There are just too many unknown factors.

I've got a tag number and I'm betting that MI6 is going after all of the different families who buy black market contraband, but I just want Mom and her friends. I also don't know how the Chinese government figures into all of this. I mean how can an operation this big, happen right under their nose? I think we should follow the big fish," Chris said and stood up.

"So how do we do that?" Natalie asked.

"We find that black Mercedes. We've got four hours," he replied.

"Hi, kids, just thought I would check . . . where's your brother and Natalie?" Mr. Alexander asked.

"They're out by the fountain. Probably kissing," R.O. responded without looking up form the video monitor.

"We don't have a fountain," Mr. Alexander answered back and left.

R.O. never moved and Heather was still asleep.

"We have an alert. Two civilians loose in the building. We've got to find them now," Mr. Alexander ordered as he talked into his cell phone.

Chris and Natalie were walking along the street trying to figure out how they were going to find a tag number in a city that they had never been to before, when all of a sudden a police car pulled up next to them and stopped. They pretended not to notice until they heard a voice.

"Mr. MacGregor and Miss Crosswhite, you are quite skillful at eluding even the best of my people," the voice announced.

"Major Chen," Chris said as he turned around.

"Would you both please accompany me for a brief ride?" he asked and opened the back passenger door.

Chris just nodded and led Natalie to the car. Once inside, the car sped away and merged into traffic.

"Mr. MacGregor, your father is worried about you and the other children," Major Chen said.

"No need to worry, we're doing fine," Chris said.

"I would say that is a definite understatement for someone who flies a Chinese army helicopter across a nation as vast as ours. Who helped you do that, Mr. MacGregor?" Major Chen inquired as he looked over the seat toward them.

"Nobody. I did it," Chris responded.

"Yes, it was Chris, alright," Natalie butted in.

"Then you won't mind coming with me to resolve an issue I was having a problem with?" he asked.

"Certainly not. I mean, if we said we wanted out right now, would you let us?" Chris answered.

"I think you know the answer to that question," Major Chen said. "It was a bit of luck that I saw you walking down the street like that. With six million people in this city, I find the two of you next to a warehouse and a garden. What a coincidence."

The police car made a right turn into an underground parking garage and screeched to a stop as a car pulled out in front of them. Chris opened the door and jumped out and dragged Natalie behind him. A policeman in the front seat bailed out behind them and grabbed Natalie's right arm, yanking her back and onto the ground. Chris swung his backpack and made contact with the policeman's head and knocked him backwards. He pulled Natalie up just as Major Chen reached them.

"Run, Natalie. He wants me," Chris yelled.

Major Chen reached for his gun and drew it but Chris stepped forward into the barrel of the gun.

"You won't kill me," Chris said defiantly.

Natalie kept on running and disappeared into the crowded street.

"You are a lucky young man, Mr. MacGregor. Under any other circumstance, you would be dead right now," Chen said. "Back into the car!"

Chen helped the driver up and shoved him behind the wheel. He drove deeper into the garage and parked the car they were soon on the elevator headed up to the nineteenth floor. When the bell rang, signaling their arrival, Chen pushed the gun into Chris's back and prodded him out of the elevator.

"I have a new guest. This is Chris MacGregor," Chen announced to Ku Jong Wu.

"Mr. MacGregor. How lucky can we be?" he asked and walked over to Chris and took his backpack and tossed it to the floor. "We should, perhaps, unite mother and son."

"You have my mom here? I demand to see her," Chris said.

"Demand. That will work for now. Later you won't demand, you will plead, Mr. MacGregor," Wu fired back.

"Bring her out," he said to two men.

As Mavis stumbled into the room, Chris's face went pale with fear and anger.

"Mom, what have they done to you?" he asked and tried to go to her.

"Chris? Is that you?" Mavis asked in response and looked up in a blank stare. Her shirt was soaking wet.

"Let him go to her," Wu ordered.

Chris ran to her and braced her.

"Mom, you're burning up. Your face," Chris cried and felt tears welling in his eyes.

He turned to Chen and Wu.

"You'll both pay for this," Chris sneered.

"No, you have it backwards. You'll pay for her. You see, when your mother dies, we will still have you," Wu laughed.

"What if I buy her back from you?" Chris asked and led his mother over to a window. He looked down at the city turning on its lights.

"Buy? And what would an American boy have that we would want?" Wu questioned and lit a cigarette.

"May I," Chris replied and pointed at the backpack.

Chen nodded toward one of the guards who picked it up and rummaged through it looking for weapons. When he found the field knife he handed it to Wu.

"Such a feeble attempt at bravery, Mr. MacGregor," Wu said.

"Now may I have the bag?" Chris asked again.

"Give it too him," Wu said as Chen watched curiously.

Chris dumped the contents of the bag onto a table next to him and found the stuffed sock. Without picking it up he looked at Ku Jong Wu and Major Yufan Chen.

"Have either of you ever heard of the Fuo River Buddhas?" Chris asked.

"How silly you are, Mr. MacGregor, an American boy asking us if we know of a legendary Buddha. There are literally thousands of legends in China's great history. Yes, we know of the Fuo River and the legends that abound in that part of the Tibetan Plateau. I will humor you. I guess I should ask, why?" Wu quipped.

"I found the Buddhas, both of them, and I'll trade them to you for the release of my mother," Chris declared.

"Oh, Chris, I'm so sick. I've got to lie down," Mavis moaned from beside him.

Chris took the sock and slowly turned it upside down, and the miniature statue of Lord Buddha slid out into his left hand. The gold glistened in the light. Both men were expressionless in the presence of its beauty. Chris tossed it to Major Chen who caught it and then holstered his gun. Wu walked over and together they studied it closely.

"But we now have the Buddha. What do you have to trade?" Chen asked.

"The matching Buddha. There are two. I hid the other earlier today, hoping for this meeting," Chris responded.

"Yes, in the legend there are two Tienlong who watch over the Lord Buddha's cave. Why wouldn't there be two statues as well? It's told that the four faces of Lord Buddha watch over his life story and that these are made of pure gold," Wu acknowledged and caressed the Buddha.

"The four faces are mounted on four life-sized Buddha and now that I think of it they were gold." Chris's mind was in overdrive trying to complete the deception. "The walls in the cave are painted with a mural of the Life of Lord Buddha," Chris said. "I've been there. I've touched the walls, brushed the dust off of the tall Buddha, and today, hid the matching gold Buddha."

"It is as he says," Ku Jong Wu said to Major Chen. "Possessing this holy shrine will give our new government great status among the people. They will know we are truly the destined leaders of China."

"Where is the cave?" Chen demanded. "Where is the other gold statue?"

"The symbols that tell the story are in your hand," Chris replied. "The wall over the hiding place was decorated with a dragon."

"It must be Fucanlong, the dragon who protects treasure. It is his pearl that we proudly wear," Wu said

Both men turned the Buddha over and over.

"Nothing. We find nothing," Wu said angrily.

"May I show you?" Chris asked and held out his hand.

Chen tossed him the gold statue. Chris caught it and turned toward his mother who was now staring at him and frowning deeply. They made eye contact, and Chris stared at her just long enough for her to notice a spark in his eyes. The corners of her mouth turned up. Out of the blue, Chris swiveled around like an athlete with a shot put and slammed the solid gold priceless artifact into the plate glass window, shattering it into a million pieces. The three men ducked avoiding the flying glass that was propelled through the air. In one swift move, Chris grabbed Mavis, locked her in a giant bear hug, and jumped through the window of the nineteenth floor suite.

Sailing through the air, they impacted the bamboo scaffolding on the eighteenth floor with their weight propelling them through floor after floor until they came to a stop on the sixteenth. Each consecutive floor of soft bamboo had acted as a shield for the next floor.

"Oh, honey, I'm in pain. I can't breathe," Mavis cried with her arms wrapped tight around Chris.

"Mom, you can breathe. Go slow," Chris comforted.

"Yes, but I think I broke a rib," she said.

"We're alive, Mom. We're alive," Chris said firmly for her to hear. "But we've got to get up and get off this scaffolding platform before they find us."

"I know, honey. I know. I'm just so weak," she said.

Chris got to his feet and avoided looking down to the ground from that height. He pulled her up slowly and put her arm around his neck and kicked some of the debris away. He led her across the scaffolding until he came to a one-man steel construction elevator. He stepped in it and wrapped the safety belt around the two of them. Holding Mavis in one arm, he reached out and pulled the handle on the gravity brake and released the miniature one-man elevator. Slowly the vehicle began to move downward to the ground.

"Honey, how did you find me?" Mavis whispered into his ear as they stood tied together.

"I never gave up, that's how," he replied.

"Oh, Chris, I love you," Mavis said and coughed.

"Breathe slowly, Mom," Chris said.

The elevator reached the ground and Chris unfastened the safety belt and pulled Mavis out of the small vehicle.

He took two steps and noticed a brown object covered in mud from the bare ground around them.

"Hang on, Mom, I'm bending over," Chris said. "I think I've got a bad rib too."

Chris reached down and picked up the muddy Buddha and looked at it as four police cars drove up to the building with sirens blaring.

"Oh, no," Chris thought but he knew he couldn't run.

"Mr. MacGregor," John Alexander said as he stepped out of the second car with Natalie behind him. "Don't you think it's time you introduced me to your mother."

Epilogue

"Chris," Jack yelled down through the tunnel.

"Yeah, Dad," Chris replied.

"I'm lowering your mom now. Are you ready?" Jack asked.

"Ready," Chris replied.

Jack and two men from the People's Liberation Army lowered Mavis on a tight, climbing rope into the root hole on the side of the mountain. Heather dangled on a rope next to her and repelled slowly into the darkness of the cave below. After three weeks of recovery for the infection from the gunshot wound, three bruised ribs, and a concussion, Dr. Mavis MacGregor was again ready to face the challenges of the world and her adventuresome family.

"Are you doing O.K., Mom?" Heather asked.

"Fine, sweetie. I'm just about recovered, so don't worry. I wouldn't miss this for the world," Mavis answered and winked at her.

"Coming through," R.O. hollered as he bounced off a couple of boulders and repelled by quickly.

"Slow it down, Ryan," Mavis yelled as he zipped by.

"Mom, we couldn't have done this before the Chinese army cleared out the roots. It was so tight, we could barely squeeze through," Heather commented as they slowly descended into the bowels of the mountain.

"I just can't believe we ate Thanksgiving dinner after you guys went through all of this, and your father and I didn't have a clue. Oh, my," Mavis said.

"Mom, are you alright?" Chris shouted from the cave below.

"Doing good," Mavis replied.

After two more minutes of slow and guided descent, Mavis finally touched bottom, and Chris and Natalie grabbed her harness and steadied her touchdown.

"What do you think, Mom?" R. O. asked, walking up with a miner's hat and lamp on, which the army insisted that all of them wear.

"I think I'll go nuts if I ever let the four of you out of my sight again," Mavis said and smiled. "But then again I wouldn't want to cramp your style. I mean, defying death on a kayak trip was a random idea, of course."

"Oh, Mom. We've got Chris. He always takes care of us," Heather laughed.

"Let's see, a grizzly in Alaska, a sunken boat, kayaking a Class IV river, a wild helicopter ride across China. Did I miss anything?" Mavis asked.

"How about surviving a Saharan sand storm and trekking across Africa?" Heather added. "Then Chris let us ride sea turtles in the Caymans."

"Of course, approaching wild animals without fear, that's our Chris," Mavis said and then kissed him on the cheek. "But we love him because he's Chris."

"No family meetings without me," Jack said as he repelled to the bottom followed by Dr. Fei Ran Zuo, archaeologist at Peking University and a specialist in Buddhist artifacts.

"Greetings again everyone," Dr. Zuo said as she took off her repelling harness. "Chris, if you will lead the way."

Each explorer picked up a bright battery-powered lantern from the supply bundle the army had sent to the bottom. The packs also contained fresh water bottles, food, emergency climbing gear, medical supplies, and digital video equipment to capture the exciting moment. The camera operator reached the bottom of the cave and grabbed the lightweight camera as the MacGregors moved out.

"These cave formations are amazing, son," Jack said.

"This is the first time I've seen it clearly. Before we only had old lamps from the cave and our lighters. We missed all the stalactites hanging from the ceiling," Chris replied.

"You guys are amazing," Mavis said to Natalie.

"You have yet to hear the entire story of the Wolong Pandas. I mean there was this state of the art tourist center and research facility and they took us to the wilderness among dozens of mountain peaks. It was like Colorado four times over. It was so beautiful," Natalie recounted walking next to Mavis.

"I want to meet David and Ginna Bloom and thank them personally," Mavis said. "Maybe we should fly to Wolong before we leave China next week?"

"That's fine with me as long as I get a new down coat. Mine is lying in the marshes in The New Territories," Heather added.

"I've been recuperating for three weeks and I still learn something new every day," Mavis said and put her arm around Natalie.

"No complaints from me," Natalie said.

"Hey, Mom, we're coming to the winding stairway. It's really cool. We slept on them for a few hours after we escaped the earthquake," R.O. pointed out.

"I think that was the other staircase, little brother," Chris said.

"It was definitely a four point five," Jack said. "I asked the Ministry of Geology and they confirmed it. Good guess, Chris."

"Science camp, what can I say?" Chris replied, as he was the first to step into the narrow stairway and descend further.

A few minutes later they were all standing on the back of the stage in the cave. Dr. Zuo moved to the front of the group for the historic moment. She carefully walked between the full-sized Buddha and stepped from the stage into the large oval room.

The bright lanterns lit up the room like it had not been seen in over a thousand years. The pinks and yellows of the mural were more vivid than the kids remembered with their light sticks and ancient lanterns.

"How beautiful," Mavis gasped as Jack helped her down from the stage.

"Here's where I crashed into the wall and discovered the gold Buddha, Mom," R.O. said and walked over to the hole and pointed. "And here's the dragon."

Dr. Zuo moved slowly around the room reading the Chinese characters. She finally stopped in front of where another dragon had been painted on the wall. She reached down to her utility belt and retrieved a small pick hammer. Carefully, she knelt on the floor and started chipping away at the mural making small holes and then gently pulling the ancient plaster away. After ten minutes of the tedious work, she reached into the hole and pulled out a second gold statue of the Lord Buddha.

"Wow," Chris exclaimed. "I had a hunch it was there. After we saw the first dragon I looked directly across the cave on the opposite wall and there was another. We didn't have the time or energy to dig for it."

"You were very right, Mr. MacGregor. Fate and maybe Lord Buddha was on your side at that moment," Dr. Zuo replied and stood up and dusted off the beautiful figure.

"It looks different from my Buddha," R.O. said and walked over to it. It has a smile on its face and mine has more of a sour look, like what Heather gives me all the time.

"Whatever!" Heather said and rolled her eyes.

"When I turn thirteen next month, I will celebrate being born under the sign of Dilong, the earth dragon. Since I discovered it, what's my cut, professor? R.O. asked and turned to Dr. Zuo.

"The gratitude of the people of China. It's only fitting that the discoverer is a son of the dragon. It's a great honor. This statue looks different because it portrays another face of Lord Buddha. It's the happy face that Lord Buddha wears in the mural when he finds eternal peace. Peace that we all will find," Dr. Zuo answered.

"It's magnificent," Jack said. "May I?" He reached out for the statue and Dr. Zuo handed it to him. "What happens now?"

"We take them back to Beijing where they will be shown to the people. Then we will open this cave as a shrine and maybe people will come here to learn more about Lord Buddha. That will be many years from now though," Dr. Zuo said. "It's a relief that the secret society that used the _sign of the dragon_ as their emblem, has been brought to justice. Several Tai-Pan will spend many years in prison for their plan to overthrow the government," Dr Zuo informed. "Where did your colleagues go?" she asked Mavis.

"Nigel and Julian went back to England. Scientists at Peking University now have all of the fossils. The _Caudipteryx zoui_ will be on traveling display for a few years, as it should, for all to enjoy," Mavis responded. "And my friends get the professional credit for discovering her."

Jack handed the gold Buddha back to Dr. Zuo and walked over to Mavis.

"Mission complete," he said.

"Right you are, honey," Mavis answered back.

"Where to now?" Heather asked.

"I think this family could use a nice warm vacation while I investigate some South Pacific atolls. A few of my zoology colleagues want to measure marine growth on battleships from World War II. How about Micronesia for a month? We might even venture off to Hawaii," Jack said.

"Warm weather at last!" Heather rejoiced and smiled.

"You've got my vote. I could use more diving time," Chris added.

"Ditto that, Dad," R.O. said.

"How about you, Natalie?" Jack asked.

"Is that an invitation?" Natalie replied softly.

"Yes, it is, and why don't you stay for the rest of the year if you want?" Mavis answered back.

"You don't have to ask twice. I can miss one semester of college without any problems, and I'm sure my parents won't mind," Natalie said with a beaming smile on her face.

"Then it's a go. South Pacific here we come!" Jack announced, and they all cheered.

REVIEWS FOR THE MACGREGOR
FAMILY ADVENTURE SERIES
Cayman Gold: Lost Treasure of Devils Grotto
Book One

VOYA • Journal for Librarians • August 2000
"Science fact and fiction based on folklore intertwine in this fast-paced story of pirate gold and adventure. In an increasingly rare story line, the family is intact, with parents who are intelligent and involved in the lives of their children. . . . surely will appeal to older teens—mostly boys—looking for a blend of adventure and a bit of romance."
—Pam Carlson

KLIATT • Journal for Librarians • May 2000
"In this quick-moving adventure story, teenagers who are expert scuba divers bump up against modern-day pirates. . . . The author, an environmental biologist and college professor, shows his love and fierce protectiveness of natural resources and endangered species. This story is fun to read while making teens aware of environmental issues."
—Sherri Forgash Ginsberg,
Duke School for Children, Chapel Hill, NC

Elephant Tears: Mask of the Elephant
Book Two

VOYA • Journal for Librarians • December 2000
". . . portrays the teens' relationships with each other and with their parents as wholesome but realistic . . . respectfully depicts the native Africans and their tradition without glossing over their problems . . . descriptive narration is admirable—family-friendly realistic wildlife adventure."
—Leah Sparks

KLIATT • Journal for Librarians • September 2000
". . . the author weaves an exciting adventure while stressing the importance of protecting the earth's dwindling

resources and endangered animals. It is a powerful, enlightening novel that remains exciting without being didactic."

—Sherri Forgash Ginsberg

Falcon of Abydos: Oracle of the Nile
Book Three

"Written for all ages, *Falcon of Abydos* is a thrilling adventure story in which the MacGregor family becomes entangled in an ancient Egyptian mystery stretching from the heat of the Sahara to beneath the surface of the Red Sea. . . . An engaging, action-packed, and memorable techno/thriller for young readers."

—*Midwest Book Review, "Children's Bookwatch"*

KLIATT • *Journal for Librarians* • *March 2002*

"This is the third adventure for the traveling MacGregor family. We find them in Cairo, unearthing secrets that could change the face of the Middle East forever. The series consists of . . . action-packed stories . . . [that] make important political and environmental statements as well as providing pure entertainment. This story is loaded with historical facts, laced with romance and humor; a definite purchase for your library."

—*KLIATT*

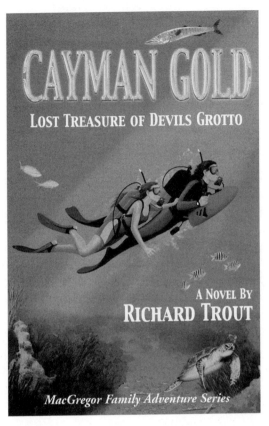

CAYMAN GOLD

LOST TREASURE OF DEVILS GROTTO

A NOVEL BY
RICHARD TROUT

MacGregor Family Adventure Series

Suddenly faced with the task of saving a lost Spanish treasure embedded in protected coral reef, the MacGregor teens rely on their courage and scuba-diving skills to explore and investigate the waters and beaches of the Cayman Islands. This first novel in the techno-thriller *MacGregor Family Adventure Series* involves sinister pirate forces, strange sea creatures, and hospitable natives, as well as issues of endangered species and environmental management. Meticulously detailed yet quick-paced, this novel is an introduction to the enterprising MacGregor clan, who have just entered what will be a full year of worldwide escapades. As with each Richard Trout book, the themes of family and wildlife conservation are apparent throughout each adventure.

In this second novel in the *MacGregor Family Adventure Series,* zoologist Dr. Jack MacGregor again strives to protect the earth's dwindling resources and endangered animals, pursuing an international cartel that is exploiting elephants in East Africa. The family's three teenagers, Chris, Heather, and Ryan, become part of the action and team up with native Africans and a seasoned American aviator to save the animals and bring the exploiters to justice. Traversing the landscape of Serengeti, Amboseli, Masai Mara, and Mount Kilimanjaro, the MacGregor teens learn about African culture and wildlife through the eyes of their new friend, native Kikuyu Samburua. This is another stimulating, action-packed journey that will appeal to all ages with its contemporary perspective of culture, environmental management, and solid family values.

FALCON OF
ABYDOS
ORACLE OF THE NILE

MacGregor Family Adventure Series

A Novel By
RICHARD TROUT

This time the globe trotting MacGregor clan lands amidst the shifting sands of the Sahara Desert to uncover a secret that could forever change the history of Egypt. Just when Egyptologists believe that the last of the great discoveries have been made, the MacGregor family's appearance at the International Environmental Conference in Cairo inspires them to pursue the truth about the Nile River. From a quaint shop in the heart of Old Cairo to Seti's exquisite temple, the mystery of the Falcon of Abydos is the third and possibly the most chilling challenge for the inimitable MacGregor family and their friends.

Царь Аляски: Крест Шарлеманар

CZAR OF ALASKA

THE CROSS OF CHARLEMAGNE

MacGregor Family Adventure Series

A Novel By

RICHARD TROUT

In Book Four of the *MacGregor Family Adventure Series,* zoologist Jack MacGregor, his paleontologist wife, Mavis, and children, Chris, Ryan, and Heather, are caught in a web of characters pursuing both noble and notorious goals in Alaska. Three Russian Orthodox priests seek the religious artifact the Cross of Charlemagne, while their rivals, a rogue Vatican priest and a renowned Polish archaeologist, threaten to retrieve the treasure first. Meanwhile, an ominous international team of ecoterrorists armed with state-of-the-art weapons are determined to prevent oil drilling in the Arctic National Wildlife Refuge and get rid of Jack MacGregor once and for all.